HER NAME WAS CHAS

SK HOLT

Copyright © 2025 by SK Holt

All rights reserved. No part of this book may be reproduced, stored in a retrieval system, or transmitted in any form or by any means—electronic, mechanical, photocopying, recording, or otherwise—without the prior written permission of the publisher, except in the case of brief quotations used in reviews or scholarly works.

This is a work of fiction. Names, characters, places, and incidents are either the product of the author's imagination or are used fictitiously. Any resemblance to actual events, locales, or persons, living or dead, is purely coincidental.

ISBN:

9798993765303 (Paperback)

9798993765310 (Hardcover)

For my wife, who waited for me in the glow of the baby food aisle at Kroger as I found the courage to begin this story. Thank you for being brave right along with me.

And for anyone who has ever felt broken for loving who you love. You are not alone. You are seen. You are lovely. May you find the strength to trust yourself, without measure.

A NOTE TO THE READER

This story contains sensitive themes and situations that some readers may find difficult. Please be advised that the narrative includes elements of **emotional and psychological abuse**, **religious trauma**, **infant loss,** and **homophobia**. Reader discretion is advised.

While the characters you will meet—Chas, Alex, Kip, Mara, and others—are products of my imagination, the events of this story are deeply rooted in real experiences. This work of fiction is inspired by the lived realities of members of the queer community, including personal accounts of navigating faith, family rejection, and the often-painful journey toward self-acceptance and love.

The profound beauty of finding one's chosen family, including the challenges and triumphs, is not merely a narrative device; it reflects the courage and resilience of real people. My hope is that by sharing this story, I can bear witness to the strength of those who have had to build their own lives and redefine what it means to be seen and loved.

With love,

SK

PART ONE

CHAPTER 1
CHAS, 2006

Chas Montgomery lay on the floor of her sunlit bedroom, hoping against hope that maybe, just maybe, she could find a way out of the appointment her parents had made for her.

Three weeks earlier, her mom had walked in on her kissing her best friend, Jess. That had led to one attempt at running away, zero contact with Jess, three weeks of being grounded, and now, the appointment. She had no choice in the matter. All that was left to do was get off the floor and go down to the car.

As Chas stomped down the stairs of their historic downtown Savannah home, her mother, Susan, packed a bag with her current book—one about a Christian family who moved to Cambodia to do mission work for their Southern Baptist church. Susan wasn't happy about taking time away from her family any more than Chas was. Chas had two younger brothers who also needed her, but given the recent events, Susan saw no other option; this had to be done.

Half an hour later, Susan and Chas pulled up to the Old Brick Church. Of course, this wasn't their church, which didn't have the resources to help with Chas's situation, at least according to the pastor. But luckily for Susan, he could guide her to a place that did. Susan parked the car and paid for street parking. Returning to the vehicle, she adjusted her seat and prepared to dive into her book while she waited for her daughter to finish with the appointment.

Only, Chas didn't move.

"Would you like me to walk you in, honey?" Susan asked.

"No," was the only reply Chas could give. She couldn't tell her mom that she was scared, felt wrong, or just didn't understand why this was necessary. So, Chas got out of the Volvo, walked up to the side door she had been instructed to go to, and knocked once.

"Welcome to Restorative Hope," said the man who opened the door. "I am Henry, and I am here to guide you away from sin and back to the path of spiritual wellness." Henry looked to be in his mid-to-late thirties and was tall and very fit. "Restorative Hope is a wellness program for teens and adults working through their sinful nature and choosing to turn away from it."

Chas was led down a hall and a flight of steps to the basement of the old church. The basement was dank, and the lighting was fluorescent, giving it all the appeal of a prison cell —or so Chas assumed. She had never been in trouble a day in her life.

At sixteen, Chas had only ever known what her parents and teachers had taught her. Unlike most girls her age, she devoutly loved her mom and never fought or argued over the rules set before her. But now, things had shifted. Ever since that kiss with Jess, her mom hadn't looked at her or talked to her the way she had before. It was as if the act of kissing someone made her mom believe an alien had inhabited her daughter's body, and she didn't know how to engage with this alien version of her daughter. Chas knew it wasn't the actual act of kissing someone that had caused this monumental shift, but rather *who* she had been kissing—specifically, a girl.

All her life, Chas had looked up to her mom. Susan was the shining example of the ideal Christian woman. A pastor's wife, she came from old Southern money and taught at the Christian school that Chas and her brothers attended. Theirs had been an idyllic life before the kiss. Weeknights were spent carting Chas and her brothers to and from various sporting events, and weekends were for family time, and of course, Sunday was for church.

This Christian lifestyle was so ingrained in Chas's family that she and her brothers were all named after some vital character or construct in the Bible. After all, Chas's full name was Chastity—the virtuous state of abstaining from sex. She was the oldest, followed by David, and then Daniel. The boys were named after strong and important men in the Bible, while Chas was practically named after the rules her parents wanted her to follow.

Chas jumped when Henry tapped her on the shoulder.

"Hey, would you like to join the main group or meet with your personal counselor first?"

"Uh ... meet with my counselor, I guess," replied Chas. She was not ready for any group interactions, so maybe this would buy her some time.

"Okay, great," Henry said as he turned into the next room. "Chastity, meet Megan; she will be your counselor while you are in the program."

"Hi, um, I go by Chas. Nobody calls me Chastity."

"Hi Chastity. I am Megan, and I will be calling you Chastity because Chas is a masculine name, and we don't need to add to your confusion. I will be encouraging your parents to do the same," said Megan with a too-bright smile.

Megan looked to be in her late thirties, with mousey brown hair cut in a blunt bob and rich brown almond-shaped eyes. Her eyes, for all their beauty, never quite smiled. They watched. They judged. Her scent—rosewater and vanilla—lingered a little too strong, like a perfume masking something rotten underneath.

Chas was now wishing she had selected the group option.

"In our program, you will be expected to record any sinful thoughts or actions in a daily journal. Then, each Thursday night, you will give me this journal and attend the group meeting where you will share your struggles with your peers. I will review the events of the past week, and after the group meeting, you will have a one-on-one meeting with me, and I will counsel you to ensure you put this sinful temptation behind you. It is important to note that during this time, any one-on-one interactions should only be with males. Any female friendships can be retained, but must always be on full public display so as to prevent any further temptations. Do you understand the program as I have explained it?"

Chas decided she was in the Twilight Zone. All her life, she had primarily had female friends, and this had been encouraged to prevent her from giving herself to a boy before marriage. And now ... now she was supposed to be one-on-one with boys, and girls were off-limits. *What the hell?* she thought.

"Yes, I understand," Chas mumbled.

"Perfect!" Megan said with that too-sugary smile. "Now I will take you to the group."

Megan led Chas to the main room, which hosted a circle of chairs that were occupied by other girls. "Where are the boys?" Chas asked. "Oh, they have group separately so they can feel open to share, as you should feel open with the girls," Megan explained.

Okay, so they want her to be friends with boys and date them, but they put her in a room full of girls she knows are like her. *What could go wrong?* Chas quipped to herself.

"Everyone, this is Chastity," Megan announced to the group. Chastity didn't bother correcting her.

CHAPTER 2
CHASTITY (FORMERLY CHAS), 2006

After the appointment, Chastity returned to the car and told Susan about the program. Before she left the group session, Megan instructed her to let her mom know that from here forward, everyone should address her as Chastity (not Chas). Susan seemed pleased by the progress made during the appointment and was looking forward to putting this all behind them. She loved her daughter and wanted to ensure not only her reputation but her soul was intact as well. This really was the best thing for her, Susan was sure.

Soon, Susan was pulling the car into one of their designated parking spaces. Living in the historic district of downtown Savannah did have its benefits—no street parking and working around the street sweeper's schedule, for one thing. Their home was beautiful, stunning actually. Huge oak trees draped with Spanish moss lined the street they lived on, and the street itself was brick, not asphalt. They were just a few blocks from Forsyth Park, where Chastity played volleyball with her friends on the weekends. She loved this home; it felt safe and comfortable—exactly how a home should feel. Her bedroom was her favorite place in the whole world. She was on the third floor and had the highest ceilings with exposed beams and brick walls and original hardwood floors. This was where she and all of her friends congregated—she had the whole floor to herself and even a small refrigerator to store snacks and drinks so she wouldn't have to venture down to the galley kitchen on the main floor. Basically, they could survive a whole weekend in her room.

After her appointment at Restorative Hope, Chastity returned to her room feeling anything but hopeful. Tucked into her jacket was the journal Megan had bestowed upon her. She understood the program, and she understood what they were attempting to do, but Chastity just couldn't understand why they needed to know her deepest and most private thoughts. Unbeknownst to her family, Chastity had already grappled with this ... dilemma privately and internally. She had tried to be normal and like boys like her friends did, but no matter how hard she tried, she found herself rooting for the boys to fail so that she could help put her friends back together again and be their source of comfort. This is exactly what happened with Jess. She had been dating Blake for all of one week when she found out that he was kissing some other girl at the movie theater while she was at basketball practice. When Chastity found out, she threatened to kick Blake in the balls and then swept in to comfort her best friend.

Jess was her oldest friend, and she had never imagined it would turn into more than a friendship, but just three weeks ago, all of that had changed. Of course, her mom would walk in on her first-ever kiss with a girl. It was poetic justice, she supposed. Chastity knew this would never be tolerated, and she had pushed these feelings down, aside, and any which way she could to avoid them, but it hadn't worked. She still felt the same way she had before she was caught, only now she was dealing with embarrassment as well as the confusion of being torn between who she knew herself to be and who she had been taught to be.

Chastity sat at the end of her room that overlooked the street and had a distant view of the park. This was her favorite spot in her favorite place. It was adorned with sheets of poems she had written on her old typewriter that she had bought from a vintage shop, and in the middle of a large bay window, there was a table that had two seats where she could type when she was alone or sit with friends. Chastity placed the journal on the table and stared at it—possibly hoping it would burst into flames. Suddenly, this spot was anything but her favorite place. She desperately wanted to figure out what she needed to say in this journal to get released from the program at Restorative Hope. Maybe if she just wrote that it was a mistake, and she wasn't feeling these things anymore, they would believe her and graduate her from the program, although that wasn't likely.

Chastity picked up a pen and wrote the only thing she knew how to write. She wrote a poem about how she was feeling in this moment.

Worthwhile

Imagine this
I wake up, I am told I am beautiful, I am told I am loved, I am
sought after, I am fought for, I am respected, I am never
demeaned, I am never hurt, I am never down, I feel love, I am
loved, I am protected, I am cared for, I am no longer broken, I
no longer have doubts, I have value, I am me again, I am full, I
do not have to imagine, this is my reality.
If I were referring to a boyfriend, husband, or man, I would be
praised, even congratulated. You would be proud. You could be
happy that I am happy. I wouldn't face rejection, controversy, or
criticism. But I am not referring to a man.

Chastity

There, she thought, *that should appease Megan.*

CHAPTER 3
CHASTITY (FORMERLY CHAS), 2006

The next Thursday came faster than any Thursday had ever come before. Had it really been a week since her first appointment at Restorative Hope?

It was the same as the week prior; Chastity was dreading the appointment and lying on the floor of her bedroom, hoping she would melt into the walls of her home and never have to leave, but then Susan called out for Chastity to meet her in the car. Filled with dread, confusion, and fear, Chastity took the familiar path to the car. Aside from worrying that there was no way this program was going to work on her, and therefore, she would always be a disappointment to her mom and dad, she was also worried about the lack of content in her journal assignments. The only thing she had written in the journal was the poem on the night she had returned from Restorative Hope last week. Although the poem had made her feel slightly better, she was doubtful that it would have the same impact on Megan.

Susan completed the same steps as last time: She pulled up to the church, paid for street parking, hunkered down in her seat to enjoy some reading time, and then offered to walk

Chastity into the church. Chastity again declined and made her way back to the entrance of Restorative Hope.

Henry greeted her again and took her directly to Megan without any offer to head straight to the group session.

"Hello Chastity, it's a pleasure to see you again," Megan said in her most saccharine voice.

"Hi Megan, nice to see you too," Chastity replied, but not with the same gusto.

Megan got right to business. "Kindly hand me your journal, and then you may go to group. You remember where it is, correct?"

Chastity handed over the journal, knowing that this was likely not the type of journal entry Megan was expecting. Somehow, just knowing that Megan was about to feel as befuddled as she was brought her a small smile and a tiny slice of joy. Chastity left the room swiftly to avoid watching Megan's reaction to the journal. Locating the group of girls, she found an unoccupied chair among them. Next to Chastity was a girl who had to be older than eighteen because she had some really awesome tattoos and facial piercings. It was the kind of look Chastity would have loved to pull off, but there was no way on God's green Earth that her parents would ever allow it. She was sure that if they didn't disown her after the kiss, *that* would surely push them over the edge.

"Hi, I am Beck," the tattooed hooligan offered.

"Hi, I am Chastity," she replied before realization dawned.

"Wait, they let you keep your name even though it is masculine?"

"No, they want me to go by Becky, but I am only here because it was a condition of my parents to allow me to keep living in their house. I don't want to 'get better' or whatever it is these people think they are doing here," clarified the girl.

Before Chastity could explain that she too had a cool name that she wanted to go by, the group counselor came in and sat down in the last vacant chair. Chastity hadn't seen this woman before. She looked to be in her late twenties or early thirties and had a really interesting look. Her head was shaved on one side, and her hair on the other side was a short, blunt bob. If there was a way to look gay, this chick had nailed it. How was she going to help them not be gay when she clearly was so herself?

"Hi everyone, as most of you know, I am Stephanie, and I am the women's group counselor here at Restorative Hope. Three years ago, I was in a long-term relationship with a woman. My parents had disowned me, and I was living out of my car. This woman and I did not make it, but it was too late for me; the damage was done with my parents, and I was no longer welcome at their home. I came to this church one evening, hoping to find somewhere warm and quiet to stay for a few hours before getting in my car for the night, and I met the team at Restorative Hope. They explained to me that embracing my sin instead of turning away from it and repenting was what had ultimately led me to a path of homelessness and abandonment by my family. After some time in the courses, I began to understand the decisions I was making were not only harmful to others—they were also damning to my soul. I turned away from that lifestyle choice and have been living as an honest Christian woman ever since."

Whoa, that is a lot to unpack, Chastity thought. This woman made it sound as if someone can't be gay and Christian, but Chastity was pretty sure she was both. She loved God, and she felt she had a personal relationship with him—it was his people she couldn't quite relate to. Chastity also wondered if things would have worked out with Stephanie and her partner if her view on things were different—if Stephanie and this mystery woman had worked out, would she still feel that this was all sinful behavior that needed correction?

While Chastity was deep in thought about Stephanie and her previous life, she realized suddenly that the room was quiet, and everyone in group was looking directly at her, as if she was supposed to be answering some unheard question.

"Sorry, I zoned out. Can you repeat the question?" Chastity was mortified that she was caught out within the first ten minutes of group and clearly wasn't participating in the expected ways.

"Sure, I asked what brought you to us here at Restorative Hope?" Stephanie patiently repeated.

"I kissed my best friend, and my Mom walked in on us," Chastity supplied for this group of people she had never met. Her cheeks felt hot, and she suddenly couldn't stop fidgeting. All eyes were on her, and nobody said anything, so she kept going. "My name is Chas."

"I believe Megan told me that your name was Chastity," replied Stephanie. "Thank you for sharing, Chastity. We are glad you are here." She quickly moved on to another apparent newcomer.

After sixty long minutes, the session ended, and Chastity made her way back to Megan's office. The office had the same prison motif as the rest of Restorative Hope, with the same cream-colored walls and horrible fluorescent lighting. To add to the feeling, Megan sat behind a large metal desk with a stack of journals on one end and a computer on the other. The only thing indicating that a human worked here was a porcelain teacup rimmed with flowers sitting beside the journals.

"Please come in and have a seat," Megan said, her normally cheerful façade absent.

Great, Chastity thought, *at least we aren't pretending to be happy for no reason anymore.*

"Chastity, can you explain why there is only one entry in this journal, and it sounds less like an account of your thoughts and actions and more like a poem blaming others for your behavior?"

Well, that is direct, Chastity thought. "Actually, I didn't have any sinful thoughts or actions this week aside from the poem I wrote, so I figured I should just leave the pages blank."

"That isn't how this program works, and I am quite certain I made the rules and expectations clear during our first meeting," Megan said in an exasperated tone.

"Right, well, I will try to have more sinful thoughts this week, so that you can have some reading material for next week." Chastity was being bold if not belligerent, which was never her style.

Megan took a deep breath in through her nose and let it out through her mouth; she moved her hands in an up-down flowing motion. If Chastity didn't know better, she would have thought that they were about to engage in some sort of yoga exercise. "Chastity, I understand your resistance to the program; we have all been in your shoes. It is up to you if you want to make the right choices or continue down a path that will ultimately result in your dismissal from the program and will put a wedge between you and those you love, as well as God."

CHAPTER 4
CHASTITY (FORMERLY CHAS), 2007

Chastity turned her final journal entry in to Megan. This was her last group session and her last meeting with her counselor.

Megan stood at her place in the circle and made the same announcement Chastity had heard multiple times over the last six months. "It is with the greatest pleasure and deepest pride that I announce Chastity's completion of the Restorative Hope program. She is a model graduate and leaves us spiritually well, which is our overall mission here. Everyone, please take a moment to celebrate her achievement." Megan concluded her speech by leading the group in a round of applause.

That was it. She had done it. Chastity thanked the group and walked to the back of the room, where her mom and dad were waiting for her, pride beaming from them like sunrays on a rainy day.

The last six months had not been easy for her or her family. Being young, her brothers were not told what was going on, which prompted David to use his imagination to fill in the gaps. He announced one night at dinner, "I know what is wrong with Chas!"

"It is Chastity, honey, remember?" Susan corrected him gently for what had to be the hundredth time. David was undeterred. "She's on steroids," he announced, holding up a tampon to their dad's utter embarrassment.

Susan then had the privilege of explaining that what David was holding was not evidence of drug usage but rather "something Chastity needs as she becomes a woman."

David's face showed utter confusion. "Wait, so we are all mad at Chas—tity because she's becoming a woman? I thought that's what she's supposed to become?"

"We are not mad at Chastity, honey; we just need her to make better choices because we want her to be able to get into heaven, too," Susan clarified.

There it was, the elephant in the room, more like the elephant that had been sitting on her chest, making it hard to breathe—"make better choices." No matter what she wrote in that journal or said in group, she knew deep down in the quiet of her soul that this was never a choice.

CHAPTER 5
CHASTITY, 2015

In the years following high school, Chastity couldn't quite settle on anything. For a time, she tried the college route, but she never declared a major, and after a few years of taking basic courses, she still had no idea what she wanted to become. So, she dropped out and enrolled in a cosmetology course at the local trade school. The intention was to go back to college after a few years of working in the salon—once she knew what she wanted to do with her life—but so far that clarity hadn't come to her.

Now, at twenty-five, Chastity was working in a high-end salon in downtown Savannah near the historic district and her family's home. She wasn't able to afford the cost of living there, so she continued to live with her parents even after she had graduated and started working.

She had a great schedule and was almost always booked with regulars who would come back every few weeks for a touch-up on their color or a trim (most of the time well before it was really needed), but Chastity loved the calm of the salon, and she enjoyed the predictability of her days.

Today, though, she noticed a name on her books—the name

caught her attention for two reasons: It wasn't one of her regulars, and the name seemed familiar, but she couldn't quite place it. Brian Jacobs. Normally, seeing a new person on the books was exciting, but Chastity specialized in color and hair extensions as well as women's haircuts. Cutting a man's hair was always the worst. It took her twice as long, and she could only pray they didn't want her to do anything with a fade or a straight razor, or they would walk out of there looking like a cheese grater had been used on them instead of a razor blade. Hopefully, this was just one of those guys who needed a quick trim only.

Five minutes before 2 pm, the door to the salon opened, and Brian Jacobs walked into the room. Chastity realized right away why the name had seemed familiar. Brian was David's friend from high school, but she hadn't seen him in years. With David being four years younger than she was, Chastity never spent much time with him when he had friends over because she was typically busy with hers or was in college or cosmetology school. They never really had the same circles of friends, but she remembered Brian from his years of showing up at her house and eating all of their food with the rest of the pack of ravenous boys. But this Brian looked different from the scrawny boy she remembered. He was tall, around six-foot-four, and really well-built. Clearly, puberty had helped this guy in a big way.

"Hey Chastity," Brian said in a husky but clearly cheerful voice.

"'Hey' back to you."

"How have you been? It's been ages since I last saw you," Brian inquired.

"I am good. Just working in the salon and hoping for someone to come in and sweep me off my feet," Chastity replied.

Where did that come from? What was wrong with her? Was she trying to flirt with her baby brother's high school friend?

And if she was trying to flirt, why was she being so awkward about it? A simple "I'm fine, how are you?" would have been completely sufficient.

Chastity had dated several guys in the years since her time at Restorative Hope, but it always ended quickly. She was never sure-footed in any relationships. It always felt like too much too soon or fell completely flat and felt like nothing at all. Either way, she always found a reason to call it off after just a few months.

Brian didn't seem to notice or mind the awkward reply. He simply smiled at her and sat down in the chair she was standing behind.

In some ways, he hadn't changed at all—his eyes were still an enchanting shade of blue, his teeth were still crooked, and he pretty much seemed to be the same happy-go-lucky boy she remembered.

After an hour of awkward conversation (awkward on her part, not his), Chastity patted Brian on the shoulder and announced too loudly, "All done!"

Brian just smiled up at her and thanked her for the haircut, but he wasn't moving from her chair. "You are done now, so you can go," Chastity offered.

Brian chuckled, and Chastity swore she could feel the deep sound warm her from the inside. "Thanks, but I think you need your cape back, right?"

Oh my goodness, Chastity thought to herself, *I forgot the stupid cape. No wonder he was just sitting there smiling at me. I am a complete idiot.*

"Oops, yes, of course I do." Chastity tried to smile and laugh her way through the embarrassing blunder.

After the cape was removed, Brian got up and went to check out at the reception. Chastity was a hundred percent sure he would not be returning as a regular. If the awkward conversation didn't turn him away, that haircut surely would …

did she just accidentally give him a bowl cut? Chastity was too mortified to watch him go, so she turned to clean up her station. As she was sweeping up the last remnants of Brian's hair, she heard him clear his throat. Chastity turned around, and Brian was back at her station. Instead of saying anything, she just stared; honestly, that was probably the safer option, as she had already made a fool of herself more than once in the last hour.

"I was wondering if it would be strange if I asked you out," Brian said on a quick rush of air. Chastity noticed that he was turning a little red near the collar of his shirt, and he seemed like he might even be nervous. It couldn't be that—she was sure that she was the nervous wreck here, not Brian, who had seemed so calm and self-assured over the last hour of catching up. As she was pondering all of the reasons he couldn't be nervous, and she must be mistaken about his intentions, she realized that she still hadn't answered him, and he was just standing there waiting patiently for her reply.

"Yes! Oops, no, no, it wouldn't be strange, and yes, I accept," Chastity replied in a rush as well.

"Great," Brian seemed perfectly happy to have waited for her reply, even if it had taken her more than a minute to process everything. "When are you free?"

"How about tonight?" she offered. She could do this. She could date and find love and be a completely average twenty-five-year-old Christian woman. Her future could begin tonight.

CHAPTER 6
CHASTITY, 2015

Chastity was getting ready for her date with Brian. They had decided to take a day trip to Tybee Island, just outside town. She was excited to spend the day walking along the shore, playing volleyball, bocce ball, or any of the other beach games she had grown up with. The beach was a great place to spend a Saturday, and having Brian there would only make it better.

They had been dating for the past five months, and things were progressing perfectly. Both families supported their relationship, and they now attended church together every Sunday with her family. They shared a lot in common, which made their time together so easy. Brian was also raised in a Southern Baptist home, loved playing board games, and was great at sports. Most of their dates had involved playing some game or another or challenging each other to a round of basketball.

Chastity had started seeing her life's roadmap more clearly over these past five months. She felt certain that Brian would someday be her husband. She knew this was what both he and her parents expected, and it was perfectly fine with her, given how well they got along and how seamlessly their lives flowed together.

The only source of tension in their relationship was around the physical component. Given her background, Chastity was a virgin and intended to stay that way until she was married. Brian was not a virgin, but that didn't matter to her as long as he respected her decision to abstain until her wedding night. It was a choice she was exceptionally proud of—that she had resisted temptation and kept her morals intact to be pure for her future husband.

Although Brian was understanding and patient, he was starting to push the boundaries a bit. On their last date, he had attempted to slide his hand under her shirt. She considered letting him, just to see what it would feel like, but she felt that even this small breach of physical contact would be unfair to her future husband, whoever that might be. If she were being completely honest with herself, she was also scared to death of physical intimacy. All her friends had already crossed this line, either by having premarital sex or by marrying exceptionally young so they could have sex. Either way, Chastity was the only virgin left among her friends, and she wasn't in any rush to change that.

Chastity did get the feeling that Brian was growing slightly impatient, and she was starting to get nervous that he would try to rush into marriage just so they could be together physically. It wouldn't be uncommon for members of their church to date for less than a year and get engaged quickly. Most of them who kept their virginity until their wedding night were engaged within a few months and married before their one-year anniversary. It was this timeline that bothered her. Chastity wasn't ready for anything physical, but she also wasn't in any rush to get to a place where she could be. Ideally, she would have a year of dating and a year of engagement. By then, she was sure she would be ready to give herself to her husband.

Chastity was all set for her beach day when Brian pulled up to her parents' house.

"Hey, before we go into Tybee, I need to stop by the grocery store," he said by way of greeting.

"Okay, sounds good. What do you need? My parents may have it in the house already."

"Thanks for the offer, but it's several things. I'm going to pack us a picnic so we can just stay on the beach until the sun goes down."

After the stop at the grocery store to pick up wine and snacks for their beach day, they took the thirty-minute drive to Tybee. When they arrived, they paid for street parking and pulled a wagon she had borrowed from her parents over the beach access ramp that cut through the dunes on 12th Street. This was her favorite spot on the island; she had always come to this exact place as a kid. The sand was warm but not overly hot, and the water was cool. The sky was one of those perfectly blue skies with big, puffy white clouds that you could squint at and imagine shapes out of—the one directly in front of her was definitely a cow with a hat on its head.

Heading straight toward the edge of the shore, Chastity took in a big lungful of salty air. "So, what do you want to do first?" Chastity asked. "We could play volleyball or paddleball or go for a swim. I'm up for anything."

When Brian didn't answer right away, Chastity turned around and found him on one knee.

Oh shit was her only thought.

CHAPTER 7
CHASTITY, 2015

This couldn't be happening. She wasn't ready. Not even close to ready. Why was he down on one knee? What was she supposed to do?

"Chastity, I love you, and I want to spend the rest of my life loving you. Please, will you marry me?" Brian asked in his calm, soothing voice. It was as if he knew she would feel like a cornered animal and was doing his best to reassure her that there was nothing to be scared of.

"I ... I ... I'm not sure I'm ready for marriage, Brian," Chastity sputtered.

Brian appeared to be ready for her rejection because he had his next response ready. "I believe you are, and I also know that we are perfect and right together. I want to be your husband more than anything. Please, Chastity. Please, will you do me this great honor and marry me?"

"I ... yes, yes, I will marry you," Chastity said. She felt like her heart was going to erupt from her chest. Was this a panic attack, or was it normal to feel light-headed and like you might be dying a little when you're proposed to?

Immediately after uttering those words, Chastity heard

clapping. Her vision was tunneled on Brian and the ring he now produced from his pocket. Where was this clapping coming from?

Brian took Chastity's hand and slid the ring on her finger. She was pretty sure it was tight—too tight, like it was cutting off the circulation to her brain. Brian stood up briskly, grabbed her by the sides of her head, and kissed her deeply. She had never been kissed like that. She really wished he had waited for the kiss because she was still grappling with everything that had just transpired in the last two minutes. She wasn't even sure she was kissing him back or if she even knew how to. Ending the kiss, Brian grabbed her hand again and held it high up in the air above their heads. Why was he doing this?

It was then that Chastity's vision expanded to include the world beyond Brian and the ring. When she looked around, her entire family was coming out from behind umbrellas, cheering loudly for her. What Chastity had assumed were other beachgoers turned out to be a large gathering of her family and friends. Everyone rushed to her to offer their sincere congratulations and share in her excitement.

The only problem was that she couldn't tell if she was excited or about to be violently sick right there on the sand. Suddenly, she was very warm, and that perfect day seemed to have turned on her. It was now sticky hot, and she was sweating down her neck and back.

She just needed to calm down. This was the happiest moment in her life. She was happy. She was just a little overwhelmed. She never liked being the center of attention, and in this moment, it was as if everyone she had ever known was showering her with theirs.

Brian swept her up in his arms, and she felt better. She could breathe again, and the sweat subsided a little.

"Brian, I'm feeling flustered," she muttered under her breath so that no one else could hear the doubt in her voice.

Brian, being the wonderful man he was, said the exact thing she needed to hear in that moment.

"Don't worry, I've got you," he said, and Chastity knew he meant it with his whole heart. "Let's take a swim," Brian said, still holding her firmly in his arms.

Chastity grinned. He carried her down to the shoreline and past the waves breaking in the water to a place where it was just the two of them for a moment. Brian knew how to help her collect herself. Brian knew her and loved her. He was the answer to every prayer.

Chastity was just calming down and starting to feel some of the excitement that everyone else was feeling when Brian slid his hand up her stomach and under her bathing suit top.

CHAPTER 8
CHASTITY, 2015

Chastity was shocked, horrified, and felt completely adrift. Did Brian think that just because he had proposed, she would be willing to change her stance on intimacy before marriage?

Chastity reached for the hand Brian had placed under her top and gently brought it back into the water surrounding her. "Brian, I still have the same beliefs I had about intimacy before marriage," she stated firmly but not angrily.

"I know. I'm sorry. I went too far. It's just that I'm so excited, and I absolutely can't wait to make you mine!" Brian said that last part in an exhilarated shout, so much so that everyone on the beach began a new round of cheers for the happy couple. Chastity smiled, glad to hear that he was still on the same page and that he acknowledged his wrongdoing. She didn't feel ready for anything physical, but she knew that eventually, she would have said yes to marrying Brian, and he was ready and waiting for her now.

Chastity closed her eyes and took in a deep breath through her nose and let it out through her mouth. She wasn't ready for anything beyond kissing, but now that they were engaged, she did want to give Brian a little more of herself. So, Chastity traced her hands up Brian's neck and into his hair. She was thinking about how thankful she was that he no longer came to her for haircuts; his hair now looked perfect with gentle curls beginning to form from the sticky brine of the saltwater. Chastity had never really touched Brian—other than the traditional side hug most Southern Baptists had perfected in their young adulthood—so putting her hands in his hair was very scandalous, all things considered. Brian made a sound in the back of his throat, something that was a cross between a hum and a sigh. A rush of blood filled Chastity's ears as she savored the knowledge that she was the source of his happiness. With her hands in his hair, she gently tilted his head down to hers, gave him the beginning of a kiss, and silently opened her mouth to him. Chastity fully surrendered to this kiss, and Brian made the absolute most of it, claiming the space she had just surrendered.

CHAPTER 9
CHASTITY, 2016

It had been six months since the proposal at the beach, and time had been on some sort of hyperdrive. Months passed in what felt like weeks, and days just flashed by.

Chastity stood in the bridal suite of the church she had grown up in. She was trying to stay present in the moment. She wanted to fully remember this and not have it rush by in a flash like the last six months had.

Susan and Richard Montgomery were both elated when their daughter had said yes to Brian. Apparently, Brian had met them in the week leading up to the proposal to ask for their permission and blessing. Chastity knew her parents had expected this, and she was grateful that Brian took the extra step of not only getting their permission but also including them in the proposal day. She wanted her parents to be there. She needed them to see that she had done it; she had grown into the Christian woman they had worked so hard to help her become.

Now, she was standing in the bridal suite, looking at her reflection. She was wearing the dress her mom had helped her pick for the rehearsal dinner. It was a long-sleeved blue dress that ended just below her knees. Because it was still wintertime, she had wanted to wear a two-piece pantsuit, but her mom had encouraged her to go with the dress because it was the more elegant choice. The dress was pretty; it just didn't feel like her, but if it made her mom happy, Chastity was willing to put it on. It was just for this one night.

The wedding had been planned by a group of women in Chastity's inner circle: her mom, and grandmother, two of the girls from the salon where she worked, and several other women from her church. Chastity was so grateful for these women who seemed to relish the idea of wedding planning. She, on the other hand, despised it. All she wanted to do was go to the courthouse and get it over with, but she knew that a church wedding was expected. Her dad would be marrying them, and her mom was making the cake and decorating the venue. Brian's family didn't come from wealth, so he had been working multiple shifts at the hardware store his family ran to contribute to the wedding (although Chastity's parents were more than happy to cover all of the costs). Everything was planned down to the minute, and every last detail was covered. All Chastity had to do was show up at the appointed time, walk down the aisle, and repeat after her dad.

Now that it was time for the rehearsal, Chastity felt that same sweaty, sticky feeling she had the day of the proposal. The walls seemed to be closing in, and suddenly she wasn't in a bridal suite but a coffin of her own making.

Chastity knew she was just being dramatic. One thing she had learned from her time at Restorative Hope was that she was prone to dramatic responses, and these were almost never helpful in real-life situations (or so her counselors had told her). Chastity wasn't going to be dramatic this time. She was dressed for her part and more than capable of performing it.

Susan knocked on the door. "Are you ready, sweetie?" she asked.

"Sure," Chastity said too quickly and with too much spunk.

Susan paused, hearing something in her daughter's voice that she knew from long ago. She knew her daughter better than anyone. She loved her deeply and truly. So, she paused for the briefest of moments, leaving a space for Chastity to speak and give voice to her concerns.

Chastity had been here before. Her worries had always been the same: What if Restorative Hope didn't actually work like it was supposed to? What if she were secretly gay? What would happen if she didn't walk down this aisle to Brian?

Chastity voiced none of these thoughts and simply put on her brightest smile. "You bet," she said, walking out of the bridal suite and into the foyer, where she would wait for "Canon in D" to play. Then the doors would open, and she would walk boldly into her future without doubt and without looking back.

CHAPTER 10
CHASTITY, 2016

The rehearsal went off without a hitch. Everyone talked about how lovely her dad's service was and how meaningful this day would be for the whole family.

Chastity was feeling better since leaving the bridal suite behind. Once the doors opened and she spotted Brian standing next to her dad, it felt right to walk down the aisle to him. Early in their relationship, she had shared her lingering doubts and her time at Restorative Hope with Brian. He had never once batted an eye at her history or her concerns. He sat quietly and listened every time she needed to talk through her feelings. She knew he really was a great match for her.

Now, Chastity was saying goodnight to Brian and going back to her bedroom on the third floor of their Savannah home for the last time.

Chastity and Brian had perfected their rhythm of kissing, so it felt like a strange dance they knew all the steps to. She often let him claim her mouth without reservation, as long as he kept it to just kissing. She knew this would be her last goodnight kiss as a virgin, and she wondered if kissing would feel different after she knew what sex was like—would it seem strange to spend hours kissing if you knew you could be making love? Chastity liked kissing Brian and was sad to think that this might shift when their intimacy shifted. He had a sweet peppermint smell to him and often tasted like Red Bull. He found his rhythm in time with hers, and they would kiss until both of their mouths were red and puffy from hours of friction between them.

Brian made this goodnight kiss count. He started by tangling his hands in the curls of her hair and then cupped the back of her head. He stroked her cheek gently, and when she tilted her head to allow him access to her mouth, he simply grazed her lips with his. She opened her mouth to him and attempted to bring his top lip into her mouth to get things started, but Brian was in no apparent rush. He was enjoying the tension he was building in her. Chastity knew that she liked kissing Brian and that he liked kissing her, but she wasn't the most patient person when it came to physical touch and just really wanted to get to the good parts. But Brian wouldn't give in despite her sigh of impatience when he would not open his mouth to receive her. He simply let out a soft laugh and whispered in her ear, "Are you ready for tomorrow night? I want to taste more than your lips before I take you completely."

At this, Chastity had a true shiver down her spine that made all the hair on her arms and legs rise. "Yes," she replied while trying to continue the kiss. She wanted him to kiss her thoroughly so that she could go to bed and rest before tomorrow, but he was still holding out on her. "Are you going to kiss me or not?" she demanded with a bit of a pout. Brian laughed in earnest now and reached for her neck, firmly bringing her face directly to his. He claimed her mouth. He was everywhere she wanted him to be. She could only imagine if the kiss was this good, what it would be like to actually *be* with him. At that thought, Chastity got hot all over and started to feel like her clothes were suddenly too tight. Not this again. Why did this happen to her, this state where all of a sudden, the air was thick, and she couldn't seem to get enough of it down into her lungs? Chastity broke off the kiss, struggling to breathe through the panic. Brian misunderstood this as her being breathless from the depth and passion of the kiss.

Either way, Chastity was glad it was over for now and told Brian she would see him tomorrow. Brian gave her a knowing wink and said, "Goodnight, Mrs. Jacobs."

Chastity attempted a smile, walked into the house, and proceeded to have a full-fledged panic attack, leaning against the door she had just walked through.

CHAPTER 11
CHASTITY, 2016

It took Chastity the better part of an hour to collect herself, bringing all the shards of her soul, piece by piece, back into alignment. But once she was collected enough to move, she hastily shuffled up to her bedroom.

She would miss this room and all its comforts. Chastity sat on the edge of her bed, realizing that she hadn't even packed anything to move into Brian's house. She had a suitcase for the honeymoon (which was another source of anxiety, given that Brian kept the location and duration of their honeymoon a secret), but that was it. She hadn't packed any of her material belongings aside from clothes. She knew she was moving out, but some part of her was hanging on to the idea that this room would always be as it was in that moment. There was comfort in that. Knowing that she could come home and visit her room. Her safe place. Her shelter from the worst of life.

During her time at Restorative Hope, this room had been her lifeline. It helped keep her sane during times where she would have bet every penny she was worth that she was tipping over the edge into insanity. Chastity's poems remained on the walls surrounding the bay window and the table for two that currently held up the typewriter, as well as an old coffee cup she really should take downstairs to rinse. Chastity sat in her spot at the typewriter one last time. She wanted to write about these feelings she was having and get them out of her, but she couldn't—wouldn't—dare. The last thing she wrote about these feelings was her first journal entry that she presented to Megan, her counselor at Restorative Hope. It was her poem. The last line—"But I am not referring to a man"—echoed the feeling she was experiencing right now.

She loved Brian. Or she was pretty sure she loved him. She liked the way he smiled, and laughed, and kissed, and listened to her. She liked that they had common interests and that he had become her best friend over the last eleven months. Most of all, she liked that she could keep her parents and her brothers. If she pursued the other line of thinking, she would lose everything and everyone she loved. She could do this.

Chastity was lost in thought when there was a soft knock at her door.

"Come in," she announced absentmindedly.

"Honey, I think we need to talk," Susan said in such a soft and meek tone that for an instant, Chastity thought someone had died, but she soon realized this conversation was worse than a death announcement.

"You see, I need to have the same conversation with you that my mom had with me the night before my wedding to your father. There are some things that you need to know for ... the wedding night and the expectations Brian may have," Susan started awkwardly. "You already know that the Bible teaches us that sex within marriage is a gift from God. 1 Corinthians 7:3-5 states: 'Let the husband render to his wife the affection due to her, and likewise also the wife to her husband. Do not deprive one another except with consent for a time, that you may give yourselves to fasting and prayer; and come together again so that Satan does not tempt you because of your lack of self-control.' Chastity, that verse teaches us the importance of fulfilling our husbands' needs so that he does not stray into temptation. You know that in our faith, the husband must be given leadership of the home, and the wife's role is to submit. Ephesians 5:22 says, 'Wives, submit yourself unto your own husbands, as unto the Lord.' So, you will now be responsible for Brian's fulfillment. You will help him by being a servant to his leadership and a partner to him in life, and you will need to be ready to fulfill his needs to prevent any of his own sexual urges outside of your covenant. You should always be available to him," Susan concluded.

Oh my god, thought Chastity.

It isn't as if she hadn't heard this preaching throughout her whole upbringing, but hearing it issued so directly as another set of rules for her to become a model example of the Southern Baptist Christian woman, Chastity felt defeated. She had completed the Restorative Hope program, agreed to turn from her sinful nature, and spent her whole life ensuring she was pure, only to find that her purity had an expiration date, a price to be paid on her wedding night. Without any warning, Chastity started crying.

"Oh, honey, I know that sounds scary, and I am sorry for that. Sex really should be a great thing—it's a gift from God. Why are you crying?"

"Mom, I just don't think I can do this," Chastity said through the sobs she was failing to repress.

"Chastity, you can do this. You are a good woman, and you love Brian. This part sounds scarier than it is. I am sorry I frightened you; that was not my goal. My goal was to remind you of your upbringing and our beliefs around sex and marriage. I wanted you to know that things will likely be different once you are married and that is a good thing—a great thing." Susan's tone had changed from soft and concerned to firm and unyielding.

Chastity recognized the shift and the tone. She had heard it many times as she attended Restorative Hope. This wasn't a conversation where she would be able to ask questions or challenge anything that was said. This was a directive.

Susan patted her daughter on the head and told her to get a good night's rest and that she would see her in the morning.

Chastity was very certain there would be no rest. Her mind was a mess, and her emotions were high. On one hand, she wanted to give herself to Brian. He was kind and patient; he seemed to really understand her. Submitting to him should not be anything to be scared of. On the other hand, Chastity knew that something felt horribly off about the idea of sex and marriage as her mother had explained it.

Chastity decided to do something she hadn't done in ten years. She picked up the phone and dialed a number she still remembered from all those years ago.

"Hello," a familiar voice answered.

"Hey Jess, it's me, Chastity. I need to talk to you."

CHAPTER 12
CHASTITY, 2016

Chastity and Jess talked until the early hours of the former's wedding morning. They talked about where life had led them and how they were both doing. Hearing Jess's voice was like coming home after a really bad day. It was safe and right and transported Chastity back in time.

She could still feel the tension between them like a rising tide. Something inevitable that they both could feel coming. Chastity could practically taste the kiss from ten years ago. That kiss was a culmination of years of sharing everything. Good times and bad times, laughter and tears. Kissing Jess was a single moment of pure clarity on Chastity's part. It had just ended too abruptly, too soon.

Jess explained that over the last ten years, she had become a physical therapist and was currently working at a rehab center with adults who had suffered a stroke. Chastity learned that Jess was happy and in love with her wife of two years. She was living her truth and seemed all the happier for it. Chastity just couldn't comprehend what she was hearing. She was happy for Jess, of course she was, but Jess didn't sound like someone whose soul was suffering, damned to hell. She sounded healthy, well, and complete.

After a few hours of catching up, Jess did the thing she had always done best—she cut to the chase.

"So, Chas, what can I help you with? You said you needed to talk, so I'm assuming something's on your mind," Jess said.

"Jess, I'm supposed to be marrying a guy I have been dating for eleven months tomorrow, and I am freaking out. I'm not sure if I'm making the right decision, and I needed to talk to someone who understands what this feels like." Chastity felt free as soon as the words left her mouth. She needed this. She needed to be able to say what she was thinking, completely uncensored, and know that there would be no judgment or condemnation.

Jess was quiet for three beats of Chastity's heart. She knew Jess. She might not know everything from the last ten years, but she knew her as well as she knew herself. Jess was trying to sort through what to say and needed some time to process this big revelation from Chastity.

"Chas, I don't know how to help. When we were caught kissing, I thought for sure we would find a way to be together, but after you completed the program your parents sent you to, it was like contact with me was forbidden or painful—I'm not sure what happened, but it felt like you had changed your mind about me. I wasn't sure if I was a phase or just something fun to experiment with, but I knew myself, and I knew that I was gay. I never questioned it. It was as true as it is that the Earth is round or that the sky is blue. But I cannot make that determination for you. Only you can know what is real and true to you," Jess said sagely.

Chastity knew Jess was right, although she despised the answer. She just wanted someone to walk into the room and tell her what she should do. Should she risk it all for someone she didn't even know yet and hope and pray she had found a partner with whom she could share every part of herself? Or should she stand by her commitment to Brian, her family, and God?

This was really not something she should have waited until tonight to figure out. Completely exhausted, Chastity thanked Jess for the talk and told her that she hoped they wouldn't wait ten more years to talk again.

Jess hesitated before saying, "Chasity, I wish you well, I really do, and I am sure whatever you decide, you will make the most of it, but I don't think we should talk again. I'm in a happily committed relationship with the woman I love, and you are seeking help and comfort. I don't want to muddy the water for you as you sort through things. I will always love you and appreciate our time together, but I think this is goodbye."

Without further comment, Jess was gone, and the dial tone replaced her comforting voice.

CHAPTER 13
CHASTITY, 2016

Chastity slept for only an hour, waking up every five minutes, startled out of her fitful sleep. For someone who was supposed to be having one of the happiest days of her life, she certainly didn't look like it.

Chastity had deep purple bags under her eyes, and her hair was sticking up on all ends from the tossing and turning. Thankfully, her mom had hired a makeup artist and hair stylist who specialized in wedding updos to come to their home and get Chastity ready for her big day. Chastity had another hour or so before the team arrived. She needed to get up, shower, shave, and dry her hair, but she felt compelled to lie on this bed and rot. She had decided early this morning. She would marry Brian. She loved him. There was nothing wrong with her, and there were far more benefits to marrying Brian than there were to walking away and losing everything. Chastity had steeled herself in her decision and would not be swayed by any further "sinful" thoughts.

After an additional ten minutes of wallowing in bed, Chastity climbed out in a very sloth-like fashion and made her way to her shower. She stood in the shower, letting the stream fall down on her head, thick rivulets flowing from her hair to her breasts and down her abdomen. Chastity looked down. She had always shaved her armpits and her legs, but she had never done what she was currently contemplating. Why shave if no one was even going to see it? Chastity wasn't even sure how to shave that part of her body. Do you shave it all off or just part of it? If it's just part of it, which part? Chastity was not about to open up this conversation with her mom, so she decided to do her best. She had once heard one of her friends reference a "landing strip" when talking about their pubic hair, so she attempted to achieve that effect.

Once she was freshly showered and shaven, she stood in front of the full-length bedroom mirror in nothing but her skin. Nowhere to hide. This is what Brian would be seeing tonight. She had never thought much about her body. She always dressed modestly and, when given the option, chose pants over shorts or dresses and long sleeves over short sleeves (unless it was the dead of summer). The only person who had seen her naked as an adult was the gynecologist she had been going to for the last two years to get birth control for her heavy periods. That was hardly the same.

Chastity felt good in her skin. She was confident in her appearance. From all of her years playing sports and still picking up games of volleyball at the park, her body was slim, but she had curves in the places that most women seemed to want them. Had it been Chastity's choice, she would have had a more athletic build without curves, but she supposed this was what most people would want, so surely Brian would approve.

Chastity put on her robe and walked down the hall to the sitting room her mom had converted into a beauty salon just for her to get ready. Chastity plopped down in a very unladylike fashion and waited for the makeup artist and hair stylist to arrive.

She didn't have to wait long because three minutes later,

both ladies walked into the room. Suddenly, someone had placed a mimosa in Chastity's hands, and both women were now doting on her, getting her ready for the most important day of her life. She learned that her makeup artist was twenty-three years old, had studied cosmetology in school, and had recently gone back to get her esthetician's license. Her name was Tara, and she was the quieter of the two helpers, but she checked in on Chastity often, asking if she was okay or if she needed anything to make her more comfortable. Then there was Bess, the hair stylist, who was much chattier than her counterpart. Bess talked to Chastity even when the latter had stopped responding. Chastity soon realized Bess didn't need her to participate in the conversation to keep it going; Bess could manage that all on her own.

After two hours of non-stop prattle and hundreds of bobby pins and layers upon layers of makeup, the two deemed her ready. At some point, they had turned her chair away from the mirror her mother had placed in the makeshift salon, so Chastity had no idea what she looked like.

"Are you ready to see yourself?" asked Bess, practically bouncing on her toes with excitement.

"Yes," Chastity said with as much enthusiasm as she could muster.

"One, two, three ..." Bess turned her around to face the mirror.

Chastity looked stunning. Like "supermodel" stunning. Her hair was in a loose braid with some of her naturally curly ringlets hanging around her face, framing it. Tara had given her a smoky look with a soft cat eye that accentuated her almond-shaped eyes and pulled out more colors in her hazel irises. Chastity had never seen herself like this. Not this beautiful or this feminine. Seeing herself in this new light gave her the boost she needed. She was feeling beautiful and confident, and after last night, she knew she needed this.

"Oh, honey, you look stunning," Susan said, walking into the room.

Chastity quickly hid the mimosa glass she had emptied. Bess noticed her movement and quietly shuffled it into her bag with her other supplies. As a Southern Baptist, Chastity knew alcohol was not accepted, and she really didn't need the lecture from her mom today, so it was just easier to keep these little things hidden and to herself. Thankfully, Bess and Tara must have taken the hint, because neither of them said a word, and all traces of alcohol were long gone, packed away in some suitcase along with the hairdryer.

"Thanks, Mom." Chastity beamed. She was happy and excited. "I think I'm ready to go to the Church now."

CHAPTER 14
CHASTITY, 2016

"The ceremony was beautiful," one of the wedding guests said to Chastity and Brian as they entered the reception hall. Chastity wasn't sure if this guest was her family's or Brian's; she had seen so many faces she couldn't keep them all straight and wasn't even trying at this point. She felt like a doll being moved from place to place, smiling on command.

"Thank you," Chastity replied as Brian swept her into the middle of the dance floor.

Chastity wanted to dance, which is why the reception was being held a few blocks from the church in an old historic home that had been converted to a wedding venue. Dancing wasn't permitted at the church, but this was one of those rules that was bent by simply going to a different location. Suddenly, dancing was permissible. She was grateful for the dancing. It was something she understood, something with rules she could follow without fear of missteps.

In the months leading up to the wedding, Brian had paid for them to have ballroom dance classes so they would have a little routine for their song. It had a small lift and ended with him dipping her and planting a kiss on her lips. Chastity and Brian executed the whole thing flawlessly. The song she chose was one of her favorites: "Banana Pancakes" by Jack Johnson. This was the one real thing she had chosen for the whole day. It made her happy and felt like the happiest outlook for her future, like she was putting what she wanted for herself in a song and sending it into the universe.

After hours of dancing and revelry, Brian approached Chastity.

"Hey you, ready to get out of here?" he asked with a devilish grin.

"Can't we stay just a little longer?" Chastity pleaded.

"Sure we can, but don't you want to get to the honeymoon so we can start enjoying each other?" Brian persisted.

Chastity gave a nervous laugh. She saw the future in his eyes and felt a wave of nausea. He was ready. He was more than ready. She just wanted to keep dancing, to stay in this safe, sparkling bubble of a party where she didn't have to be a wife, just a bride. She couldn't put it off forever, and staying for thirty more minutes or five more hours really didn't make any difference at all. The end result would be her in bed with Brian tonight.

"Sounds great—we just need to let Mom know so she can gather everyone for our send-off," Chastity explained.

After about fifteen chaotic minutes of wrangling guests, everyone was lined up outside the venue in two rows, holding sparklers to light the path to their waiting car. It was beautiful, really. This might have been her favorite moment of the night. It was dark, and her path was literally sparkling in front of her. For the first time in the last six months, she felt like she was making the right choice by choosing to marry Brian. The sparkling path felt like a tangible, solid confirmation. She was an actress on a stage, and the audience was clapping for the perfect ending. It felt real, safe, and right.

They ran through the sparklers, and at the end of the path,

Brian grabbed her by the waist, put her in a dip, and kissed her. Everyone went wild for the smooth show of affection, and Brian opened the car door for Chastity.

Chastity climbed into the car, all smiles, and waved goodbye to her friends and family. The car door closed with a click that felt final. The lights of the sparklers disappeared behind the tinted window. The silence was deafening. The panic started to creep in, a cold, familiar knot in her stomach. It was happening. There was no turning back.

CHAPTER 15
CHASTITY, 2016

They arrived at the oceanfront beach house on Tybee just after 11 p.m. Brian was beaming; Chastity wouldn't have been surprised in the least if rays of sunshine had started shooting right out of his ears. She liked seeing him like this; she may have been nervous, but Brian's exuberance made her relax a little.

"I'll come back out to the car for our luggage—well, your one suitcase—in a bit," he said with a grin. "But first, I want to show you around our honeymoon home."

Chastity was grateful to see that they were staying in a somewhat local place, and it was exceptionally thoughtful of Brian to book a beautiful beach cottage at her very favorite beach. This was where they were engaged and where she had spent her summers growing up. This place felt like a home away from home, somewhere Chastity could figure things out at her own pace and be at peace.

A picture-perfect cottage, the house was perched on pilings that lifted it high into the air and allowed for parking underneath the structure. The cottage was a single story with a wrap-around, screened-in porch on the back of the house overlooking the ocean. It was exactly the type of place Chastity would have picked for herself. As they reached the open porch at the side of the house, Chastity was suddenly whisked into Brian's arms.

"Hello, Mrs. Jacobs—are you ready to see your home for the next two weeks?" Brian's voice was husky and warm and matched the feeling spreading through Chastity.

Wait, did he say TWO WEEKS?

"Brian, two weeks? We can't afford to miss that much work."

"Chastity, my love, why do you think I have been working so many shifts? I have saved enough for both of us to be off for two weeks and still have enough to cover all of our bills and even some extra for us to spend while we are here," Brian replied in a reassuring tone. He had thought of everything and had clearly been planning this since the proposal to have saved that much money.

Without further discussion, Brian shifted Chastity's willowy frame in his arms, turning to grab the door handle and push it open while holding her tight to his chest. She had to admit, this felt comforting, like a hug from her best friend when she felt like crawling out of her skin.

The door swung wide, and Brian stepped over the threshold. The house was set up with what had to be hundreds of glowing candles (the battery-powered kind that flicker) and rose petals leading from the front door all the way to what she assumed was the bedroom. A faint, almost imperceptible scent of cinnamon and lavender filled the air, a deliberate choice by Brian, but one that Chastity's overwhelmed senses could barely register. Her stomach lurched. She could pretend all they were going to do was hug and kiss, but the reality was fast approaching. Brian had waited eleven months for her, and it was time for her to keep her end of that bargain.

Thankfully, Brian knew her and loved her. He paused at the door and asked one simple question.

"Chastity, are you ready—actually ready for this?" He seemed reluctant to move forward into the house without her answering this one simple question first.

Chastity felt sick. She wanted to be with Brian. She chose this. Although she was prone to dramatic moments, this was not the time for one of them.

Chastity gave him what she hoped was a seductive smile and said, "Yes."

That was all the clearance Brian needed; he grinned wickedly and marched over the rose petals and into the bedroom. He gently set her on the edge of the bed in a seated position. Chastity had no clue what to do next. *Do we kiss? Do we undress? Do I undress myself, or does he do that?* Her eyes must have betrayed her and shown Brian the confusion and turmoil beneath the smile because he paused and sat down beside her. He took her trembling hand in his and gently traced small, calming circles on the back of her palm with his thumb.

"Chastity, thank you for waiting for me so that I could be the only person to have ever had you. I wish I had done the same for you, but I have spent the last eleven months imagining this moment, and I just wanted to say that you were worth the wait. I know this part may be scary, but it is you and me, babe. There is nothing to be afraid of. I have got you just like I always have." Brian's words were like a balm to all of the rough patches in her emotional fabric about not knowing how this went. It was Brian; he would take care of her. Chastity knew that.

"Brian, I love you," were the last words she spoke that night as he claimed her mouth.

CHAPTER 16
CHASTITY, 2016

Chastity woke up sometime around eleven the next morning. Her hair was a mess, and her eyes were puffy from the hard sleep, but she was surprisingly okay.

Last night, Brian had kept his promise and taken care of her in all the ways that mattered. He was tender and checked in often to ensure Chastity was okay and ready for the next steps.

Chastity was just recounting the events from the prior night when she felt a familiar rush of fluid from between her legs. This couldn't be happening on her honeymoon—her period wasn't due for two weeks. Chastity lunged from the bed to try to prevent any staining of the pristine white sheets on their king-size bed. That would be mortifying.

In the bathroom, she realized this wasn't her period. She knew about semen from health class, but she honestly had never thought about it beyond its use in making a baby, which she was taking birth control to prevent. Chastity wiped—this was sticky, and it smelled strange and foreign. Chastity's stomach rolled. This fresh reminder of her night with Brian brought on a new wave of emotion. If sex is a gift from God, why did she feel so uncertain about it even after she had done it?

Brian bounded into the bathroom while Chastity was trying to clean up.

"What are you doing in here?" she demanded.

"What do you mean? I've seen all of you now, babe, so there's no reason to be shy or modest. I figured you wouldn't mind me coming in to see my wife." Brian's voice sounded unsure if he had just made a horrible mistake, but his smile stayed firmly planted on his face.

"I think I'm still going to be a private person who likes their own space in the bathroom," Chastity blurted out.

Brian's cheeks turned red. "Right, of course. I'm sorry. I'll wait for you in the bedroom." And with that, he turned and walked out.

What was wrong with her? She was treating him like he had done something wrong, even though he hadn't. Chastity went over it all again in her head. She loved Brian. She had given herself to him, mind and body. Chastity was fulfilling her role as a Christian woman and now a wife. This was a good thing.

Then, why was this feeling so complicated?

"I'll just be a minute—I need to shower," Chastity called out. This sticky mess between her legs was unbearable; she needed to get clean. Really clean.

Thirty minutes later, Brian was waiting patiently on the bed when Chastity came out of the bathroom. If he noticed her splotchy face, he didn't comment on it. Chastity went directly to him, sat on his lap, and wrapped her arms around him in a hug.

"Hey, love, you know you can tell me if anything is wrong. Did I hurt you last night?" Brian asked with genuine concern.

"No, not at all. I think I'm just emotional from the high of the wedding and the bigger life changes coming, like moving in together. I'm fine. Really." Chastity leaned in and gave Brian a kiss on the cheek. Brian gently grabbed her chin between his thumb and forefinger and turned her head to him for a proper kiss. This part of her relationship was great. The kissing was never a problem. Having him kiss her the way he had before last night was a relief. Maybe everything wasn't as different as it seemed.

"I have one more surprise for you today," Brian whispered against the shell of her ear.

"Oh yeah, what is it?"

"Go to the living room and find out."

Chastity entered the living room to find what looked like a massage table looking out over the back deck and the sea beyond it. There was a robe lying on the table, and there was a woman in the room. She had strawberry-blonde hair; it was shaved on one side and cut to a short, blunt bob on the other. "Hi, I am Alex."

"Uh, hi, Alex—how can I help you?" Chastity was sufficiently confused.

Brian burst into laughter, which set Chastity's cheeks on fire. What was so funny?

"Babe, Alex is here to give you a massage. I booked two hours with her so you could relax while I went out fishing with some of my guys," he proudly announced.

Oh. *Oh no*. Chastity hadn't been alone in a room with a girl since that day with Jess and the kiss. Restorative Hope had made things perfectly clear. This was a no-no. This was going to tip her back into sinful thoughts if she wasn't careful. Brian knew about the program; why would he have her alone with a woman in a room by herself?

"Brian, can I just talk to you for one second in the bedroom?" Chastity did her best to seem elated and not frightened of herself at all.

Brian followed her back into the bedroom they had just emerged from.

"Brian, I can't be alone with girls. You know that. What am I supposed to do or say to Alex to explain this?" Chastity was clearly agitated.

"Mrs. Jacobs, I am not worried in the least about your past. You are mine, and I am yours, remember? That was a phase. You grew out of it. You married me and made love to me last night. I think we can safely put the program in the past," Brian said, sounding very self-assured.

Was Brian right? Maybe this was just the program talking loudly in her head. She hadn't even had an attraction to another woman since Jess. She had dated men and married Brian. Restorative Hope hadn't mentioned a timeline for when that rule could be abolished. Chastity realized Brian was staring at her with a look of genuine concern on his face. "Look, I feel like I keep getting it wrong—if you don't want to have a massage, you don't have to. I just thought it would be something nice I could offer to help you relax after all the excitement of the wedding. I can tell Alex to go if that would make you more comfortable." Brian's offer was sincere; she could tell.

"No, you're right. This is very sweet and thoughtful, and you are just the best for thinking of me! I think my time at Restorative Hope may have just confused me about relationships with girls, but this is a massage and not a relationship, so I have nothing to worry about. I chose you, and I know it was the right choice."

"Perfect!" Brian said, looking truly delighted. "The session is for two hours and includes a hot stone massage. I will be back in around four hours, and then we can go grab some lunch. Sound good?" Brian was again the handsome, happy-go-lucky guy she enjoyed spending time with. He was radiant with joy.

"Sounds great." Chastity's smile and enthusiasm were genuine.

With that, Brian hopped up off the bed, gave Chastity a kiss on the top of the head, and headed for the door.

"I love you, Mrs. Jacobs," he said with a cheeky grin.

"I love you too," Chastity replied.

In a couple more minutes, Chastity was looking at Alex and wondering what she was supposed to say or do next.

"Have you ever had a massage before, or is this your first one?" Alex said, breaking the ice.

"Oh, it is my first one."

"Okay, great—I am going to step out of the room for a few minutes and let you get undressed. You will then get under the covers on the table and face up to me. I will knock before I come back in so you can tell me if you are ready or not. Is there anything in particular you would like me to work on today?" Alex's demeanor was pure professionalism.

"Not really, I just want to try and relax," Chastity said.

"I am sure I can help with that," Alex said as she turned around and left the room.

Chastity knew she was going to be in the room with Alex. She had made her peace with it, but getting undressed? The same logic and rules applied. She had already been over this. Clothes or no clothes didn't matter. She was ready to trust herself to resist any temptation. She was married, so she was safe.

Chastity undressed as quickly as humanly possible to prevent any chance that Alex would come back and see her naked. She slid under the covers. They were blissfully warm—it was like sinking into a warm bath without getting wet. A few seconds went by, and as promised, Alex knocked on the door and waited for her reply.

"Come in," Chastity said.

"Are you comfortable? How is the table warmer, too hot?"

So that explains the warm sheets. Chastity thought. Out loud, she said, "It's perfect."

"Great, let's get started," Alex said with a quick smile.

Chastity was just settling into the warmth of the cover, her senses on high alert. She could hear the soft, rhythmic crash of the waves outside and the gentle hum of the table warmer beneath her. When Alex's lubricated hands finally rested on her neck, the initial contact was a feather-light pressure, professional and almost clinical, but a shiver still traced its way down Chastity's spine. As the hands slid slowly down her collarbones and then her shoulders, a profound sense of release, distinct from anything she had felt with Brian, washed over her. It wasn't passion, or duty, or fear. It was simply … peace. Chastity felt happy and at peace, and something a little more down in her gut. She felt right.

CHAPTER 17
CHASTITY, 2016

Alex was a consummate professional. She kept Chastity draped so that only one part of her body was showing at a time. First, Alex worked on her neck and shoulders, and then she folded the sheets back to reveal Chastity's left arm, then her right—all the while keeping Chastity covered and modest. The whole "being naked in a room with a stranger" thing suddenly didn't seem like such a big deal.

Her touch was gentle but coaxing. Like her hands knew exactly how to tell Chastity's body to relax. Chastity realized this was the first moment in ten years that she could feel her body and mind in alignment. She would have been upset or confused if she wasn't being coaxed so tenderly by Alex's hands to relax and lean into herself.

As Alex moved to her legs, Chastity realized she had never had anyone (even Brian) touch her with such deft motions. It felt like Alex was everywhere, but somehow Chastity was still left craving more of the contact. More of the connection. Her body began responding to the massage. Her muscles loosened, and her breathing deepened. She was fully present within herself.

After Alex finished with her legs, she lifted the covers and looked away, telling Chastity it was time to flip over onto her stomach so that Alex could have access to the back half of her body and to complete the hot stone portion of the massage.

Chastity panicked; she did not want Alex to stop touching her for a single second of their two hours together.

"I know I'm supposed to get a hot stone, but your hands feel incredible. Would it be okay if we skipped the stones and you just massaged me the whole time? We will still pay whatever it costs for the stones, of course, but I just think this is helping so much more than a stone ever could."

"Of course, we can do that," Alex said. "I'm so glad you are enjoying the massage."

"You know, I'm not sure 'enjoying' fully covers the experience," Chastity quipped. "'Life-altering' may be more like it." And then she laughed. To be specific, she came down with an embarrassing bout of the giggles.

"Sorry, I have no idea what that was about," she said once she had regained her composure.

"You have every right to be happy/giddy," Alex said. "You are a new bride; it's to be expected."

And just like that, Chastity came crashing back into herself. Her shoulders tensed, and her spine went rigid, a physical manifestation of the memories that flooded back. She was a bride to a man. Brian. She had given herself to him last night, but the touch felt full of obligation. Not that he was demanding or had said anything about his expectations; it's just that she knew her role. It had been explained to her in great detail by her mom the night before her wedding.

"Hey," Alex said softly, pulling Chastity back to the here and now. "Where did you go? Your body tensed up, and you aren't relaxing anymore. Is everything okay?"

It was like Alex was reading her mind and not just her body.

"Yes, I'm good. Sorry."

"No need to apologize; I was just checking on you. Do you need a break or some water?"

"No, I'm good, please continue." Chastity knew that if she could just feel the movement of Alex's hands across her body, she would regain the composure she had lost, stumbling around in her brain.

"Your name is Chastity, right?" Alex interrupted her attempt at Zen.

"Mmmm hmmm." Chastity let out a soft moan at the graze of Alex's hand moving down her lower back.

"Well, Chastity, massage therapists are like barbers; we don't mind if people want to talk to us during their session. If you decide that you want to talk, I'll be right here."

Chastity considered this for a few moments. On the one hand, she hadn't had a meaningful friendship with a woman in ten years. She missed the connection—the feeling of having someone she could relate with so perfectly, who would know her inside and out. She had spent the last decade masking her real voice, giving everyone what they wanted and needed her to be outwardly. She knew Alex wasn't offering to become her new best friend, but even just the offer to listen for the two hours they were together felt like something Chastity couldn't pass up.

"Actually, that would be great—it has been ... a long time since I had some girl talk," Chastity said through the hole in the face cradle of the massage table. Why had she waited until she was face down to talk to Alex? This was going to be so weird; she was practically blabbing at the floor, but the offer of a friendship, however brief, was too tempting to deny.

"Oh, I'm not so sure I'm great at 'girl talk,'" Alex said, and Chastity could hear the small smile in her voice. "But I guess that depends on what you have in mind."

Chastity filled the next hour with non-stop talking about everything she was feeling. She told Alex about how it felt strange to be married to a man when she would have bet ten years earlier that she was gay and would end up with a woman. She told her about her family and about the church she was a member of, and how the pressures there made her feel like a lightning bug in a jar. Someone was always watching and waiting for her to do something, but the only thing she truly wanted to do was fly away.

Alex continued to rub away every anxiety and every fear throughout Chastity's monologue, offering very little feedback, but a very real and present listening ear. For some reason, Chastity felt like Alex might actually understand what she was saying and the things she was feeling. Maybe it was just the skin-to-skin contact, but to Chastity, they felt connected internally.

It was almost time for Alex to go, so she started to pull the cover back up to cover Chastity's entire back. Then, she pressed the warm sheets into her back, soaking up some of the lotion that was coating her. "That will end my service with you," Alex said in her hushed tone. "Take your time getting up and getting dressed. I will go into the kitchen and get you a glass of water, and I will knock before I come back in."

Chastity was so slow to move this time, unlike the rushed undressing and jumping under the covers at the start of the session. She didn't really care if Alex came back and caught her still lying on the massage table. Instead of jumping back into her clothes, Chastity opted for the robe that was draped on the back of the dining chair next to the massage table. She wanted to keep this feeling of warmth and comfort for as long as she possibly could. She relished the feel of Alex's hands and didn't want her clothing to disrupt her savoring of every last touch.

Alex knocked and presented her with the promised water. "You need to drink plenty of water after a massage," she prompted in a rote fashion; she must have to say this at the end of every session, Chastity realized.

"Thank you for being exactly what I needed today, Alex," Chastity said with a small, almost sad smile.

Alex noticed. "Chastity, it was a pleasure meeting you today. I hope to see you again sometime." Again, all business.

Chastity agreed with the sentiment and went to grab the tip for Alex out of her purse. When she bent over to grab her cash, the tie on her robe loosened, and she realized her chest was exposed.

Alex noticed, but quickly looked away, keeping her professionalism intact.

Chastity wasn't sure she wanted her to. For a split second, an electric impulse shot through her—a fleeting instinct to say something, to leave the robe open, to see what would happen. But the thought was quickly followed by a cold wave of shame and the familiar panic. This was a sin. This was the exact "temptation" her parents had warned her about. Her hand flew to the tie, yanking it tight, a frantic act to cover herself and the unwanted feelings.

"I'm so sorry," Chastity blurted out, her cheeks burning. "That was so unprofessional of me."

Chastity saw a flicker in Alex's eyes—a brief, knowing glance that seemed to hold a world of understanding, as if Alex had seen not just her exposed body, but also her unbared vulnerability.

Alex walked over to Chastity and took her hands in each of her own. With Chastity's hands in Alex's control, the tie loosened and revealed her again to Alex.

Alex released her hands so that she was in control of the moment. She stood there for a long beat, not tying the robe, and the silence stretched between them, no longer awkward but full of a new, fragile honesty.

CHAPTER 18
CHASTITY, 2016

After a beat of silence, Alex gently reached out and re-tied Chastity's robe, but her touch lingered for a moment—too long to be casual. Chastity didn't flinch or pull away. She accepted the gesture for what she was sure it was: a gesture of care and respect, not of modesty or shame. Alex had seen her, understood her, and accepted her.

Alex started the process of collecting her things and loading them into the car. Chastity remained wrapped in the robe, but had taken up residence on a lounge chair on the back porch. Alex came through the sliding glass doors.

"Chastity, I have another appointment on the north side of the island in thirty minutes, so I need to head out, but I want you to have my number." She gave Chastity a business card that had her full name, Alex Henderson, as well as her cell phone number. Chastity tucked it into the pocket of her robe, currently unsure of what she would do with that information.

"Thank you for everything, Alex, and please, call me Chas."

CHAPTER 19
CHAS, 2016

A few hours later, Chas was still lounging on the back porch, wrapped in the robe with Alex's number tucked safely inside. She heard the crunch of gravel and loud, rowdy laughter from below the house. Brian was home, and it sounded like he had company? Great, she was still trying to process her feelings about the time spent with Alex. Engaging with Brian at this time would be hard enough, but she most definitely did not feel like entertaining guests.

Chas lurched up to her feet and made a beeline for the bedroom, closing the door. She didn't want to change out of the robe. It was the last thing Alex had touched, and it felt like a vital part of her now. She had just committed what could have been the single biggest act of defiance against her beliefs, her family, Restorative Hope, and Brian, and she had done it in this robe. She needed to hold on to that feeling, to that moment. She wasn't ready to part with it.

Brian's laughter was loud and drawing closer, along with the sounds of other guests in the house. "Hang tight, guys, I'm going to check on the little Mrs. I'll be back in a few—or maybe a little longer." Chas heard his comment and the boisterous laughter that followed.

Brian opened the door to find Chas sitting on the side of the bed in her robe, looking out at the ocean. "There's my wife," he proclaimed with the authority of a Christian man coming home to his kingdom.

"Here I am," Chas replied in a sarcastic tone.

"Hey, what's wrong? I just got back, and you already seem ticked at me. I missed you," Brian said, genuinely confused.

"Brian, I'm a private person. I heard what you said to your friends, and it felt like you were bragging about coming in here and having sex with me—that is embarrassing and I don't like it," Chas said, firm but calm.

"Look, it isn't like I'm going to whip out my dick and make you do anything. It was just guy talk, lighten up. You've been in a bad mood since we got here, and I'm just trying to have a good time," Brian said, moving closer to her. Chas caught the scent of something a little ... skunky.

"Brian, are you high?" Chas demanded.

"No, I just had a few beers with the guys. I'm not high, and you really are making this into something when it doesn't have to be," Brian said, less patient than she had ever seen him.

Chas needed to check herself. She was the one in the wrong today. She had crossed a line. Brian was right—she had been a mess since getting here and pretty much stayed cross with him for one thing or another. This was not the kind of wife she wanted to become; she could never stand the sound of someone nagging. "I'm sorry, you're right. I haven't shown you enough grace for the learning curve that we're going through, and I'm sure it seems like I'm just running around, griping at everything you do. Please don't be mad at me. I will work on my attitude from here forward," Chas said in a small tone.

"Chastity, you don't owe me an apology. I'm sorry I was short-tempered. I probably shouldn't have had so much to drink, and I'm sorry you heard what I said to the guys," replied Brian. "I'm just excited, and they all know I have waited eleven months to have you. They're happy for us—that's all."

Great, Chas thought, *all of his buddies now know my most intimate details.* If he was freely joking about coming in here to have sex with her, there was no way they hadn't talked about last night in nauseating detail. Chas thought about doubling down and again explaining why this was wrong, but she remembered what her mom had said. *He is the leader, and I am the servant to his leadership.* It wasn't worth arguing over something this trivial.

Brian didn't wait for any further explanation or comment from Chas; he came over to her side of the bed and put both of his hands in her hair and kissed her just the way she liked. There was no way Brian was going to convince her to have sex with a house full of guys waiting in the living room, but she was happy to kiss him and feel his warmth spread through her. But Brian didn't stop there; he let his hands wander past the folds of the robe onto her breast.

Chas pulled away slightly, but Brian mistook this as an invitation. He replaced his hand with his mouth. He pulled her nipple a little too strongly into his mouth, and she made a hissing sound, letting him know it was sensitive and it hurt. Brian took the hint and stopped sucking. He gave the nipple a small lick and a kiss, easing the hurt. "There is more where that came from, baby—just wait until tonight," he said with a wink.

Brian left the bedroom with Chas's mind thrown into chaos. *Did that really just happen, and is he serious—two nights in a row?* She was still sore from last night.

For a brief moment, Chas wondered if she could just leave the house and never return. Instead, she settled on putting on her jeans and a sweater, her hair thrown in a messy bun, and heading down to the beach. Chas walked through the living room, where she saw the guys lounging on the couches and making small talk. She tried to make eye contact with no one, but she heard the catcalls.

The last sound she heard before the door closed was one of the guys saying that Brian must be the luckiest guy in the world.

Yeah, Chas thought, *but what about me? I am certainly not as lucky.*

CHAPTER 20
CHAS, 2016

Chas thought about what would happen if she just decided not to go back. There would be a search party, *Dateline* would do a segment on her as a missing new bride—basically, it would be a shitshow. She knew that she had no actual intention of disappearing, but somehow the thought that she could just walk away from it all and live in a shack by the sea settled her. She was hurt and mad and honestly just disappointed. Is this what marriage was going to be like the whole time? Brian was a good guy, a great guy even, but it boggled her mind that her whole life was spent being chaste and modest and private, and now in one single night, all of that had changed. Now, she was supposed to just, what, enjoy the attention Brian was lavishing on her and pretend that this was all normal? That her sex life and most intimate thoughts were up for general discussion because she was married?

Chas felt gross and stormy and angry, and her blood felt hot under her skin, making her feel like she would burst into flames at any moment. She needed to cool down. This was her honeymoon, and if she wasn't careful, she would ruin it for both of them.

Chas had already let herself do one incredibly bold thing today—why not make it two? If her whole life was modesty, and that was being abolished in one night, she was going to be the one controlling that transition. Chas stripped off her sweatshirt and her jeans and was left standing on the beach in the moonlight in the wintertime in nothing but her underwear. There was nobody to see this act of defiance, but she knew that this was something she was controlling. What would happen next was her decision.

As Chas stood in the moonlight, the salty breeze was cold and damp on her skin. She needed to make a choice. Just standing here in her underwear on the beach in the dead of winter was bold, but it wasn't enough to cool the raging inferno happening beneath her skin. She was boiling. Raging. Chas was pissed. She looked up to the sky and knew exactly who this anger was addressed to.

"God, why would you make me this way if it's so sinful to act on my feelings?" Chas said quietly into the air. "Is this some sort of test to see how much I can withstand?" She could see her breath steaming as she spoke to God. She had prayed for answers for years. She had looked for those answers everywhere, and when she found Brian, she was sure he was the answer. But why would answered prayers feel more wrong and unnatural than the sin? Her parents would say that sin is designed to make you want it, and that is how you know it is the wrong thing. But if the right thing feels wrong, and the wrong thing feels right, how is anyone supposed to function at all?

Chas looked up at the stars, hoping for an answer but knowing she wouldn't get one (or at least not one she could understand clearly).

She was close to the edge of something—something she wasn't sure of. Instead of standing here and working through all of the thoughts and feelings over the past twenty-four hours, Chas took off, running directly into the water.

The water hit her like a block of ice straight to the gut. This was crazy, and she knew it. If anyone saw her in the middle of this tortured state, they would have her taken away for intense psychiatric care. Maybe she needed it.

She was thigh deep when she heard Brian's frantic call from down the beach.

"Chastity Montgomery Jacobs! What in God's name are you doing?!"

This would be the moment to turn around and just lie, say she had to pee and didn't want her clothes to get wet, or something equally lame.

Chas couldn't bring herself to walk back out of the freezing water. She pushed forward deeper into the icy waves. Her teeth were chattering furiously, and her breath was coming out in short puffs now. The water was past her navel. Brian was now yelling. He was practically screaming at her.

"Chastity, get out of the water! This isn't funny; this is dangerous!" Brian's fury was rolling off him in waves as big as the ones around her.

Chas just pushed out further. The water was neck-high now, and the cold had numbed her body, making her feel disconnected from the sting. The ice water began to feel less like a threat and more like a comfort on her burning skin.

All that was left to do was to go under.

Chas took another short puff of breath and submerged herself completely—to Brian's utter horror. He was about to watch his new wife drown.

Below the surface, Chas was free.

CHAPTER 21
CHAS, 2016

Chas wasn't entirely sure what she hoped to accomplish with this stunt. She knew she couldn't wade in the water forever, and if she stayed out there much longer, Brian was likely to call the police or an ambulance.

Chas surfaced for a breath of air and heard Brian's ongoing shrieks for her to come out of the water. She didn't reply, nor did she stay above the water where he could see her. She dipped back down below the waves for one last moment of peace before she would need to head back to the shore.

By this point, all of Brian's friends had heard the commotion and come out onto the beach. They were all standing there in total shock. Two of them had their hands in their hair as if they might yank it out, one stood with his hand over his mouth, and then there was Brian, running frantically back and forth in a short line. Chas would have laughed at the picture if she hadn't been busy trying to figure out what to say when she eventually emerged from the water.

Chas understood that this was about to be rough, but at least she wouldn't be the hot-headed one this time. Brian was clearly losing it, and she was feeling nothing but relief. Chas was sure that the moment her toes left the icy grip of the sea, she would be back in that all-too-familiar cycle of not knowing what to do, asking for help and answers that wouldn't come, and then pushing everything she wanted aside to ensure she was doing the Christian thing. The right thing.

Chas started to make her way back toward the shore. Brian looked instantly relieved to see her motion shifting from going deeper to pulling back toward him. Chas looked directly into his eyes. She was not ashamed of her behavior. She would not look down or give him the satisfaction of thinking that she had come to her senses and knew what she was doing was wrong. What feels right to one person isn't always the right thing for someone else. Her late-night winter swim was needed for *her*. He could choose to understand or not, but she would not be explaining herself or backing down.

When Chas was only knee-deep in the water, Brian realized she was in her underwear, and given that those were white, she was basically nude on the beach. Brian told his buddies that he needed to call it a night and that he would catch up with them later, and sent them on their way. By the time Chas was out of the water, Brian's friends were gone, and it was just the two of them.

Brian looked like he might cry or yell some more. Instead, he remained quiet, waiting for Chas to say something. Anything.

But Chas didn't feel like talking. Everything she had to say was somehow wrong. She didn't need his permission to go for a swim, even if it was the dead of winter, and it was dangerous. Chas's teeth started to chatter. She attempted to lock her jaw tight so she was in control of this situation, but that only caused her other body parts to twitch and shake.

She was cold, verging on hypothermic, and instead of worrying about her safety, she was having a battle of the wills with her husband, seeing who would break first.

Brian broke first. Without speaking, he simply walked up to

Chas, scooped her up in his arms, and walked back into the house. Chas thought he would set her down once they reentered the home, but she was mistaken. Brian carried her into the bathroom and set her down on the toilet. She was shivering all over in earnest now. Brian turned on the shower to a subtly warm temperature (but not hot), stripped off all of his clothes, picked Chas up again, and walked into the shower with her in his arms.

Chas was shocked. She expected anger or fighting. She wasn't ready for kindness and what looked like understanding from Brian. She felt like she was losing it, and in some ways, she wanted him to fight with her, so she had reason to want to walk away. But instead, he stayed right there in the shower, letting the water warm her, slowly increasing the temperature of the water every few minutes until Chas stopped chattering and was simply lying in his arms like a wet mop.

Shutting off the shower, Brian stepped onto the bathmat, dripping along the way. He didn't bother with a towel for himself, but instead set Chas upright in front of him. She wasn't cold anymore, but she felt more naked than ever before. Turns out, if you want to feel more naked than being naked, all you have to do is put on wet, see-through underwear, and suddenly you're the most naked thing ever to enter the world.

Brian still hadn't spoken. Neither had Chas. They would probably start fighting any minute. *Good*, Chas thought. She was ready for a fight. Brian reached behind her back with one arm and popped the button on her bra so that it was hanging freely from her arms. Chas was feeling very vulnerable. She wasn't sure what headspace she was in. Her act of defiance was to avoid this very situation, but she somehow found herself here despite that attempt. Brian placed his fingers on either side of her hip bones, tracing below the underwear line. He slowly pulled the saturated garments off her.

Chas was now properly naked. She started to feel cold again, but she was quite sure that her skin was still flushed with warmth.

Brian no longer looked panicked or angry. He looked hungry. Chas reminded herself that this was her responsibility. She had already put him through hell tonight; the least she could do would be to give in to this non-verbal request.

As Chas was starting to feel self-conscious, she noticed Brian was ready for her. There was no denying or wondering what he was thinking.

Brian still hadn't spoken, so Chas broke the spell. "Brian, I know you're mad, but I just had to do that for me."

Brian stepped forward, his expression still and unreadable. He put a hand on either side of her neck, his thumbs rubbing gently along her collarbones. The touch was the same as Alex's. Her body, without her permission, stopped its shivering. "Chastity," he said, his voice a low, final whisper. "I told you I don't want to talk about it." He said it like a threat, not a warning. She knew he had no idea what he was doing or the power that he held in that moment. Her heart was beating rapidly in her chest, but she didn't know if it was out of fear or excitement. Maybe it was both? Her mind was going back and forth, but her body had already made a decision for her.

She wasn't ready when his mouth claimed a whole new place on her. But she remembered her vows. She remembered her promise, and so she silently offered herself up for his enjoyment.

CHAPTER 22
CHAS, 2016

It had been one week since they said their vows and six days since her nocturnal swim. In that time, Brian and Chas never spoke about the swim again. It was as if her defiance was washed down the drain the night Brian had tentatively showered her to bring her body temperature back to normal.

Chas was feeling exhausted from the honeymoon. What started out as something so thoughtful—bringing her to the beach she loved—now felt almost like a strange form of punishment. The beach was empty day after day, and Brian kept leaving her to go fishing with his buddies, only to return at night and have her perform her wifely duties. She had performed something every night. She was so sore now that she thought she might have to tell him she needed a break from their lovemaking. She felt like she was quickly losing her "best friend" status and was now a figure solely for sexual fulfillment.

She knew Brian would die if she voiced these doubts aloud to him. He wasn't doing anything wrong. He was hungry for his wife in a way that felt insatiable. The only problem was his hunger wasn't being matched—at least not internally. Chas had figured out a perfect system. She would be in the robe when he arrived from his day of fishing. Brian would shower, and then he would come to bed still sticky with the warm steam of the shower rolling off him. He would claim her in whichever way he wanted for the evening, and then she would immediately get up to shower and try to prevent that foul rush of fluid from coming out in her underwear or on the sheets.

She hoped that this drive and desire would taper off. It was called the honeymoon phase for a reason. Maybe it was wrong to make him wait the whole time they were together before marriage. Maybe that had created this insatiable lust he seemed to have for her. She could tolerate the sex—maybe could even like it someday if they would take breaks and let her soreness subside, but what she was finding intolerable was the fact that she seemed to have shifted from someone he wanted to do things *with* to a plaything he wanted to do things *to*.

Chas was sitting alone in her robe (which was now her daily attire) on the back porch, thinking it all over, when she saw someone walking along the beach near the ocean's edge. They were a fair way down the beach and headed in her direction, but she knew. Somehow, she knew this was Alex. She wasn't sure if it was intentional or if Alex lived nearby and was just out for a walk. She didn't care. It was Alex, and she was coming toward her.

Chas jumped up and realized she was a mess. Aside from being in the same robe Alex had left her in six days ago, her hair was a mess of curls that went every which way because of her frequent showers and then not taking the time to dry her hair afterward. She mostly just poured herself into bed after her nightly shower and fell quickly and soundly asleep. How could she salvage the look? Chas grabbed her favorite pair of jeans and a Stevie Nicks T-shirt, threw her hair in a messy bun, and took off down the steps toward Alex.

Chas couldn't breathe. But this was not the kind of breathlessness that felt like an elephant was sitting on her chest, the kind she felt when Brian arrived home each day. *This* was the kind of breathlessness where she was having trouble remembering to breathe because her thoughts were wholly consumed by someone else.

As Alex came closer, Chas could see her smile. She could see the same muscular arms that had massaged away all of her tension that day. She could see the hands that had gently tied her robe back for her. Alex's face was exactly as she remembered it. Chas hadn't noticed her eyes last time … they were green, but not Kelly green. They were the green of the ocean she went swimming in a few nights ago. Calm, deep, and fierce.

"Hey Chas, how have you been? I wasn't sure if you would still be here or if your vacation had ended already." Alex smiled as she approached her. Was she real or just in Chas's head? Chas noticed Alex's use of the word "vacation" instead of "honeymoon" and was instantly grateful for her intentional choice of words.

"Alex, hi, I'm so happy to see you. We're here for one more week." Chas was so relieved to see Alex that she didn't even care that she was audibly out of breath when she spoke.

"Wow, that is a long … vacation. Well, if you are staying in town for that long, we should grab a bite to eat or a coffee or something." Alex's offer was like a lifeline.

"I would love that." Chas's excited reply came without hesitation.

"Okay, great, we will plan for it." Alex sounded like she was ending the conversation, but Chas was desperate to keep it going.

"Would you like to come up to the house?" Chastity knew this was bold and could be off-putting, especially since Alex had clearly offered to see her in a public space, and Chas was now offering to bring her back to a very private place where they had already crossed a line.

"Chas, I like you, a lot, but I'm scared that if I come up there, things are going to go in a direction that may hurt one or both of us." Alex's voice was full of pain.

"Right, I completely understand." Chas felt deflated. She tried not to let it show, but she knew Alex picked up on every shift in her emotions the instant they happened.

Alex raised her hand haltingly and tucked a rogue curl that was blowing in front of Chas's face behind her ear. The touch was so delicate it made Chas feel a strange pull low in her abdomen. How could Alex have this effect on her just by touching her hair?

"If we stay outside and on the porch, I would love to spend some time with you," Alex offered, seeing the hurt and struggle Chas was dealing with.

Chas beamed. She wasn't trying to make anything happen, but she needed Alex like she needed air. The two walked back up the steps to the screened-in back porch. Chas chose her favorite lounge chair, and Alex picked the spot facing her. A safe distance away, Chas noted, a little disappointed.

"So do you live around here?" Chas asked.

"Uh, no, actually, I live on the north side of the island," Alex replied.

Chas's heart was racing. She could feel the blood rushing around in her gut and between her legs.

"Well then, Alex," Chas said with a raised eyebrow, "why were you on the beach near my house?"

A beat of silence stretched between them, thick with the unspoken question. Chas waited, her breath caught in her throat.

"I needed to see you."

Alex had given voice to the feeling Chas was too afraid to express. Alex needed to see her as much as she needed to see Alex.

CHAPTER 23
CHAS, 2016

Chas and Alex spent hours together that day on the porch. Chas wanted to feel her hands even if just to hold them, but she knew that reaching for Alex in that way would likely just push her away.

Their conversation flowed naturally, and it gave Chas the sense of connection she had been longing for. Chas mostly wanted to listen to Alex and learn everything she could about this person who seemed to encompass all her thoughts. Alex shared that her dad had passed away several years earlier, but that her mom was living on the island as well, just a few streets down from Chas's beach cottage. Alex and her mom were not particularly close until her dad's death, but since then, they had had a much stronger connection.

Alex explained that their bond grew exponentially when she came out as a lesbian (six months after her dad passed away). Her mom's reaction was one of pure joy for her daughter. Alex's mom was one of those who went out and bought all of the pride paraphernalia and was currently flying a pride flag at her house in support of her daughter, according to Alex. Chas thought that she sounded like every queer person's dream parent.

"What about God and sin? Are you at all worried about your soul or the eternity they say you will spend in hell?" Chas could not believe she had just asked that question. It sounded harsh and judgmental, all of the things she despised about her church and how they treated people who were different.

Alex handled it with great grace and tact. "Well, I actually do believe in God—I just don't believe in organized religion. I think that each person's relationship with God is meant to be intentional and personal to them. I talk to God often and pray and ask for guidance, but he has never once made me feel like I'm going to hell or that I'm wrong for being who I am. Only Christian people have done that, actually. But God … never."

What Alex said felt profound. Why hadn't Chas come to any of these conclusions for herself? She only felt bad about her "sinful decisions" when someone human had told her to. God had never given her any internal feeling of wrongness. In fact, the only time she felt "wrong" on the inside was when she was following "the rules" that were set before her by the church.

Alex saw or felt the shift in Chas with this new revelation. "Chas, did something happen to you with the church?"

Chas felt her face go flush and her eyes pricking with tears. *Oh great, this is a good first look ... Hi, come over and talk to me for hours, and I will burst into tears.*

Alex noticed immediately. She stood up, crossed the space between them, and grabbed Chas's hand. Chas was so startled by the sudden movement that her feelings scattered temporarily, and she was solely focused on that one point of connection between them—their hands. Alex's hands felt amazing. They were soft (probably from all of that lotion she had to rub on people every day), but they were larger than hers, which felt tiny in comparison.

Alex was tugging Chas out of her seat and down the back steps towards the ocean. "Where are we going?" Chas said, breathless from the sudden change.

"I had a feeling you may want to tell me more, but that you would need connection and grounding to get through whatever hard thing happened. You don't have to tell me, but I'm here, and I want to know if you want to share. I'm going to hold your hand until you either ask me to let go or finish your story. I know the water's cold, but I find that it centers me. I wanted you to be able to be near it or touch it if you needed the comfort."

Chas couldn't believe what she was hearing. Alex was drawn to the sea, but she was drawn to it even when it was cold and others would avoid it. Did Chas somehow feel this connection the night she was driven into the sea by her own madness?

Chas was very comfortable putting her feet in the water— she knew they would go numb soon after entering and that the feeling would shift into a pleasant one. She knew that feeling the initial icy sting against her feet would help her be present in her body in order to tell her story to Alex.

Chas wasn't sure how, but Alex knew her. Not in the way you know someone after years of friendship and time together. She knew her soul. Whatever Chas was made of, Alex was made of the same matter.

The sun was setting over the marsh, and Chas was standing in the water holding Alex's hand when Brian's car pulled into the driveway. Chas didn't hear the crunch of gravel over the sound of the sea.

Chas opened her mouth to begin to share her painful truth about Restorative Hope, her parents, and Brian, when Brian called out from the back porch.

"Chastity, can you please come here now?" It was a directive.

CHAPTER 24
CHAS, 2016

Brian made his way to the water's edge, unwilling to wait for Chas to conclude the conversation with Alex in any natural way. He wanted this to be awkward for her. Chas looked up at Alex, helpless. Alex simply smiled, gave her hand a squeeze, and said, "I need to get going anyway; see you around, Chas."

"Her name is Chastity," Brian said through clenched teeth.

"Hi, Mr. Jacobs, I was just walking the shoreline when Chas—tity and I ran into each other," Alex supplied, hoping to ease the palpable tension a little.

Chas hated the way the name "Chastity" sounded in Alex's voice. It felt wrong coming out of her mouth. To Alex, she was Chas.

"Right, well, have a good rest of your day," Brian said, remaining direct and unwilling to yield. They were done with the conversation now.

Chas was mortified at his behavior; he was treating her like a child. Chas only got out the words "Bye, Ale—" before Brian grabbed her by the elbow and directed her back to the stairs. He wasn't hurting her, but she was being physically maneuvered.

She was done with that. She got to the bottom of the steps and jerked her arm out of his grasp.

"Chastity, why was that masseuse here? Why were you holding hands? Why were you looking at her like that? And why on this Earth were you in the water again after the other night? I thought we settled all of that." Whatever emotion Brian was going through was not something Chas could understand. She couldn't tell if he was angry, hurt, or confused.

"Chastity, answer me, dammit; if you're going to act this way, then I at least deserve a reason."

"We're just friends, nothing happened. She was holding my hand because I was about to tell her about some of my past, and I felt a little shaky while I was recounting everything that led me here." There was no point in lying. It would do no good, and Brian did deserve the truth.

"Chastity, the look you had was not a look of friendship. I think we need to call your parents and have an emergency session at Restorative Hope."

Chas could not believe what she had just heard him say. Her stomach dropped as if she had been chucked off a high-rise building. That would have been preferable to this.

"No. God, please no. Brian. I can't do that again."

"Chastity, it won't be like last time. You made it through the program, and you got married. We knew there may be stumbling blocks along the way. Your mom told me when we started dating that Restorative Hope saved you. It brought you back to them. Now, I'm not comfortable with the way you were looking at her, and we need to put an end to this behavior before it spirals out of control."

"I said I can't." Chas was sobbing. The sobs wracked through her body, so strong she began to dry heave.

"Do you want to be married to me?"

The question was so simple and so direct. She had been internally grappling with that question since the proposal. She knew that although her feelings on God and her soul had started to change—that wouldn't matter to her parents. Their feelings would always be completely the same. She felt something deep and true and right with Alex, but she couldn't lose everyone and everything she had worked this hard for.

She didn't do all of this for nothing.

"Yes—yes, I want to be married to you, Brian." Chas was resolute in her answer.

"Then we're going to Restorative Hope and getting the first appointment they have available. I'll go with you, but I'm not staying married to some lesbian. You have to work through this if you want to be with me." Brian's tone was final.

Chastity's heart broke, and she knew in that moment she wasn't going to get a chance to say a proper goodbye to either Alex or Chas.

CHAPTER 25
CHASTITY, 2016

Chastity stayed in the bathroom all night. Brian didn't try to talk to her or offer any comfort. She cried awful, silent tears until her eyes burned, and the tears stopped falling. She curled up on the bathroom floor and slept fitfully there.

When she woke up the next morning, she had no idea what time it was. In the mirror, she looked as awful as she felt—at least that was in alignment. It felt like nothing else in her life was, or ever would be again. Chastity was running her fingers through her messy hair, trying to wrangle the curls into her signature messy bun, when she heard voices. She put her ear to the door; the voices sounded further away than the bedroom, but they were definitely inside the house.

Chastity couldn't believe it. Brian must have invited his friends over for another day of fishing, leaving her behind to suffer alone. *If I am going to make sacrifices in this relationship, so is he.* Chastity got most of her hair in the bun and stormed out of the bathroom, ready to give Brian her own little ultimatum. She flung the door open and walked straight into her dad.

Richard Montgomery. Chastity stopped dead in her tracks, all the fire leaving her immediately.

Her mother came through from the front porch, clearly having just gotten off the phone. "Chastity, Brian gave us a call and let us know what's been going on this week; we're all very concerned about you and want to get you the help you need." The look on her dad's face was enough to make her want to do anything to make this right. It was a look of disappointment she had only ever seen once before.

"Dad, I …" But what was she going to say? *I'm sorry?* She wasn't. *I shouldn't have?* She didn't really do anything other than hold a girl's hand—it was even less physical than last time.

"Chastity, I've called Restorative Hope," Susan announced, interrupting her thoughts. "They are asking that you go in today for an emergency one-on-one session with Megan."

Chastity couldn't take it, not one more second of this. She threw up bile all over the floor.

Brian quickly stepped in to help his ailing bride. He saw how the fire that had been in her eyes the night before had now been replaced with a pale, sick fear. He couldn't lose his wife to some sinful impulse, not after he'd waited so long. "Chastity, honey, this is for your own good, and we are only doing this to help you. You know that, right?"

She knew that was what they believed, yes, but adding that clarification only made things worse. Chastity nodded and proceeded to run back to the bathroom, where she was sick again. Her body was not coping with the news any better than her mind.

Brian quietly entered the bathroom after the heaving subsided and brought her a wet rag for her mouth and one for her forehead. "Chastity, I know I said I would go with you, but they are asking for your first session to be one-on-one. They said I may be asked to participate later. I just didn't want you to think I didn't WANT to go with you. I do. I'll be right outside waiting in the car so that we can head out of there as soon as you're done."

Great, just like mom used to, thought Chastity.

She still hadn't laid eyes on any clock, so her concept of time was skewed. She lay her head on the side of the toilet, savoring the cool of the porcelain against her cheek, when Brian spoke again.

"Chastity, I know you aren't feeling well, but we do need to go to make it to your appointment on time. The drive takes forty-five minutes, and session starts in one hour."

So, it was noon. She had one hour, and then she would be right back where she started.

CHAPTER 26
CHASTITY, 2016

In a few more minutes, Brian and both her parents were in the car, hauling her back to Restorative Hope. Her mom and dad were in the front seats, talking about someone at church who just had a baby and the meal train they were setting up for the happy mom. Meanwhile, Brian sat in the seat next to hers, staring out of the window, looking just as miserable as she felt.

Chastity didn't speak during the entire ride.

When they pulled up to the church, the routine of it came flooding back. Her mom got out of the car and paid for street parking. Chastity didn't see her book, but she felt sure that she had one in her bag and would be bringing it out for a bit of light reading while her daughter was getting purged of sin, or whatever they believed this ... session would do for her. The only thing different now was that her audience now included Brian.

"Honey, you've had a big day—do you want me to walk you to the door?"

The same offer as the last time she was here.

"No," came the same reply.

Chastity got out of the car without looking back. She heard a car door shut that sounded further away, but then she felt Brian grab her hand. "Hey, I love you. I know you'll fight through this. You're stronger than your demons, Chastity."

She supposed that was meant to be a pep talk—she really didn't know or care.

"Right," was her flat reply.

She turned from Brian and headed for the door. She knocked once, and the door was opened. Only this time it wasn't Henry. It was Megan herself. She was nine years older than the last time Chastity had seen her, but the only change was a few gray streaks in her otherwise mousy brown hair. The sugary smile was as sickening as she remembered.

"Chastity Jacobs, I had hoped our paths would not cross again in this way," Megan said, with the intentional sound of disappointment leaking from her.

"Yeah, me too, Megan."

Megan led her back to her office—it was the exact same. Had Chastity been prone to flashbacks, this would be jarring.

"I want to hear all about what's going on so that we know where to begin. Your mom tells me that you got married a little over a week ago … have you been intimate with your new husband?"

Chastity stared at her blankly. *Okay, surely I heard that wrong.* Last time, Megan had wanted an account of all her impure thoughts, and now she was asking for an account of her marital sex life? This woman was perverse.

"Yes, I have." *No point in lying; they will just hold me hostage here until I come out with whatever they want anyway.*

"Great! That is so exciting—the first intimate encounters can be so crucial to someone who struggles with their sinful sexual nature like you do. Can you tell me a little bit about how those encounters went? What did you do exactly? How did it make you feel?" asked Megan, as if she were asking Chastity about her favorite soup. She seemed nonchalant about the most private moments of Chastity's life.

"I liked it. A lot." Chastity lied a little on that one. It wasn't awful, but she wouldn't say she liked it either. She was meeting the responsibility, but that answer wouldn't win her any points or get her out of here.

"Chastity, we went through this last time—I know it's hard to open up at first, but the sooner you do so, the sooner the program will work for you, and you can move on with your happy life."

Chastity didn't respond—there wasn't a question in there, and she wasn't sure what else Megan was looking for.

"Did you have intercourse? Or did you do other sexual things together?"

God, I'm going to throw up again. No, no, I can do this. I've done it before. This is no different. Say the things they want to hear, and you leave.

"We did both. He put his penis in my vagina. He also put his mouth on my vagina. I haven't put my mouth on his penis yet." Chastity supplied these clinical terms in the driest voice she could muster.

"Okay, well, that is wonderful. Which of those did you like the best?"

"I guess I liked his mouth on my vagina the best."

Megan looked concerned. She looked down at a notepad and scribbled something Chastity couldn't read. For a long moment, neither of them said anything.

Megan broke the silence. "Chastity, I need to ask you something personal, and I want you to reflect before you answer me."

"Okay …" What could this be?

"Chastity, do you enjoy his mouth on your vagina because you can pretend it's a woman's?"

"Excuse me?!" Chastity had been calm so far; she had gone

along with this for the sake of saving her marriage and her family, but this was too far.

Now, she stood up to leave.

"Chastity—I'm thinking that your intense reaction to that question may be telling. I think there is more to that than you may have acknowledged yourself."

When Chastity didn't say anything, Megan continued. "I have a homework assignment for you … I want you to journal the sexual experiences you have with your husband throughout the next week. I want to know what was done and how it made you feel. After I get your account of everything, I will ask him to join us and see if he feels the same way about the encounters as you do."

"What? Why? What good can come of that?" Chastity demanded.

"I need to ensure that you are experiencing intimacy in a Christ-like way. That you enjoy the act of serving your husband, and that you are prioritizing that over your own selfish longings."

"I just told you I liked it. I told you what we did, and I told you that I liked it. What more can you possibly want?"

"I have given you your assignment—you can now go to group."

Chastity felt her heart rate rising to a fever pitch. She was going to scream or cry or throw up or possibly all three for good measure. "I was told I was having a one-on-one session and that this was a single session." Chastity had been holding on to the single thread of hope that this was just a one-time visit to make sure she got back on the obedient path.

"I don't know why you were told that—your program is restarting effective immediately."

Chastity got up from her seat and went to group. She had only two choices that she could see: leave now and never come back, lose her family, and lose Brian; or stay and do what was asked and have everyone go back to the way they were—happy with her, proud of her, loving her.

Is there even really a choice when you compare the options?

CHAPTER 27
CHASTITY, 2016

Chastity completed group feeling even more out of place than the last time. Most of the people in the group were in their teens and in high school, the same age she was during her first stint in Restorative Hope. Now she was older and married to a man. Would she look like a failure or a success to these young women? she wondered.

Once group concluded, she set her course to exit the building as swiftly as possible, but when she was about ten feet from the door, her path was intercepted by Megan. What new and fresh hell was this woman going to inflict on her now?

"Chastity, here's your journal. Please pick up where you left off."

Chastity was shocked to see Megan hand over her journal, the same one she had last time. *She keeps these things? For what purpose?*

"Also, I met your family and your husband while you were in group. They explained to me that you committed this infraction with a woman at the beach during your honeymoon. I'm directing them to discontinue the beach house stay, and you will be returning home with Brian, away from any temptation to continue down this path." With that, Megan smiled that same sticky-sweet smile and turned on her heel, returning to her office.

Chastity's mind was a blank canvas of terror, all thoughts wiped clean by a single, shattering truth. Her family, her husband—they were going to spend their lives oppressing her "for her own sake." There would be no middle ground. There would be no room for anything Chastity needed. This life she had chosen over her own desires and truths was going to close in around her for the rest of her life. She was going to become the scream trapped inside her chest. A fire smoldering behind her ribs, a slow burn of agony that left no room for air.

Chastity never knew what her breaking point would be or what it would feel like. When she was younger, she had imagined a physical rip exposing all of her internal organs. It turns out the feeling ... the feeling was a quiet stillness deep within her soul. She was no longer uncertain or afraid. It was like the first view of the shore when your head appears above the water. It was the closest to God she had ever felt. It was as if this internal voice was *him* all along, trying to help her find herself and be true to that. God made her, and he did not make a mistake by having Chastity be gay.

CHAPTER 28
CHAS (FORMERLY CHASTITY), 2016

With her journal from nine years before tucked into the crook of her arm, Chas walked out of Restorative Hope for the last time.

Brian was waiting on the sidewalk, midway between the church and the waiting car that would surely take her to her grave. Brian must have registered that something was different because he approached Chas more tentatively than he ever had before.

"Chastity ..." Brian was clearly the unsteady one now.

"My name is Chas."

"Wait? What? I thought they told you that you couldn't go by Chas." Brian's tone shifted from tentative to confused.

"Nobody can tell me what my name is, Brian. It's MY name. I'm done making myself change for those around me." Chas started to walk down the sidewalk.

Brian chased behind her frantically. "Chastity, I love you, I don't want to change you."

Chas stopped and turned to face him. She could see on his face that he actually believed those words. How he could be so cut off from reality, Chas didn't know or care. This wasn't going to lead to a fight; you have to *want* what you're fighting for, but she no longer did.

Chas didn't speak. She just turned her back on Brian and continued down the sidewalk at a brisk pace. When she got to the end of the sidewalk, she saw her mom and dad beaming from the car window, ready to collect their soon-to-be-perfect daughter and her perfect Christian husband. That wasn't happening. Chas walked past the car without looking back.

Chas heard the car doors open, and she heard her parents' confused and rushed tones aimed at Brian. Chas was crossing the street when she heard her dad's low tone penetrate the air between them. "Chastity, get in the car. I'm taking you to Brian's house. Now."

Not talking was an effective exit, but one that would only cause confusion and further discourse as her family tried to catch on to what was happening. To Chas, it was clear as day. She had accepted herself, in her skin, as she was always meant to be, but everyone else was looking for Chastity to have returned from Restorative Hope.

Chas turned around. She didn't owe anyone anything more than she had already given, but she loved her family, and if there was ever a hope that someday in the future they could make amends, she wanted to leave space for that possibility. Chas crossed the street and faced her father.

"Dad, I love you, and I will always love you, and I know and believe that you love me, but your love is not what I need right now. I'm leaving Brian." Her dad attempted to interrupt, but Chas plowed forward, undeterred, dropping her voice to a lower pitch and tone, forcing him to stop talking in order to hear her. "I'm not going to repeat this, so you may want to listen to me now ... this is not up for discussion or debate. I know the cost of this choice is to lose everything, including you. I have accepted this. I will always hold the door open for you if you want to reconnect in the future. I'm not trying to change you or your beliefs, but I'm done changing mine to suit yours. I love you and Mom, but I love me more."

And with that, Chas pulled out her cell phone and opened Uber.

PART TWO

CHAPTER 29
CHAS, 2016

Chas had to enter an address so the Uber app would allow her to select a driver. She knew she wasn't going to her parents' house, and she knew she wasn't going to Brian's either.

Megan had said that she was not returning to the beach house for the remainder of her honeymoon. Well, the part about not returning for the remainder of her honeymoon was true enough, but she was, without a doubt, going back to the beach house. Chas punched the address into the app and waited for her driver to come and collect her.

Chas's parents and soon-to-be ex-husband remained standing by the car, huddled together like a flock of seagulls picking over a fish carcass. She was just glad she was no longer volunteering for carcass duty. Chas supposed they were waiting for her to change her mind or offer something else as an explanation for her behavior. Neither of those things would be happening, Chas knew, but she was done with the talking portion of this new, uncharted course in her life. It was time to take action.

Thankfully, the Uber driver pulled up within three minutes of Chas placing the order. She opened the door and climbed in.

She could see Brian walking toward the car with a look of shock and disbelief plastered across his face.

"Could you please start? My crazy ex is trying to come up to the door, and I don't think either of us wants that," Chas said to the driver, trying to spur them into action.

The driver was a woman who looked to be about her age and simply said, "Ugh, that's the worst!" as she sped off from Brian's outstretched arm.

Chas had no idea what the rest of her plan looked like. She had made the decision. She knew it was right. But that was as far as she had gotten. *Okay, hard part's over,* she thought. *Now I have some time.* Technically, she knew she only had a week before she had to find a new place to live. This was a rental, after all, and even though it was the off-season, Chas knew that staying at this house for a prolonged period would drain her small savings account within a week. Chas had never really had to worry about bills or a place to live. The plan was to live with her parents until she could move in with her husband. These were all very realistic things she needed to sort through.

Just not today. Today, Chas was going to enjoy the freedom —no longer temporary for times when she was alone, but true freedom, every day for the rest of her life.

Forty-five minutes later, the Uber driver pulled up to the beach house on Tybee. Chas had already paid her on the app, so she didn't have to worry about that, but she was pretty sure she didn't have any cash for a tip. "I'm so sorry," she rushed to explain. "I wasn't thinking—I don't have any belongings." The woman just looked over her shoulder and winked at Chas. "No worries, hun—this one's on me. You've had enough to worry about today." Chas thanked her for her generosity and understanding and exited the car.

She climbed the stairs to the door on the open-air front porch. She realized she had no idea what was actually waiting for her beyond this door. She knew Megan told her family she should not return to the beach house, but had they made the trip back during her session to collect her belongings, or would the cottage look exactly as she had left it, with her family planning to return at some later time? Chas opened the door and found the house was empty of any of her belongings.

"Fuck."

So, she was going to be starting literally from scratch. That was an overwhelming thought. Not only did she not have a place to live, she also didn't own any underwear, a toothbrush, or have any food stashed away in the house. This should have caused one of her panic attacks, but it didn't. She knew she didn't have these things, and for now, she was perfectly okay with that.

Chas walked into the bathroom and saw the only thing left from her time here. Her robe.

CHAPTER 30
CHAS, 2016

Chas knew she had made a life-altering decision today, so she wasn't quite sure if it would be fair to bring Alex into the mess, or if she should sit with herself for a while and make sure she was taking measured and thoughtful actions going forward. Chas wasn't even sure if Alex was the right person to call. They had only met twice, and nothing had even happened. Would Alex think that Chas had left Brian for her? That wasn't what had happened. Maybe Chas could explain it to her in a way that didn't make it sound like Chas had made a completely rash decision for the possibility of being with Alex when they hadn't even discussed Alex's feelings toward Chas.

She was caught somewhere between feeling excited at the prospect of a future she got to determine and scared speechless for the same reasons. She knew she needed to figure out how to access food and her bank account. She would also need clothes, a toothbrush, and a hairbrush; the list was long. Work wasn't expecting her back for another week, so at least she didn't have to figure out everything today. She had seven days to get herself sorted before the realities of the world would snap her out of this mesmerizing daydream.

Chas wanted to be in her robe. She knew that just sliding it on over her clothes wasn't what she craved. She craved the contact of the robe on her skin.

Chas stripped down bare and slid the robe around her. She didn't bother tying it; she savored the air on her body. She had only ever let the robe fall open once before—with Alex. At the thought of Alex, she felt a pang of longing deep inside her, so strong that she audibly gasped for air.

Chas knew there was something there, but she was a mess. A living tornado. Bringing someone else into the mix—especially someone as calm and grounding as Alex—would be unfair. But the fact that Alex was calm and grounding made her second-guess her decision to hold out on the phone call.

Chas slid her hand down into the pocket, checking to make sure Alex's number was still there. It was. Perfectly safe right beside her.

She would think on it for a while longer, she decided, but she needed to set some sort of timeframe, or she knew she would just lie around in the robe for the next week, hoping someone was coming to save her without taking the necessary steps to regain her life. Six in the morning tomorrow, Chas decided. She would have made her decision to call Alex by six.

For now, Chas really needed food, but she had no desire to get dressed again and go out looking for anything. The house was a rental, but surely someone over the months or years had left something in a cabinet somewhere. Soon, Chas was raiding the kitchen, and every cupboard was coming up empty—pots and pans, check; olive oil and spices, check; plates and cups, check. When she got to the fourth and final cabinet, she was thrilled to see a jar of peanut butter. Chas grabbed the jar and tilted the top to face her. It didn't expire for another eight months. Success! Chas grabbed a spoon, her jar of peanut butter, and headed onto the back deck to listen to the waves and eat her fill.

The sun was finally setting on this day when Chas finished eating the peanut butter. She had cleared almost half the jar, leaving enough for later tonight and possibly tomorrow morning when she woke, but Chas knew she couldn't live off this one jar of peanut butter forever. Chas stood up to take the spoon and the peanut butter inside, but something in the sea nearby caught her eye. The sea looked like it was glowing in patches, in glittering shades of blue and green.

Chas went to investigate. She didn't bother closing her robe; twilight was in full effect, and nobody was around on the winter beach to see her anyway. She walked down to the place where the ocean met the sand. Something was definitely glowing, but what could that even be? Chas stripped her robe and hung it on the end of the stair railing leading back to the house. She waded into the water; it was as cold and jarring as last time, but she was not afraid. This water wouldn't hurt her. Chas felt it rising past her knees, her thighs, and coming up to her navel. She was past the area where the waves were breaking, and the water was eerily still. Chas was standing in a pool of glowing—*What is that?* Chas scooped up some of the glowing water and saw that she was holding several small jellyfish. Only they weren't stinging, just glowing.

The more she moved into the water, the more these little things glowed. They were different sizes, some as small as the tip of her pinky finger and some as big as a golf ball. They were flashing a soft blue-green light as she turned circles in the water. She was meant to be here. In this moment, these glowing little blobs of goo were just for her. Chas relished it.

After about twenty minutes of wading in the water and turning circles, Chas was very aware of how cold she had become. The water no longer had its sting, and she was pretty sure everything below her knees had gone completely numb. Chas walked out of the water and directly into the warmth of her robe. It was as heavenly as the sheets the day Alex had given her the massage.

Alex.

Chas didn't need until six the next morning to figure this out. She was going to call Alex. Alex had always understood her. Today would be no different.

Chas went up the stairs and found her phone lying on the kitchen counter. She reached for the card in her pocket. She pulled out the card, but when she attempted to place the call, nothing happened. That is when Chas noticed the top-right-hand corner of the screen: "No service."

Her parents had disconnected her phone.

CHAPTER 31
CHAS, 2016

Right. Once Chas realized what was going on, she wasn't the least bit surprised. She had forgotten that she was on her parents' phone plan. It wasn't as if she was mooching off them—they got a better deal for a family plan, and she paid her portion of the bill. This was just one more way they could punish her for her choices now that they couldn't punish her in other ways. It was a brilliant move on their part.

Okay, so like it or not, it was time to make some decisions.

The sun had gone down, but it was still relatively early—only 7:30 p.m. There was a local bar with rainbow umbrellas in its décor, not too far up the road. She had seen it several times while coming and going from the cottage. It was easily within walking distance, and they would likely have a phone. If she explained in very vague but effective detail that her situation was dire, maybe they would allow her to use the phone and call Alex.

Chas went back to her clothes. She slung the robe over the foot of the bed and dressed swiftly. She didn't have to hurry—she knew the bar would be open for a while, but she didn't know Alex's sleep schedule, and she didn't want to call at an unreasonable hour.

Chas walked the five blocks over and three blocks inland to arrive at the bar. A hostess told her to pick anywhere she liked. A few people were scattered across the place, but it was mostly empty. The hostess was young, maybe high school–aged or a little older, and she had an eyebrow piercing and two surface piercings that gave her cheeks dimples. Her hair had pink highlights, and a floral tattoo ran down the length of her arm (or what Chas could see of it). She seemed open and nice. Somehow, seeing her outward show of defiance of conventional norms immediately set Chas at ease, almost like it meant Chas could come as she was without fear of judgment.

"Um, actually, I have a favor to ask."

"Okay, shoot," the pink-haired girl said from behind the hostess stand.

"I really need to borrow a phone. I left my husband and my whole life behind today, and wasn't thinking properly and forgot that my parents had my phone line on their plan," Chas stammered. "I just came back up from walking on the beach and found that they had disconnected it." Why she was telling the pink-haired girl all of this, she didn't know. Clearly, she wanted to talk to someone.

"Whoa, that's harsh. Normally, we don't allow customers to make phone calls, but Kip is behind the bar, and they'll be understanding after what you just told me. Let me go tell them, and I'll flag you over." And with that, the pink-haired girl bounded toward who Chas assumed was Kip.

Kip was one of the most beautiful humans Chas had ever seen in real life. They had raven-black hair that was cropped short and an athletic build without being bulky with muscles— Chas would describe them as androgynous and devastatingly perfect.

The pink-haired girl (Chas really needed to ask her name)

was waving at Chas and signaling for her to come join them at the bar.

"I filled Kip in, and they say it's completely fine to use the phone," her unnamed friend stated with a broad and open smile.

"Thank you both for this—it really means a lot. Also, I'm so sorry, but I didn't catch your name."

"Oh, it's Mara."

"Thanks, Mara, and thank you too, Kip."

Kip smiled and passed Chas the phone. She realized this next part was going to be a little awkward. She couldn't leave the bar with their phone, so she just stood a few feet away as she dialed the number from the business card Alex had given her. Chas was acutely aware of Kip and Mara looking in her direction, but she had come all this way and had little choice now. She needed help, and she had already decided to call Alex before she realized the predicament she was in.

The phone rang for three long beats.

"Hey, Kip, what's up?" said Alex.

"Hey, Alex, it's me, Chas. Something has happened, and I need help. Can you come get me?"

"I'm on my way," was all Alex said before ending the call.

Chas immediately realized her mistake—she didn't even tell Alex where she was, but wait ... Alex had thought she was Kip. So Alex knew where she was. How was she connected to Kip?

Chas brought the phone back over to Kip.

"Can I get you a drink?" Kip offered.

"Honestly, I would love one, but I don't have any money right now. I left everything behind, but thank you for the offer. Once I have access to my money, I'm sure I'll be right back here, begging for a drink," Chas said with a smile. She knew it was true. This was exactly the kind of spot she would like to spend some time in, and having a drink publicly for the first time was going to feel amazing.

"You sound like you've had a hell of a time. Why don't you

let me get you a drink and some food, and you can pay me back someday by picking up the tab when we hang out?" Kip responded warmly.

"Kip, you have no idea how much that would mean to me right now."

Kip smiled and grabbed a laminated menu from the back of the bar.

"Pick anything you like as far as food and drink go, but I do need one thing in return."

"Okay ..." Chas was curious.

"I'd like to know your name."

"Oh." Chas let out a hearty laugh. "Sorry, I should have introduced myself first. I'm Chas."

"Chas?" Kip said it like they recognized it somehow, but Chas was quite sure she had never seen them in her life. She would surely remember someone as remarkable as them.

"Yes ... Do you know someone else named Chas?"

"Nope," Kip said with a knowing grin that Chas had no clue about. "What can I get you, Chas?"

CHAPTER 32
CHAS, 2016

Chas ordered a mango margarita and a chicken sandwich. Kip brought the mango margarita over first, along with chips and guacamole that Chas hadn't ordered but was endlessly grateful for. She was starving; it turned out the peanut butter hadn't held her over as long as she had hoped.

Chas settled into a seat at the end of the bar, a perfect vantage point to watch for Alex's arrival.

Kip was standing in front of her on the other side of the bar. Soon, she was the only patron left, and most of the other dinner guests had departed. There were a few stragglers, but for the most part, it was just her and Kip. Mara was around somewhere, but Chas couldn't see her at the moment.

Kip leaned casually against the bar. "So, Chas, how long are you going to be in Tybee?" They didn't strike Chas as the type of person who made small talk; what were they trying to get at?

"Well, at least one more week, but who knows after that. I love it here. I may just try and find a way to stay forever," she said with a smile that didn't quite reach her eyes.

Chas shoveled chips and guacamole into her mouth, one bite barely cleared before the next went in. She was so hungry that she was stuffing her cheeks like a chipmunk. When did she last eat? Was it yesterday? She couldn't recall.

As Chas reached for another chip, Kip's expression changed. Their eyebrow rose first, then they gave a big smile to someone walking in, and then Kip turned their back to the seat Chas was sitting in.

Chas looked up to see who had caught Kip's attention, and there she was: Alex.

Alex looked concerned but not frightened. She saw Chas and glanced at Kip, subtly rolling her eyes at their back. Her pace quickened as she made her way to Chas.

"Chas, are you hurt?" Alex quickly scanned her for any signs of physical damage.

Chas was confused for a second. Why would Alex think she was hurt? Then she remembered: the last Alex had seen of her was Brian grabbing her by the elbow and dragging her away. And then Chas had called the next day, saying that something had happened and she needed her. *Okay, it doesn't look or sound great when you put them together.*

Chas shook her head. "No, I'm not hurt." Then, for some unexplained reason, she started to cry. It wasn't a full-body or sobbing cry, but a more unsettling kind. Chas was sitting there silently, letting the tears fall onto the bar. This was just great. She wasn't even sad about leaving Brian or her old life. She was a little scared, but not enough to justify this reaction. What was happening to her?

Alex gently raised her hand to Chas's face, using the back of her finger to divert some of the tears. The move was so kind and so gentle, and it felt like it was full of love. Chas's breath stumbled.

Alex remained quiet, waiting for Chas to collect herself and explain what had happened.

Chas couldn't think of how to frame the situation so that she didn't sound on the verge of a mental breakdown. It was a lot, and they were in a public space. Chas was sitting, and Alex was still standing.

"Do you want to get out of here so you can talk to me?" Alex offered.

"That would be great." Chas sighed as another silent tear snaked down her cheek. "But this really nice bartender offered me food, and it hasn't come out yet. Maybe I can get it to go?"

"Way ahead of you," Kip said, returning with the chicken sandwich already boxed and bagged as a to-go order. Chas really didn't deserve this type of kindness from a perfect stranger.

"I also threw in a few brownies and more chips and guac since you seemed to like it so much," Kip said with a chuckle.

"Thank you so much, Kip. I won't forget this, and I promise to make it up to you someday."

"Chas, I have no doubt that you'll keep that promise," Kip said as Chas stood to leave.

"See you soon," was their parting line.

Alex waited for Chas to make her way around the chair, to-go bag in hand. She gave a tight smile to Kip and a wave to Mara, who had reappeared from somewhere in the back, and then placed her hand on the small of Chas's back.

Chas felt it again. All of her tension was leaking from her; it was being siphoned out at their exact point of contact.

Once they exited the bar, Chas stopped.

"Is everything okay?" Alex prompted.

"Yes, I just don't know which car is yours," Chas said, a little embarrassed that she had called this person asking for help, yet she didn't even know what kind of car she drove.

"Oh, no worries. I'm the yellow Jeep just over there." Alex pointed to the Jeep Wrangler diagonal to where they stood.

She gently applied some pressure to Chas's back, not to guide her or push her, but just enough to let her know that she was still there, and the contact between them was not broken.

Alex walked up to the passenger door and moved some beach towels off the seat to make room for Chas, who climbed in and rested the food on her lap. Then, Alex climbed into the driver's seat.

Chas was busy thinking about how she already missed the contact between them when Alex brought her back to the present.

"Chas, would you like to go to your place or mine?" Alex's offer was completely consistent with everything she had always shown Chas—that Chas had options here. She was just as much in control as Alex. She knew that if she had requested they drive to Savannah to Brian's house, Alex would have obliged.

"Can we go to your place?" Chas's heart was hammering like a drum.

CHAPTER 33
CHAS, 2016

Ten minutes later, the Jeep pulled up to a small, single-story house on the north end of the island. The house was perfect. It was a small green cottage with a palm tree in the front yard next to the driveway. Chas couldn't see the full backyard, but she could see string lights peeking over the wooden fence and a red umbrella propped open.

Alex hopped out of the Jeep and walked around to Chas's side. She opened the door for Chas.

Something so simple—opening a door. Chas had never had anyone deliberately open a door for her.

She got out of the car, food bag in hand, and Alex quickly replaced her hand on the small of her back.

When they reached the door, Alex walked right in.

"You don't lock your door?"

"Normally, I do, but I was in a hurry."

Chas was touched. Alex cared more about her and her well-being than she had realized.

"Thank you for coming, Alex."

"Let's get you inside and settled."

Chas stepped through the doorway and took in the room

around her. The door was wooden with wavy, translucent glass that let light in. Two couches formed an L-shape—one was white, and one was gray. The walls were a soft beige, and the lighting was warm. There was a chair in the corner with a blanket draped over the back and a stack of books at its foot. The pillows were mismatched but somehow coordinated, and the TV was over the fireplace—which was filled with unlit candlesticks of various sizes and styles. Chas loved this room. It was as warm, welcoming, and peaceful as Alex was. Chas could immediately see this being a place she would love to spend time in.

Alex led Chas through the living room into the adjoining dining room. It was small and quaint, with a packed bookshelf lining one wall and a vintage-looking dining table in the center. It was wooden with ladder-back chairs. Alex pulled out a chair for Chas.

Chas sat and paused. She felt like she owed Alex an explanation.

"Go ahead and eat. You looked pretty hungry when I arrived. I'll be right here. I'm not going anywhere. Oh, wait, I lied—would you like some water or a drink? I think I may have beer or maybe milk, but I'll have to check the expiration date." Alex was rambling a little. It was charming.

"Water would be great."

Alex walked through the open doorway that Chas could see led to the kitchen. It looked small from where she was sitting. She could see that the counters were white, the cabinets were a sage green color, and the tile for the backsplash was tan. There looked to be a vintage-looking table or island in the middle.

A few seconds later, Alex returned with the water, an empty plate, and a fork, knife, and napkin. Chas was busy ripping the to-go bag open, like she couldn't get to the food fast enough. She needed to remember to slow down and eat like a normal human, or Alex would think she was some sort of beast that needed a trough and not a plate.

Chas ate as slowly as she could manage, which was still twice as fast as she normally would have eaten. She cleared the chips and guac (offering Alex some, but she declined), ate all of the chicken sandwich, and ate one and a half brownies.

There was no talking. No chatter. Just comfortable silence between them. Alex waited patiently as Chas downed the entire meal.

Eventually, Chas finished eating and wrapped the last brownie and half of the one she had started eating in one of the paper napkins supplied by Kip. Alex collected all of her trash and took it back to the kitchen.

When Alex came back, she stretched out her hand, an open invitation. Chas grasped it and stood up. Alex led them back into the living room. She didn't make a move to sit, so Chas picked the gray couch against the wall of windows and sat down. Alex positioned herself on the white couch immediately to Chas's left, close enough to touch but not touching (much to Chas's displeasure).

It was time to talk. Chas was comfortable. Alex had been calmly waiting. Chas looked into Alex's eyes and knew that no matter what she said, it was going to be okay. She wasn't alone. She wouldn't face this alone. Chas began to tell her story.

"Yesterday evening, when Brian found us on the beach, he became very upset with me. He told me that he was taking me back to a place that I didn't want to go. He involved my parents, and when I woke up this morning, they had decided to take me to this place despite my wishes. I think returning to this place broke something inside me. I realized I could no longer meet the expectations of everyone else. I couldn't keep up the facade I had been curating since high school. So, once my appointment was over, I walked out, walked up to Brian and my parents, and told them I was leaving. My parents are both very religious—my dad is a pastor—they would never accept the choice I was making, so I knew in that moment I would be cut off from everything and everyone I loved, but I just couldn't ..."

Chas didn't finish her sentence. She wasn't sure how to. "I couldn't keep living that way" were the honest words here, but it sounded dramatic and cliché, so she just left the sentence hanging. Chas knew that was a very abbreviated version of events, and she was sure Alex would have questions, but it was a good synopsis of the last twenty-four hours.

If Alex was surprised, she didn't let on.

"Chas, I'm so sorry this happened to you. You didn't deserve any part of that. I do have some questions, but I don't have to ask them if you'd rather I not."

"No, go ahead—I need you to know, well, everything."

"What is this place you didn't want to return to?" Alex's first question itself was a doozy. Chas was quite sure that, based on the story Alex had told her about her own mom, this whole conversion therapy thing was going to seem radical and a little psychotic.

"It was a church program called Restorative Hope. It's a conversion therapy program where they take in young men and women and make them express all their most intimate and private thoughts and actions in an effort to humiliate them into submission. I was sent there in 2006 when my mom walked in on me kissing my friend Jess. The program makes you keep a journal detailing all of your 'sinful' thoughts and actions. The counselor then reads these weekly and asks you to recount your feelings around these events. They quote an obscene amount of scripture that pertains to the specifics of whatever you wrote in the journal. If you wrote that you were attracted to a woman, they would quote scripture explaining the covenant of marriage between one man and one woman. If you wrote that you enjoyed masturbation, they would quote scripture about sexual purity and self-control and the use of the body as a temple. It was hugely degrading and very confusing as a younger person. I was made to believe that my choices were damning me to hell and that I could only be a successful Christian if I complied with the rules of the program, which were rooted in biblical teachings. I went there weekly for six months." Chas stopped for a breath. She was calm. She wasn't crying, and she didn't feel like crying. It felt good to tell someone who wasn't rooted in the same religious doctrine what had happened at Restorative Hope.

Chas hadn't been watching Alex's face while she told her story, but when she looked up at her to try and gauge her reaction, Alex was crying soft, silent tears.

"Chas, I'm so profoundly sorry."

Chas felt safe and seen and understood. She wanted to keep going with her story.

"After I completed the Restorative Hope program in 2007, I dated only men. I wasn't allowed to be alone with women during or after the program. If I was ever interacting with them one-on-one, it had to be in a public setting on 'full display' to keep my actions in check. So when Brian booked my massage with you for the morning after I was just married, I panicked. I hadn't been alone with a woman in more than nine years. I felt like being alone with a woman was the thing that was going to cause me to 'fail' or 'fall into temptation.' I told Brian all of this the morning you arrived—when I pulled him back into the bedroom before my massage. He told me that he wasn't worried and that my last infraction was nine years ago, so it was likely a phase that I had grown out of. I was unsure, but what he was saying seemed accurate, or at least accurate enough. I completed the program. I married a man. Being alone with a woman shouldn't be a problem anymore. But ... during the massage, something happened. I realized that the program hadn't worked. All it did was make me mask myself. Having your hands on me was the single greatest moment of my life to that point. I knew at that point I was gay, and my choices were limited. I could lose Brian and my family and risk it all to be myself, or I could stay. I decided to stay and that I would make the most of it.

"The night of your massage, I kind of lost it—I stripped into my underwear and went deep into the sea. Brian and all his friends saw me, and he freaked out. I thought we would fight and it would end right there, but all he did was take me inside. Six days later (yesterday), you were walking along the beach, and I knew I had to go to you. When Brian caught us holding hands, you saw him grab me and take me upstairs. He told me he was going to tell my parents, and he was going to take me back to Restorative Hope. I begged him not to. I told him I couldn't do it. I couldn't go back to that place. I slept on the floor of the bathroom, and when I woke up, he had my parents in the house, and they were all taking me to Restorative Hope. I had my appointment there today at one. My old counselor was there and told me that she was forbidding me to come back to the beach house and that I was to go home with Brian and journal all of our sexual encounters and how each one made me feel. She wanted to make sure I was 'experiencing intimacy in a Christ-like way.' I finished the session, and I even did group, but when she told me I was not coming back here … I think it again broke something inside of me. It was not a breaking like a shattering, but more like the snapping off of a tether I had been straining against for too long. I walked out of the session and told Brian and my parents that I was leaving and that I was done trying to be something I am not. I came back to the beach house (it was already rented for the rest of this week), and they must have come while I was in session and removed all of my belongings, thinking that, like a good girl, I would just do what the program told me to do—like last time. I went for a swim and … Alex, did you know there are jellyfish that glow in the water? Anyway, I decided, when I got out of the water, I was going to call you, but when I went to call you from my phone, my parents had disconnected me from their plan. So I walked to the bar, met Kip and Mara, and they were nice enough to let me call you. You know the rest from there."

Alex had stopped crying by the end of Chas's story. The look on her face was something Chas couldn't recognize.

"I know that is a lot, and so much of it is embarrassing. I completely understand if you think of me differently now—I was a coward and foolish to think I could make it through life faking it." Chas offered.

"Chas, no. You're not foolish, and you're not a coward. I don't look at you differently. I— I'm looking at you in admiration. I don't know how you made it out, but I'm so very thankful that you did. What happened to you was wrong and perverse and should never happen to anyone, queer or hetero, it doesn't matter. It should not happen to anyone."

Alex took a beat to catch her breath and regain her calm.

"Chas, would you like a hug?"

Chas let the tears flow once more and nodded. At last, she was safe.

CHAPTER 34
CHAS, 2016

Alex stood up, and Chas stood up in response. Alex reached her arms under both of Chas's and embraced her. Body to body. No space between. A full embrace of everything Chas had said, all that she was. Alex's hug was like a reset—it tilted the world on its axis, and in that moment, everything felt different from before. Chas had the distinct feeling that life for her would always be separated into two parts: before this moment and after.

Alex didn't let go until Chas loosened her grip and created a sliver of space between them.

"Chas, would you like me to take you home, or do you want to stay here? I have a spare bedroom."

Chas was quiet. She knew she wanted to stay, but she didn't want to be alone. It wasn't just the attraction to Alex (although that was very present). She wanted to absorb her comfort, her peace, her calm, and let it ground her.

"Alex, I ... I would like to stay, but I have a favor to ask. If it is too much, you can just tell me so, and I promise I won't be hurt, offended, or mad. If I promise that this isn't anything it shouldn't be … Is there any way you would feel comfortable staying with me tonight? Like in the same bed, or even on the couches in the same room. I just don't want to be alone."

CHAPTER 35

CHAS, 2016

"Chas, you don't need to promise me that this isn't anything 'it shouldn't be.' I don't know what this is yet, but I do know that whatever's between us, it's not wrong, and there's no 'shouldn't be' when it comes to you and me."

Chas was stunned. Not because of what Alex had said, but because of how true it was. Chas knew this wasn't wrong, and she knew that whatever was between them, they would figure it out together.

Alex offered Chas her hand.

Chas latched on, intertwining her fingers with Alex's.

Alex led Chas back to a bedroom down the hall.

"This is my room, or I should say, our room, for tonight …"

Chas's heart sank. She shouldn't be thinking about the future with Alex right now in this moment; she wasn't even officially divorced, her life was messy, and she had a lot of self-discovery to do. But hearing that it was just their room for tonight sent a shard of doubt through her.

Alex sensed the shift in Chas immediately.

"Chas, I'm only saying 'for tonight' so that you can decide tomorrow where we land. I will welcome you here in this bed for as long as you want to be here, but I know you have been through a lot in the last forty-eight hours, and I don't want you to feel like you have to make any long-term decisions you aren't ready for."

Chas's doubt evaporated as quickly as it had appeared. She relaxed. How did Alex know everything she was thinking and feeling? She had never experienced that level of connection with anyone—even after years and years of friendship with Jess and a year of being with Brian; neither of them could read her thoughts and emotions the way Alex could after only three days of knowing her.

Chas let out an audible sigh of relief and smiled up at Alex.

"Thanks for that."

"Always."

Alex stood at the foot of the bed and seemed to hesitate.

"Is something wrong?"

"No, not at all. I just don't know which side of the bed you like."

"Well, it isn't all about me ... what side do you like?"

"You first."

"Not going to happen."

"Okay, on the count of three, we each say right or left, and we will go from there."

Negotiating with Alex was fun and brought a smile to Chas's face.

"Okay, one ... two ... three... Right," Alex said at the same time as Chas said, "Left." It was perfect. Chas somehow knew it would be.

"Great," Alex proclaimed. "Okay, we need to get a few more things situated before we can turn in for the night."

Chas realized their fingers were still intertwined. Neither of them had let go. Chas had stopped focusing on their point of contact during the bed debate and now realized that holding

Alex's hand felt just as normal as breathing air or drinking water.

Alex led them out of the bedroom and into the bathroom. She dropped Chas's hand and reached up to the top shelf of what looked like a built-in cubby that housed towels, toilet paper, and the like. When Alex brought it down, she had a small box of miscellaneous items. She was pillaging through and found what she was hunting for.

Alex pulled out a purple toothbrush and a green one. "Which color?"

"Purple, please," Chas replied with a giggle. After the day she had, she never guessed she would be standing here picking out a toothbrush in Alex's bathroom.

Alex passed over the toothbrush and returned to the mystery box. After another minute of rummaging, she produced a toothbrush cover and a tube of toothpaste.

"If you don't love this kind," she said, indicating the toothpaste, "we can go out tomorrow and get you something else."

"This is perfect, thanks." Chas was feeling everything all at once. She had never had anyone take care of her this way. The simple little things she had always done for herself. Alex was providing so much more than hygiene products.

Then, Alex produced two towels and passed them to Chas.

"Two towels?" Chas asked.

"One for your body and one for your hair."

Chas noticed the slight bit of pink that crept into Alex's cheeks when she mentioned Chas's body.

"That's incredibly thoughtful. Thank you."

"Sure thing. Okay, I'm thinking you may want a shower, so I'm going to give you some privacy. I'll just be in the bedroom if you need anything." Alex turned and exited the bathroom, sliding the door closed behind her. Chas realized the door was a sliding style, but then she noticed something she hadn't expected … the door was made of panes of glass. The glass was fogged out, but she was sure that if she was standing in front of it, anyone on the other side (mainly Alex) would be able to see her silhouette. Chas felt flush at the thought. Alex had already seen her breasts the day of the massage. It isn't like she hadn't seen Chas mostly naked anyway.

Chas stripped down and tried not to linger near the door too long. She stepped into the shower and fiddled with the knobs—neither was marked hot or cold, but she would figure it out.

"Oh," came Alex's voice from beyond the door, "hot is on the left and cold is on the right."

It was going to take some getting used to—having someone this intertwined with her thoughts. It was a little jarring when you were used to having an entire inner monologue just to yourself, but now someone seemed privy to all of these sacred, secret thoughts. Although the shower temperature was hardly a sacred thought.

"Thanks!" Chas called back.

Chas got the water to the right temperature—nearly scalding and fogging up the entire bathroom in a matter of minutes. She stood in the shower. She had gone through what felt like every emotion in the human arsenal, and she felt raw. The heat of the shower on her skin made her think of the cool of the ocean. She wondered how far from the ocean Alex's house was. As the hot water settled into her skin, she felt exhausted. Even her bones were fatigued. She wanted to stay in the shower forever, but the longer she remained, the more exhausted she felt. She needed to rest.

Chas finished washing her hair and rinsed off one last time. She reached out of the shower curtain and grabbed the towel for her hair—she twisted it around her head and flipped it onto itself like a strange ponytail. Then, she wrapped up in her towel and stepped out onto the bathmat.

Shoot, Chas thought. She had forgotten she had no clothes. She wasn't about to get back into the clothes she had worn all day, and she really didn't want to put back on the same underwear. This was awkward. Should she ask Alex for PJs and underwear? That seemed super weird, even with how close they felt. Maybe she should just ask for PJs and go commando. That made her flush with a fierce red staining her cheeks. Sleeping commando in Alex's clothes may be even worse than asking for her underwear.

Chas was being silly. Nothing had bothered Alex so far, so why make it weird now? Chas opened the door and came into the bedroom, wrapped in her towel.

Alex's eyes bulged like she thought Chas might drop her towel right then and there. But Alex would not drop eye contact, as if looking down might signal Chas to bare it all. Chas smiled a sly grin.

"Alex, I don't have anything to wear to bed. I'm sorry, but I was hoping I could borrow something just for tonight."

"Ha!" Alex blurted a laugh. "Sorry, I was … I don't know … Anyway, yes, you can. Here, let me get you some shorts and a T-shirt."

"Sounds great," Chas said. She would just go commando. Asking for underwear felt strange.

Alex produced the garments, folded in a neat pile.

"You can dress in here, and I can step out if you like?" Alex offered.

"You can stay. I will just turn around," Chas said. Not sure exactly when she became a little nudist whenever she was around Alex.

Alex flushed. "Okay, I'll turn around too."

"Okay, if that makes you more comfortable," Chas said over her shoulder.

"I mean … I …"

Alex seemed to keep getting stuck at the same part.

"You …" Chas prompted Alex to go on.

"I'm comfortable with being here if you're comfortable with me being here." Alex worded that very carefully, Chas noticed.

"I'm fine with it," Chas said confidently.

Chas turned around and dropped the towel. She wasn't sure if Alex was watching or if she had turned around. Either way, she was surprisingly comfortable with it. Chas heard the squeak of the bed as if Alex was climbing into bed. She bent over to slide the shorts on.

"Uhm," Alex coughed, "would you like any underwear? It's totally fine if not, but I thought maybe I should offer."

So, she *was* looking.

"I'm good without them, thank you, though." Chas was shocked at her answer. She was feeling bold. She didn't want any extra layers between her and Alex.

"Okay, right. Sounds good." Alex sounded like she may still be choking on her spit.

Chas pulled on her shirt and realized that her nipples were hard and very noticeable through the shirt. *Hmm, okay, well, nothing to do about that*, Chas thought as she turned around.

Alex was not lying in the bed but rather sitting on the end of the bed, less than three feet away from her. She was looking directly at Chas.

Chas blushed, seeing Alex's gaze drop slightly to her chest and quickly returning to meet her eyes with a rush of pink creeping up her neck.

Chas crossed the distance to stand in front of Alex. She wasn't expecting anything, she told herself.

CHAPTER 36
CHAS, 2016

Time literally stopped. Neither woman moved a muscle. Their eyes were locked in a silent conversation only they could hear.

After an unknown amount of time, Alex moved. She had been sitting on the edge of the bed with her arms resting on her legs. Her movement was subtle, one that would have been casual if it weren't happening in this moment. Alex spread her legs, leaned her torso back slightly, and propped herself up on an arm (now outstretched behind her).

Chas removed the towel from her head, her damp curls dropping around her face and grazing her shoulder.

She walked over and stood between Alex's legs.

"Chas, I'm sorry, but you'll have to lead this. I'm not sure what … I'm not sure how far …"

"Don't be sorry. I want to lead." Chas didn't know where this confidence was coming from. She had no idea what she was doing, but simultaneously knew exactly what she was doing. She hadn't had time to establish her own desires since deciding to choose herself earlier in the day, but she knew the desire for Alex had been there before today and would be there tomorrow.

Chas removed one of her legs from between Alex's, placing it on the outside of her left leg. She was straddling Alex's leg but still standing. Chas leaned down slowly, allowing time for Alex to change her mind and stop her. Alex didn't stop her. Alex scooted back onto the bed, pushing with her feet and staying on her elbows. Chas followed her, still straddling Alex's leg and resting her weight on her outstretched arms, hovering above Alex. Alex's shirt was a little big on Chas, and when she was positioned this way, the neck swooped down and allowed Alex a perfect view of her chest and her still-hard nipples. Alex made a soft whimper in the back of her throat. If the tension between them had been any more taut, Chas was sure the universe would have collapsed in on itself.

Chas lowered her head and brushed a kiss across Alex's mouth—soft, barely there, a whisper of a touch. Alex reached up for one of Chas's curls, tucking it behind her ear and smiling up at her. Chas lowered her mouth again, but this time there was no whisper between them. Their lips collided. Alex's lips were warm and soft and perfectly fit with Chas's. Chas opened her mouth to allow Alex entry, but she didn't take it. Alex simply sucked on Chas's lower lip, holding it gently between her two lips. Chas moaned, loudly. Alex gave a wry grin, keeping Chas's lower lip between her teeth.

Chas wanted more. She needed more. Chas ran her hand over the plane of Alex's stomach. She could feel Alex tense at the touch, but not in a negative way, she realized. With Brian, Chas had tensed more times than she could count, preparing her body for something unwanted. This tensing was more of a cramping wave, beckoning Chas to do more—to touch more. And Chas was happy to oblige. She slid her hand under the lower edge of Alex's T-shirt while moving her mouth to her neck. Chas breathed her in. She smelled like citrus and very slightly of something like vanilla, but without being sweet. She smelled like sunshine. Chas kissed Alex's neck just below her ear while moving her hand further up the length of Alex's stomach. By now, Alex's skin was prickled with goosebumps. Chas could directly see the effect she was having on her. Alex's eyes were open, looking into Chas's, but she couldn't help herself; she looked down at Chas's shirt to view her torso. She had seen her before, but this time it was not a passing glance but a full, appraising, long look. Alex was drinking her in. Chas allowed her to drink her fill.

When Alex's eyes returned to Chas's, Chas let her hand roam further. She was well past the navel now and needed to decide how much further she would go. She wanted to have all of Alex this minute, but she knew that they needed to wait. Today was not the day for everything all at once, but for more of a release of the pent-up tension between them. Chas sucked gently on Alex's neck, followed by a gentle scrape of her teeth, and then a lick over the already damp spot.

"Chas," Alex whispered like it was a prayer and not her name.

Chas grinned against Alex's neck. "Alex, will you touch me?"

"Yes. Where?" The reply was immediate.

"I want your hands on my breasts." Chas's voice was calm and sure, but she felt a rolling fire beneath her skin—a hard and crashing burn that needed the oxygen to stay alive. Chas was the fire, and Alex was her oxygen.

Alex grinned. "Gladly."

She shifted to the side, and Chas slid down onto her elbows and then lay flat on her back. It was Alex's turn to be on top, not in control but rather responding to Chas's spoken desire. Chas knew she could stop this at any point she wanted … but would she? She wasn't sure.

Alex gently and reverently raised Chas's shirt to expose both breasts, her nipples hard and starting to feel sore from the strain against her skin. Alex positioned her body the way Chas had moments before, straddling one of Chas's legs and angled to the right side of Chas's body so she could still see her, but the contact between them was almost full body.

Chas could feel a wet spot forming on her shorts. Her body had never done that before. She thought about being embarrassed if Alex noticed, but then decided she was done with embarrassment; it no longer served her.

Alex traced small circles around Chas's breasts, then onto her breasts, and then finally grazed her aching nipples. Chas arched her back at the touch, signaling the need for more. Alex obliged and cupped her breast, aching and full, in her hand while replacing her mouth on Chas's. Chas opened again for her, and this time Alex took it. Tentative at first, small licks and flicks on the roof of Chas's mouth, then more insistent tongues colliding.

Chas was panting heavily between kisses. Alex's grip was firm on one breast, and then she switched to the other, knowing Chas needed her touch everywhere.

This dance between them felt like the most natural thing in the world, as if one was created for the other.

Alex sat up slightly (still straddling Chas's leg), stripped her shirt, and deftly removed her own bra with one hand. Chas lost all of the thoughts and sensations in her own body (beautiful as they were) and found her attention landing firmly on Alex. Damn, she was beautiful.

Her short hair was mussed from removing her shirt, and her stomach was strong and flat—none of the curves Chas had. Her breasts were unbearably perfect. Chas wanted to taste the skin there. Alex must have seen or read the desire in Chas's mind because her nipples rose to a peak, and she leaned back down, allowing Chas to make the next move. Chas cupped Alex's breast and grazed her thumb across that firm, demanding nipple.

"May I ..." Chas hoped Alex knew the intended question—she wasn't sure she could ask it out loud.

Alex positioned her body in a way that gave Chas the access she craved.

Chas reverently and methodically licked, kissed, and sucked on Alex's breasts. Alex came undone, letting out a moan of her own now. Chas started with one breast and then moved to the other, cupping the breast she left behind so that Alex could feel her everywhere. Chas raised her leg slightly between Alex's, allowing her friction against her thighs.

Alex was panting now.

"Kiss me, Chas."

And so she did.

CHAPTER 37

CHAS, 2016

Chas woke to the smell of sunshine. Alex.

She opened her eyes to find Alex watching her. "Good morning, gorgeous," Alex said lovingly.

They hadn't had sex or gone any further than taking off their shirts, but it was still the most intimate moment of Chas's life.

"Hey you," Chas croaked back groggily.

Of course, Alex would sound beautiful, and she would sound like a bullfrog.

"I canceled all of my clients today, but I will have to go back to work tomorrow. I figured you may need to go shopping for a few things, and we probably needed to make some decisions."

Chas knew Alex was right, but she was really enjoying this little fantasy bubble she found herself in.

"Thank you for taking the day off to help me."

"You bet! But first, breakfast!" Alex announced as she leapt out of the bed.

Okay, so Alex is a morning person. Noted.

"I'm not hungry," Chas playfully groaned and tried to pull Alex's pillow over her head. Alex appeared at her side, swift and quiet as a cat, and pulled the pillow off Chas's face. "Okay, sleepy, you just stay right here, and I'm going to go cook us something and bring it back to you."

Breakfast in bed? Another thing she had only seen in movies and on TV.

Alex left the room, and the next thing Chas heard was the sounds of a coffee maker.

Chas must have dozed back off while waiting for Alex to return because it was the smell that woke her … fresh-baked bread and bacon.

Alex huffed a small laugh. "You really are a sleepy muffin. Would you rather I take breakfast to the dining room and let you sleep a little longer?"

"No!" Chas practically choked out the reply. Did her voice get more froggy?

Alex set a tray on the foot of the bed and sat beside Chas. Chas pulled herself up in the bed to take a look at what Alex had whipped up that smelled so lovely. Avocado toast with crumbled bacon and some dark drizzle—probably some kind of balsamic sauce. Two cups of coffee and two cups of orange juice. And on the corner of the tray, a small vase with a very beautiful but unusual-looking flower.

"Alex, this looks amazing. Thank you!"

"Happy to do it. I love to cook."

"Well, that's perfect. I love to eat," Chas said with a bright smile, relieved that her voice was returning to its normal pitch and tone.

They ate the toast and drank the coffee and orange juice; all the while, their feet were touching under the covers. Chas was happy. If you had told her twenty-four hours ago that she would be happy today, she would have bet you anything that you were wrong.

"Alex, what is that flower?"

"It's hellebore. It grows in the backyard and blooms in the late winter and early spring. It's one of my favorites because of its defiance. A flower growing in the winter. It's like someone told all of the flowers they needed to bloom in spring, and the hellebore decided to do whatever she wanted. It made me think of you."

Alex was right. Chas realized she had been told to bloom in the spring, and here she was in the winter, blossoming into her true self.

CHAPTER 38
CHAS, 2016

After breakfast, Alex offered to take Chas wherever she wanted or needed to go. Practically, she needed to accomplish the following tasks: get access to her money; get a new phone; go to the DMV and get a replacement license; get new clothes; and make some decisions about what to do next. She had six days left at the beach cottage, but she needed to have a plan for where to go after.

The first three were the most complicated tasks and took the bulk of the morning and early afternoon. Alex told her that it might be easier to get the phone first and then go to the bank because they might need her to have access to emails, but without money, Chas was worried if she could even get a phone. To her immense relief, she didn't need any actual cash today. She opened her own account and phone line and would be billed monthly for the service, with the cost of the phone built into the monthly sum. At the bank, they set her up with Google Wallet (on her new phone) and had a new card being shipped to Alex's house in the next three to five business days. The DMV took the longest, and the wait would have been miserable if it hadn't been for Alex. Instead of being grumpy about the long and arduous wait, Alex decided they should play a game. There was a vending machine next to where they were sitting. Alex decided that they would play a game of which snack to eat next, and then whoever was the last one would obviously get the worst snack and would lose the game (the worst snack, of course, being the old, stale honey bun).

After the more stressful and/or mundane tasks of the morning, Chas was relieved to have some time to go shopping. She had access to her money now, and while she only had about $2,000 in her account, she knew that she would be returning to work next week and would be making more money soon. Knowing her funds were somewhat finite, Chas decided to be frugal with her choices. She just bought items for a sort of capsule wardrobe: underwear and bras, socks, two pairs of jeans (one light and one dark), several plain T-shirts of various earth tones, a few graphic T-shirts, a pair of khakis, a pair of dress pants, and a pair of flats. The salon she worked at didn't have a dress code as long as everyone wore closed-toed shoes and put on their apron with the salon logo over their clothes—so, it really didn't matter. Chas had her favorite pair of Adidas shoes on when she left, so with the addition of these new clothes, she was set for a while. All of this came to just under $500, so she still had some fallback money.

After a day full of chores, Alex was driving them back home when a realization hit Chas.

"Shit."

"What is it?" Alex looked concerned.

"Sorry, I made that sound worse than it was … I just realized I don't have a car for when I need to return to work next week, and if I take Uber all the way to Savannah, it's going to cost an arm and a leg."

Chas realized her mistake as soon as the words left her mouth.

"Not saying I'll still be at your place by then," she rushed in to say. "I just thought I might try to find something to rent on the island."

Alex was quiet for a moment.

"Chas, do you … do you really want to live somewhere else? Because I'm happy to have you stay at my house. You can have the spare room if you don't want to stay in the one we were in last night."

Chas noticed Alex didn't call it "her room."

"That is the nicest offer anyone has ever made me …" Chas started.

Alex's face fell, expecting Chas to decline.

"And I'd love to stay—under two conditions."

Alex's face returned to its bright, natural state. "Okay, Chas, name your terms," she said with a toothy grin.

"One, I get to pay half of the mortgage, and two, you have to promise that if we don't work out or things change for you, and you don't want me there any longer, you will tell me."

"Deal."

"Okay, well, I'll need to know what I owe you for rent this month so I can keep that in mind when I go look for a car. I want to make sure I have enough saved that I can pay the first month now."

"Zero dollars would be due this month," Alex said with a truly wicked grin.

"Alex, you promised …"

"I promised you could pay half the mortgage, and you can. I don't pay a mortgage. My grandfather on my dad's side left me the house when he passed away last year. It was supposed to go to my dad, but he passed away before Grandpa, so it came to me. I had been living there with him for a few years while his health was failing, and after he passed, I found out that it was mine and that he had paid the house off years earlier—he lived there for most of his adult life."

"You little sneak!" Chas exclaimed.

Alex just grinned wider.

"Okay then, I get to pay all of the utilities and groceries."

"Nope, that wasn't one of the two conditions," Alex said with an all-out laugh.

Chas rolled her eyes.

"Okay, smartie, but I won't be a freeloader or someone you have to care for. I want to do this together."

Chas flushed—that statement assumed a lot. It was clear that Chas was not speaking in terms of a roommate situation. She was including so much more than bills in that statement.

Alex's exuberance softened, and her smile relaxed.

"Chas, I would love to do this together. Whatever this is. I am in."

CHAPTER 39
CHAS, 2016

When they arrived back at Alex's house, Chas was famished. She realized that throughout the day, she and Alex hadn't stopped for lunch or any snacks—despite the vending machine game. She hadn't had anything after her avocado toast this morning.

"Hey Alex, I'm hungry, and I would love to take you out to dinner. It's the least I can do after you helped with everything today."

"Chas, are you asking me out on a date?" Alex was clearly baiting her.

"Why, my dearest Alex, I believe I am. Let me try again, a little more properly. Alex, would you please allow me to take you out tonight?"

"I believe I will," Alex said with an extremely thick, faux Southern accent.

They both burst into a fit of giggles.

"Okay, how do you feel about going back to that bar you picked me up from last night? The food was amazing, and now that I have some money, I would really like to return and pay Kip for their kindness."

That reminded Chas of something.

"Last night, when I told Kip my name, they seemed to recognize it, and when you answered my call, you thought I was them. Is Kip a friend of yours?"

Alex's smile brightened even further. Chas loved seeing her face light up. It was like the sunshine she smelled of was actually taking over her whole being.

"Actually, yes. Kip and Mara are two of my best friends. They are really more like what I imagine people have when they have siblings." (So Alex was an only child, Chas noted.) "Kip and Mara came to the island in situations not too unlike yours … Kip was disowned by their family when they came out as non-binary, and Mara was living with friends and couch-surfing, because her mom kicked her out for being pan. For being a very small island, we have a lot of 'diversity' in the LGBTQIA+ arena."

All that made sense, but Chas still wanted to know a little more.

"So why did Kip know *my* name, Alex?" Now, Chas was the one doing the baiting.

"I may have mentioned you." Alex was feigning nonchalance.

"Just mentioned me?"

"Probably only once," Alex replied with a laugh.

"I somehow doubt that," Chas said with a wink.

"In truth, I did tell Kip and Mara about you. The night I gave you a massage, I went to the bar and got blitzed drunk. Kip had to drive me home and tuck me into bed. I couldn't stop talking or thinking about you. It felt like I left you in a house with something wrong. It felt like I left a piece of me with you. I didn't handle it well. I was convinced I would never see you again, and it felt like something was being ripped away from me, even though I had only spent a few hours with you."

Chas knew and understood the exact feeling. That was the night she had found herself in the ocean.

Alex looked a little ashamed of the confession.

"Alex, the night you massaged me was the night I went into the sea. I was dealing with the exact same emotions and feelings. You weren't alone, and neither was I."

Alex pulled Chas into a hug. She really did give the best hugs. Chas was being scooped up, but not being picked up and moved around as Alex pleased, just held tightly while she remained on her own two feet.

"I would very much like to meet Kip and Mara officially if you think they would be at the bar tonight," Chas offered. "If not, we could always invite them to meet us for dinner."

"They are at the bar. They've been texting me all day, asking me to bring you by," Alex said with a smile.

"Let's go surprise them," Chas said.

Alex extended her hand, Chas intertwined her fingers with Alex's, and they left for the bar.

CHAPTER 40
CHAS, 2016

Once they reached the bar, Alex came around the car to open the door for Chas, but she had already hopped out and was making her way to the back of the vehicle. Alex held out her hand, and Chas took it. They had held hands the whole drive to the bar (granted, that was less than ten minutes), but it was the first time since last night that they had had sustained contact.

Chas savored every second of it but didn't want Alex to feel like she needed to show up holding Chas's hand if she wasn't ready to publicly be a couple. Chas slowed a little and relaxed her grip. Alex stopped and turned to look at her.

"Chas, do you want to hold hands?"

"More than anything, I just wasn't sure if you wanted to 'go public,' or if you would rather take it slow. I don't know anyone on the island other than you, so I won't have to explain anything to anyone, but I wasn't sure if you were ready."

Alex squeezed her hand, leaned in, and planted a kiss on Chas's forehead. Then she leaned in further and kissed her lips, then her cheeks, and then her hand that was intertwined with Alex's.

"I have wanted to have this," Alex gestured at their intertwined hands, "my whole life. I don't know what the future looks like, but I know that I have wanted to feel this way and never have before. For me, it's worth putting everything on the line. You aren't a temporary part of my life unless *you* want to be. I want you. I want to be with you."

Chas's heart stumbled again. Alex seemed to have that effect on her whenever she gave a voice to what Chas was thinking and feeling.

"I don't want to be temporary. I don't know what it looks like either, but I want you and want to be with you, and I can't imagine any day from here forward without you."

Alex smiled and squeezed her hand, and they continued to the bar.

When they walked in, the bar was empty, but most of the tables in the open seating area were full. Mara was at the hostess stand and broke out in the biggest, brightest smile when she spotted Alex and Chas approaching.

"The famous Chas," Mara said with reverence.

"The best friend, Mara," Chas replied in the same tone.

"Aw, did you tell her I'm your best friend, Alex, darling? Kip is going to be *sooo* jealous," Mara said with obvious delight.

"Kip!" Mara called over to the bar. "Guess what? Alex told Chas I'm her best friend!"

"To be fair, Alex said you were *both* her best friends," Chas clarified.

"Let's just leave that part out for ol' Kipper over there," Mara said with a conspiratorial wink.

Chas chuckled, and Alex said, "She's always like this. Don't bother trying to tame that one; you can't."

"Alex, darling, that may be the kindest thing you've ever said about me." Mara beamed.

Alex gave Chas a look that clearly said, "See what I mean?" and Chas laughed.

"Mara, love, we'll be at the bar if you have some spare time and want to pop by," Alex said as she headed for Kip at the bar.

Alex pulled out the seat for Chas and then sat down beside her. Kip came right over. "I had a funny feeling I would be seeing you again sooner than later." Kip's gaze swept over Chas.

"You could have told me you were Alex's best friend," Chas said, feigning being cross with Kip.

"Oh, I'm not Alex's best friend. That honor is reserved for Mara, love," Kip said this in an intentionally loud voice so Mara would hear.

Chas looked over and caught Mara sticking her tongue out at Kip. Chas snorted, which appeared to please Mara from across the room.

"They really are like siblings," Chas said, still laughing.

"So, does anyone want to fill me in, or would you like me to guess where we are in this little love story?" Kip was direct. Chas really liked that about them.

"Well, I can't speak for Alex, darling," Chas began, quickly adopting the same term of endearment they used, "but for me, it was the first touch, and I knew something was different. My story is long and complex, but I found myself not being able to function without her. It took just three days of knowing her for me to find and know myself."

Chas was looking at Alex the whole time, and Alex was holding eye contact for the entire story. Alex was here, looking deeply into Chas's eyes, knowing that this was the way she could support her best—by seeing her. As she had always done since day one.

Chas broke eye contact to look at Kip, who was now sobbing silently. "It's just so beautiful," they said.

Alex barked a laugh. "Kip, you always were a softie for a good love story."

Alex paused and looked at Chas, looking slightly panicked.

But Chas had caught the words: "Love story"—they were a love story.

Chas slid one hand up Alex's jaw, cupping her fingers behind Alex's head around her ear.

"I'm really enjoying our love story." Chas kissed Alex right there in the middle of the bar, with everyone around and no one around at all.

CHAPTER 41
CHAS, 2016

Chas was still enjoying her kiss at the bar when Kip started clapping loudly.

"Y'all listen up now!" they called out, voice dripping with a dramatic Southern belle flair. "We're buyin' a round for the whole bar—'cause my best friend has finally found love, bless her heart!"

Mara rolled her eyes at the "best friend" part, and Alex grinned, relaxing her hand on Chas's leg and handing Chas a menu.

"Kip, do you have time for a break so you can join us for dinner?" Alex asked.

"Oh, Alex darling, I would love to, but I'm just the busiest beaver over here, keeping all these lovely patrons well-hydrated."

Alex looked down the bar.

"Kip, we're the only ones at the bar."

"Well, lookie there. You're right! Looks like I'm free as a jaybird."

Chas was loving this interaction. Her cheeks hurt from

smiling at the three of them. It was like watching three siblings all vying for each other's attention.

"Chas, baby, what do you want to drink? Mango marg like last time?" Kip offered, continuing the southern drawl.

"That would be great!" Chas giggled.

"Okay, let me get that going, and I will put in the order for chips and guac (since I know you love them), and then we can sit and chill." Kip had dropped the accent by now. Too bad, Chas liked the southern belle version of them.

"They can be a lot," Alex whispered in Chas's ear, "but you will love them."

"I already do," Chas whispered right back.

Alex gave her leg a squeeze of gratitude. Chas realized this was a big moment for Alex. What if Chas didn't like Mara or Kip? What if they didn't like her? It would have put Alex in the worst position. Thankfully, that was not something anyone needed to worry about. She could see Alex settle in and just enjoy their time together.

They had a feast—Kip must have ordered one of everything on the menu. Chas got her very own order of chips and guac (she really did love Kip), and they shared everything else. There were crab legs, shrimp, and chicken wings, and nachos, and some sort of hamburger, Kip cut into four pieces, and a bunch of sausages cut up with dipping sauces to pair with the little meaty bites. Chas had never seen so much food, and she was more surprised at the fact that they ate it all between the four of them. Mara couldn't sit down because she still had to perform her hostess duties, but she ran back and forth from the table every chance she got, stealing food off of Alex's or Kip's plate and then running away laughing like a wild banshee.

Chas was falling in love. Hard. But it wasn't just with Alex. Chas was loving this life, her new friends, Alex, and herself.

CHAPTER 42
CHAS, 2016

When they returned to Alex's house later that evening, Alex opened the door for Chas. Chas was still on cloud nine from the night with the three friends. She couldn't remember a single night of her life that had felt more authentic and grounded in reality, instead of some fantasy version of herself she had manicured.

Her breathing was light, and her heart was full.

Chas walked into their bedroom to get ready for bed with a huge smile on her face. "Well, shit …"

"Uh oh," Alex said, laughing. "What did you forget now?"

"Hey, how did you know?" Chas demanded.

"You typically curse when you realize you forgot something vital," Alex stated as if that were the most obvious thing in the world.

"Huh," Chas said in a musing tone. "Okay, well, yes—I forgot to get PJs today. After all that shopping, I thought I had everything I needed."

Alex walked up behind Chas and brushed her curls aside, seeking out her ear. "I rather hoped you'd find yourself wearing mine again," Alex whispered, her breath caressing Chas's ear and sending chills everywhere. Chas's breath caught in her throat.

She was ready and wanted to take things further, but was it too soon? Would Alex think she was just rebounding?

Alex kissed the dip on her shoulder where her collarbone created a hollow. "Chas, whatever it is you're worried about, you can share it with me, and we can work through it together."

"I just don't want you to think you're a rebound or that I am moving too fast, and this is the type of person I am, that I just go from being married to having a girlfriend overnight."

Alex moved to face her. "I don't think that. I think you were married out of obligation, and then you found your match in an unexpected place, and now you are authentically pursuing that. It's beautiful, and I am happy it's me."

That was all Chas needed to hear.

"Alex, how do you feel if I ask you to make love to me? Are you ready for that, or should we wait?"

Alex's eyes were soft and warm and didn't change when Chas posed the question.

"Chas, I'm ready as long as you are."

"I'm ready." Chas was completely breathless, so the words came out as a gasp and not a whisper.

"If you change your mind, just tell me to stop. I'll do the same," Alex said in a breathy voice.

Then, she reached out and touched the hem of Chas's shirt. Chas nodded, urging Alex to take the next step. Alex pulled the shirt upward, and Chas lifted her arms. Alex dropped the shirt on the ground and placed a strong arm behind Chas's back, supporting her. She placed her hand flat on Chas's back and released her bra clasp (Chas needed to learn how to do that move—it was hot). Alex came back around to face her and gently lifted the bra off of Chas's shoulders, down her arms, and then allowed the bra to drop to the ground to join her shirt. Chas felt exposed in the very best way. It was the same feeling she had in the robe on that first day, allowing Alex to see her. Her nipples peaked from the cold and her desire. Her breasts felt heavy.

Alex took off her own shirt and used her one-handed trick to remove her bra. Now, Chas was free to gaze upon Alex as Alex was gazing upon her. Both women stood together, not touching, but just getting to know each other's bodies in precise detail. Chas noticed the color and shape of Alex's nipples, different from her own but perfect and hard and waiting for her touch.

Chas bridged the space between them and grazed Alex's nipples with her searching fingers. Alex leaned back her head, and her breathing shifted from her stomach to her chest. Chas loved watching Alex's body respond to her touch. It was validating in a way she didn't know she needed. Chas leaned in and kissed the space between Alex's breasts, gently pulling Alex's nipple into her mouth and sucking lightly. Alex was panting now. When Chas was done licking and sucking, she kissed the wet peak and stood back up to face Alex.

Alex reached out for the button on Chas's pants. Chas nodded her consent and encouragement. Alex tenderly unbuttoned and then unzipped Chas's pants, pulling them down slowly but leaving Chas's underwear in place. Chas stepped out of her jeans and left them with the growing collection of clothes on the floor. Chas froze. She hadn't shaved her legs or her pubic hair since the night before her wedding. Her personal life had been such a whirlwind that she just hadn't thought of that part.

"Alex, I … I haven't shaved, and my legs are going to be prickly."

"That doesn't matter in the least to me, but I can understand if that's bothersome to you. Do you want me to stop?"

"I really don't want you to stop. I just needed to say it."

"Chas, your body is perfect. It doesn't have a single flaw and never will have one in my eyes. Body hair doesn't bother me, no matter where it's growing. You should do what you want as far as that goes. I don't have any expectations. I just want it to feel right for you."

Chas breathed deeply—not quite a sigh of relief, but more a deep breath before plunging into a place she had never been but was desperate to go.

Alex took off her pants. Then Alex reached for the waistband of her own underwear. She paused again, letting Chas decide if this was going further. Chas was suddenly hungry in a way she had never been before. She completely understood books and movies using that term for this sensation. She wanted Alex. In her mouth. Inside of her. Filling her up while allowing her to drink her fill of her. If hungry was what normal people felt, Chas was sure she was starving. Chas nodded, but instead of allowing Alex to remove her own underwear, she stepped forward and replaced Alex's fingers with her own. Now it was Alex's turn to nod.

Chas didn't hesitate further. She gently and expectantly pulled down Alex's underwear, exposing her completely. Chas's mouth literally started watering, and that same wet spot from the night before was showing through her own underwear. Chas stood back up after helping the underwear off Alex's hips. Alex looked down at Chas's underwear and noticed the wet spot spreading through the fabric. Alex groaned deep in her throat and reached for it. Chas let her feel the wet patch she had created. Alex gently rubbed her fingers up and down on the fabric, tracing the lines of Chas's vagina. Chas could feel her barely graze her clit. It sent a shock wave through her body. If Alex wasn't careful, she was going to undo her before her panties were even removed. Alex seemed to relish the reaction and did it again to watch Chas shatter a little. Alex grinned, and Chas grinned back. Alex traced her fingers back up the front of the now very wet underwear. She kissed Chas's cheek and slid Chas's underwear to the floor. Both women were bare.

It was the most alive either of them had ever felt.

CHAPTER 43
CHAS, 2016

The next morning, Chas didn't wake to the smell of sunshine as she had before. She woke to the utter, quiet stillness of being alone. This realization jolted her out of sleep, and she sat up in bed a little disoriented. She looked over to Alex's side of the bed, but it was empty.

A note was lying where Alex had been.

Chas,

I had to go to the other side of the island for my first appointment, so I had an early start to the day. I've left a muffin and coffee on the kitchen counter for you. If you need anything, just text me, and I'll respond asap. There won't be one minute today when you won't possess my thoughts. Last night was amazing. You're amazing. I adore you.

With Love,

Alex

Chas flushed a deep red, the color overtaking her neck and cheeks as she thought about their shared night, mentally replaying every moment as she lay in bed. She craved Alex. She had a feeling that their days would be filled with fun and laughter, and their nights (with any luck) would be filled with lovemaking and whispered secrets.

Chas wasn't exactly sure what she was going to do today. She did know that she needed to buy a car at some point. That was the last thing she had to tackle before the week ended, and she had to return to work. At some point, she would need to meet a lawyer to work on getting her divorce finalized, but that was a problem for future Chas, if she'd ever heard one.

Chas had slept in nothing but Alex's T-shirt from the day before. It still smelled faintly of her—sunshine.

Chas padded into the kitchen and demolished her muffin and coffee. When did she become so ravenous? It was like the toll of the last few days was requiring more and more food. The muffin was a heavenly cinnamon muffin that tasted like fall. The coffee was rich and had just the right amount of cream and very little sugar. This was bliss.

After Chas finished eating, she went back to the bedroom, made the bed, and put on underwear, a new pair of jeans, and a graphic tee. She threw her hair into a messy bun and put on her favorite pair of sneakers before opening Uber on her phone. The closest car dealership with used cars and financing was in Savannah. It would cost her a bit to get to it, but she really needed a car, and she wanted to go back by the beach cottage one last time to collect her robe and her old journal. She didn't want the journal for sentimental reasons, but it held her most private thoughts, and she couldn't stand the idea of someone else finding it.

Ten minutes later, the Uber pulled up to Alex's house. On the way to the car dealership, Chas texted Alex.

"Morning, beautiful, thank you for the note, the muffin, and the coffee. I devoured them all. Can't wait to see you when you get home." Chas paused before sending. *Is that last line too presumptuous? Home?* That implies it was *their* home. But Alex had made her feelings clear. She wanted them to be together. She wanted Chas for as long as Chas wanted to stay. For now, at least, it was their home. Chas hit send.

Forty minutes later, the Uber stopped at the used car dealership. Chas had no idea what she was doing or even if she was going to be able to purchase a car, but the online advertisement ensured that they would work with potential customers if their credit score was good and they had a variety of financing options available. Instead of walking around and getting attached to any one car in particular, Chas decided to head straight into the main office and ask for assistance. An older gentleman with a bow tie came right up to Chas as she entered the door.

"Hi, my name is Bart. Can I help you today?" Bart said with a salesman's grin—slightly cheesy but well-practiced.

"Yes. I don't know if I'll qualify to buy a car, and I was hoping we could check on that and set a realistic budget before I browse. I'm going through a rough breakup, and I need a way to get myself around."

"Okay, let's take a seat and see what we can do."

Bart spent the better part of an hour asking Chas questions —what her income was, how long she had worked at the salon, what debt she had, and so on—and clicking away on his keyboard, punching in her answers in some system she couldn't see.

"Do you want to put down a down payment?" Bart asked.

"I can. I have $1,500 today, but that would pretty much drain my savings. How much would I have to put down?"

"Oh, you wouldn't have to put down anything if you didn't want to. Down payments bring down your overall cost, so they're often recommended, but based on your situation, I would suggest maybe $500, so you can keep some pocket money."

The longer she sat with Bart, the more she liked him. He was about her father's age, she guessed, and he seemed genuinely helpful and considerate of her situation.

"Okay, after I put in all of the numbers, it looks like your credit score is a little lower than we typically like for financing. You wouldn't happen to have anyone willing to co-sign, would you?"

Chas shook her head. She was not about to call Alex and ask for that.

"I thought maybe not when you said you were on your own after a breakup. Okay, I'm actually the owner of this dealership, and I have a daughter about your age. I would want someone to step in and help her out if she were in your position. So, tell you what, I'm going to waive the issue of you not meeting the credit requirements and do a manual override so we can get you that financing."

"That's really so kind of you!" Chas exclaimed in gratitude. "I promise you I will make every single payment on time. You have my word."

"Okay, after everything, we can do a car for up to $17,000. That's a pretty strong number, and we have several cars available in that price range. Do you want me to take you around the lot and show you which ones fall within that budget?"

"That would be great!" Now, Chas allowed herself to get a little excited. Even if it wasn't some fancy car, it would be hers.

Bart spent another hour walking Chas around the lot and pointing out all of the cars within her price range. By the end of the tour, she had narrowed it down to two cars: a blue 2017

Volkswagen Jetta or a white 2019 Hyundai Sonata. Bart offered to take her on a test drive of both so she could make an informed decision. After riding around in both vehicles, Chas had decided: She was going home with a blue Jetta today!

The paperwork took what felt like an eternity, but Bart assured her this was all part of the process and apologized for the lengthiness. At the end of it all, Bart had keys for Chas. Chas picked up the keys, thanked Bart for his help and kindness—she had grown rather fond of him over the last three hours—and then headed out for her first real ride in her new car.

Chas stopped at a drive-thru for a quick and cheap bite to eat and then made her way back to Tybee. She needed to swing by the beach cottage, and then she could go back home. *Home*— such a simple, wonderful word and concept. This stop should only take a few minutes, and then she would be all set to finish the week in her fantasy bubble without any further life-changing interruptions.

Chas bounded up the stairs, eager to get back to the Jetta and then home. She opened the front door and rushed past the kitchen, heading straight into the bedroom to collect her robe. The odd thing was … she swore she had left it at the foot of the bed, but it wasn't there. Chas went to the bathroom, thinking she may have put it back where it had been hanging previously. No luck. Chas walked back to the kitchen and then headed into the living room toward the back deck.

"Looking for something?"

The voice sent a jolt straight through her. It was an all-too-familiar feeling. A scream was trapped in her chest and trying to escape, but her immediate response was to suppress it. Only one person had that effect on her. Brian.

CHAPTER 44
CHAS, 2016

"Where have you been? Off fucking that dyke?" Brian's tone was dripping venom. He was sitting on the couch next to the sliding glass door that led to the back porch. Her robe was draped across his lap, and the journal was placed on top of it. He looked like he hadn't showered or slept in days.

Chas realized she hadn't told Alex where she was headed or what she was doing. Alex had no idea she was here. Chas couldn't whip out her phone and start texting without risking more problems.

Chas had her phone in her hand. She subtly opened the text thread with Alex and hit Talk to Text. "Brian, what are you doing back here at the cottage? I just came by to get some things. I'm not staying."

Chas looked down at the phone to make sure it had captured that message and then hit send. She could only hope that Alex would get the message and come here to find her.

Brian had never been violent. She didn't think he was going to start now, but she couldn't ever know for certain what he would be capable of when he was wounded. Chas needed to tread lightly, try to work her way out of the situation with calm, precise steps.

"Where is your car? I didn't see it outside," Chas queried. Maybe small talk would allow a more natural exit.

"I parked it further down the road and paid for street parking, so if you did come back here, you wouldn't see it."

Smart—that's exactly what she would have done.

"Right. Well, I'm going to pick up my journal and robe and go," Chas said with a calm she didn't feel.

"Like hell you are," Brian replied with an ugly sneer.

"I asked you a question. Where have you been? Have you been fucking that dyke? Did you like it, Chasity? I read your journal, and from what you wrote, I bet you did like it. It's unnatural and wrong, so of course you would like it; you're a pervert."

"I stopped owing you an explanation of my whereabouts the moment you shipped me back to Restorative Hope." Chas wasn't going to rise to the rest of his comments. She would not give him that satisfaction.

Brian stood up and threw the robe and the journal on the floor.

Chas decided he could have them. Neither was worth the price of coming near him. Chas turned and rushed for the front door.

Not fast enough.

Brian had her in a familiar grip: her elbow in his fingers.

Brian had never been violent, but on multiple occasions, he had coerced her into moving, either by picking her up or grabbing her. These were things she hadn't registered when she was submitting to him, but now that she was free, it caused her blood to boil.

"Get your hands off me, Brian," Chas said with a lethal calm now.

"You are my wife!" Brian's scream was chilling. "You are MY

wife," he stated again, emphasizing his possession of her. She didn't follow that doctrine anymore, so he could state it all he wanted—it didn't make it true.

Brian's grip was hurting now; it was surely going to leave a mark.

"You are MY wife, and you have been off fucking a dyke!" Brian was positively screaming in her face. "Your parents are disgusted by you, you know? I told them I would come back for you, and they told me I could have you if I wanted you, but they were done. Nobody wants you like this, Chastity. You are being an unfaithful little whore, and it's even worse because it's with ... with a woman. You know the scripture. You know you're going to hell. I'm going to save you from yourself. We're going to Restorative Hope, and you're going to *obey*."

Chas couldn't take it. She spat directly in Brian's face. Brian released her arm and backhanded her across the face a millisecond after the spit. Chas fell to the ground.

"What the actual fuck do you think you're doing, you son of a bitch?" screamed Alex.

She came. Thank God she came!

Brian looked as if he might try to murder them both, but Alex was ready for him. Alex was holding up her phone, camera facing Brian and Chas.

"We are live-streaming you, you little fucker. I'm not about to let you get away with touching her again. The police are already on their way here, so you can decide if you want to stay and wait for them or go. Either way, they *will* be catching up with you."

Chas was stunned—mostly by the slap she had just taken to the face. The force of it sent fireworks shooting across her eye, and it felt like her eye should be bulging out of its socket.

Alex took slow, deliberate steps toward Chas. Brian had positioned himself between them.

"You will move and let me get to Chas."

"Her name is Chastity, and she is mine."

"She is her own person, and I have asked nicely for the last time. You will move away from her."

Brian was undeterred. As Chas attempted to rise and go to Alex, Brian seized her by the hair. "You have lost it, Brian!" Chas screamed, clawing at his hand and trying to draw blood. The sound of her scream shattered any remaining restraint Alex had. Brian, preoccupied with his grip, didn't see Alex marching toward them until he looked up and she punched him in the face.

CHAPTER 45
CHAS, 2016

Hours later, they arrived home. They had spent time with the police, and charges were filed. The police took pictures of Chas's arm, which was already showing a bruise, and her face, which had taken the worst of it. Her eye was now swollen shut. She hadn't seen it yet, but she knew it looked bad by the way Alex kept checking on it every few minutes.

Alex helped Chas out of the car. She had only been manhandled and then hit in the face, but her entire body ached as if he had thrown her down a flight of stairs.

"Chas, where do you want to go once we get inside? Do you want me to help you get situated on the couch, or the bed, or something else?"

"Alex, I want to shower. Everything hurts, and I just want to feel clean."

"Okay, I'll go start the shower, and then we can get you in there."

Chas loved her even harder for saying *we*. Chas knew she was going to need help with this—her body wasn't moving normally—but Alex saw it, and Chas wasn't going to have to ask for help. It was being provided without a request.

Alex brought the shower to a warm, pleasant temperature. Not the normally scalding temperature Chas usually preferred, but something calmer. Safer.

Then she brought Chas into the bathroom. Chas sat on the toilet, utterly exhausted by the walk from the couch to the bathroom. Maybe a shower wasn't a great idea.

Alex helped Chas out of her clothes and wrapped her in a towel. Then Alex undressed herself.

Alex offered her hand, and Chas pulled herself up to standing. Alex led them into the shower. She helped wash Chas's body, sensing her discomfort with movement and knowing she wanted to feel clean. She gently scrubbed her with a loofah that smelled of eucalyptus.

It was then that the tears started flowing down Chas's face. They were silent but caused full-body shudders. Alex wrapped her arms around Chas and stayed with her in the water.

CHAPTER 46
CHAS, 2016

Alex tenderly dressed Chas in her shirt, a garment that still held the day's warmth and the faint scent of sunshine. Chas sank into the fabric, the familiar smell enveloping her in a sense of peace she had never known. Even with Alex gone, her lingering scent was a silent, powerful caress.

Chas must have drifted off because she awoke to voices coming from the hallway beyond the closed bedroom door.

"I will run him over with my car!" Mara's tone was dead serious, and her voice was raised.

"Shhh—Mara, we all want him to pay, but who gives a shit about him? We need to care for Chas. Alex, what can we do?" This was Kip.

A new flood of warmth rushed through her. Alex had called their tribe, and they had come.

Chas stood up on shaky legs and made her way to the door. When she opened it, the three stopped their chatter, and Alex looked at Mara a little crossly for clearly having woken Chas.

Mara didn't catch Alex's look. She was busy staring directly at Chas's eye. Kip was giving her a full toe-to-head appraisal, starting at her feet and making their way up, checking for any other signs of damage. When Kip's eyes landed on her face, their eyes darkened, eyebrows pinching together, and they made a face Chas hated to see on her usually cheerful friend.

Mara turned away and headed for the kitchen without another word. Kip opened their arms, a silent offer of a hug. Chas knew Kip wouldn't be offended if she didn't take it, but she wanted to have her friends' offered comfort.

Chas crossed the space, still wobbly, and leaned into Kip's chest. Kip was much taller than she had realized—a solid head and a half taller than herself and at least half a head taller than Alex. Chas leaned her head against the base of Kip's throat, feeling the warmth of her friend replace the coolness of the air she had been standing in. Kip smelled of something smoky and woodsy. It suited them perfectly. Kip's hug was so different from Alex's, but just as reassuring. Instead of feeling scooped up, like she did with Alex, she felt Kip wrap their arms around her shoulders, gently resting their head on hers. Chas took a deep, settling breath.

"Thank you for coming."

"There isn't anywhere else I'd be right now, Chas baby." Kip's use of her pet name from the other night brought a small smile to her lips. Even that movement hurt a bit, but it was worth it.

Mara returned, stomping back down the hallway. Chas peeked up from Kip's embrace to find Mara standing there with a bag of frozen peas.

"We need to get ice on that eye, Chas. It's pretty rough, and I know it can't feel great. Do you want to come to the living room and sit, or can we get you settled back in bed? We wanted to see you, but you don't have to stay with us and entertain; we're completely fine if you want to be tucked back into bed."

Mara wasn't offering the kind of sweet reassurance Kip had provided but something else entirely. Chas was learning that Mara showed her love through action. She saw the eye, and although it had clearly sickened her to see her friend looking this way, she had sprung into helping, not dwelling on the emotions but on what Chas physically needed.

This trio of humans who had found their way into Chas's life was a perfect blend of empathy, compassion, care, and kindness.

In that moment, despite her day, Chas knew she was profoundly lucky.

CHAPTER 47
CHAS, 2016

It had been six days since the incident at the beach cottage. Alex, Kip, and Mara had taken care of things in the days after. They had brought her Jetta back to Alex's house, retrieved her robe and journal that had been discarded at the house, and checked out of the cottage on her behalf.

Today was her first day back at work. The bruise, now a purple splotch, was beginning to fade into a sallow yellow-green color around the edges of her eye. Alex and Kip had practiced covering it as best they could the day before in a dry run, preparing for this morning. Kip showed Chas how to blend the concealer first, then the foundation, and followed by a fairly thick covering of eyeshadow to make it less apparent that this eye was different.

All things considered, it had worked remarkably well. If you knew she had a black eye, you could see its edges through the mask of makeup, but if you didn't, Chas just looked like she might be trying out a new emo/goth look with heavier, darker eye makeup.

Chas and Alex had talked through the option of just leaving it open and not trying to hide it. She had done nothing wrong, and she was not ashamed of the bruise—it was a reflection of Brian's poor character, not her own. But ultimately, Chas decided she wanted it covered. She didn't want her regulars to worry, and she wasn't ready to talk about it with people outside her tribe.

Alex had an early morning, so she was already gone when Chas got up to start her day. Chas's first client was at 10:30 a.m., so she needed to leave by 9:30. She hadn't had to make this drive yet. It should take thirty minutes on a good day, but if traffic into Savannah was bad, it would take longer.

Chas applied her makeup the way Kip had taught her and put on her Adidas shoes, her darker blue jeans, and a plain, mossy-colored T-shirt. Her hair was up in a messy bun—she spent too much time on her makeup to dedicate any time to her curls. Chas appraised herself in the mirror. She was supposed to be coming back from her two-week honeymoon with her husband. Instead, she was coming back from her liberation and the first week of falling deep in love with Alex. It was like an entirely new person was returning to her salon, one who looked like Chastity but was definitely and confidently Chas.

She knew confidently that she was in love with Alex. They had said the words "with love" and "love story," but she hadn't expressly said that she was in love with Alex yet. She was ready, but she wanted the timing to feel organic and meaningful. She and Alex hadn't been intimate beyond soft, caressing kisses since the fight with Brian. Chas knew it wasn't that Alex didn't want to, but that Alex wasn't preoccupied with sex when Chas was recovering. Chas could determine when she was ready, and she knew Alex would be ready to match her.

Chas collected her belongings. Earlier that week, Alex, being Alex, had asked her what she needed to return to work. Chas really didn't need anything special; her station had all of her tools, so luckily, they weren't lost in her escape from her former life. The only thing she really needed was a water bottle to keep at her station so she could take a couple of gulps between clients and maybe a snack. Alex heard her mention this, and that same day, when Alex returned from work, she had an Owala water bottle and a box of granola bars.

Chas was ready. Or as ready as she would ever be. She grabbed her keys, her water bottle, and a granola bar and confidently walked out to her Jetta.

When she opened the door, she found a note from Alex propped up in her seat. This had become a thing between them —every day, Alex left her a note somewhere. Sometimes, they simply said "Good morning, beautiful." Other days, they contained a small inside joke or a recount of something funny from the day prior. Either way, each day, she was on the lookout for her note. Today's note read:

My dearest Chas,

Just a quick note to say I'm thinking of you as you start your day. Remember that you are brave, beautiful, confident, and perfect. You have every right to continue pursuing the wonderful woman you've become, and I'm so proud to watch you choose yourself every single day. I can't wait to see you tonight, to hold you, and to hear all about your day.

Yours,

Alex

Chas smiled and climbed into the driver's seat. Alex's note had bolstered her confidence, and she reversed out of the driveway.

Thirty-five minutes later, Chas arrived at the salon. Her

stomach had started to knot on the way there. People would definitely be asking about her honeymoon, and nobody would know she had left Brian—her coworkers and her clients alike. She hadn't worked out what to say when they cheerfully asked her to regale them with tales of love and happiness. She had plenty of those stories to tell from the last week, but none that included Brian.

Still, Chas got out of her car and marched into the salon, her head held high.

CHAPTER 48
CHAS, 2016

Another week had passed since Chas had returned to work at the salon. The first day had gone by quite uneventfully. People asked, and she provided a brief explanation: She and Brian were no longer together. She didn't include the aggression he had shown or her relationship with Alex in her stories. It wasn't that she was ashamed, but that she wasn't seeking anyone's approval or permission. She didn't need to explain herself; she simply needed to state the fact that she was not staying married to Brian.

Today, Chas was headed back into Savannah, but not to the salon. She was meeting with a lawyer she had contacted last week to discuss her next steps. Chas was relieved to be taking this step here and now. The bruise was mostly gone, but she had brought the police report as well as her journal from Restorative Hope (with Megan's perverse notes in the margins of her own accounts from 2006). She wasn't sure if this would be helpful, but most people hadn't heard of Restorative Hope or their methods—the program wasn't exactly advertised on billboards and flyers. Chas hoped it would help her explain some of the events that had led her to this position.

Alex had offered to come, but Chas knew she could take this step on her own.

Chas entered the tall brick building on the edge of the park; it felt familiar, as she'd had a view of it from her old bedroom window. She checked in with the receptionist and then sat down on a comfy leather sofa next to an old fireplace that was clearly ornamental now.

"Chastity Jacobs," a man's voice called from the hallway. Chas's stomach curled in on itself. She needed that not to be her name. It wasn't her name.

"It's Chas," she corrected the man.

"Hi Chas, my name's Brian." Chas's curled-up stomach dropped through the floor.

This Brian was tall—over six feet—and had what some would refer to as a dad bod. He had a handsome face with kind, soft brown eyes and a five o'clock shadow. This Brian was not the Brian she was escaping, she reminded herself.

"Hi," Chas managed to breathe out.

Brian walked her down the hall to his office. He motioned for her to take a seat on the opposite side of his desk while he sat behind his computer screen. Brian moved the screen, which was on a swivel, so that he could see Chas without looking around the monitor.

Chas had selected this lawyer's office because their website had come up when she had searched for "LGBTQIA+ safe lawyers near me." She didn't even know that you could search for supportive businesses before. Brian's practice had come up: "Stern and Sons—serving Savannah since 1986." Chas had looked over the website and noticed that on their homepage, they had a list of previous and existing clients, and she saw the words "proudly supporting and protecting members of the LGBTQIA+ community." Chas had scheduled an appointment immediately.

"So, Chas, tell me a little about yourself, and what brings you in today," Brian began in a gentle but professional tone. "I see that you're seeking a divorce lawyer, and I'm happy to help with that, but I'll need to know the case history. If you're comfortable, I'll take notes on my computer while you share, and then we can come up with a game plan together."

"Yes, that would be fine," Chas said. Then she told this Brian about everything that had happened, starting back with her first experience at Restorative Hope.

Brian sat patiently, listening and taking notes. Chas wasn't emotional when she recounted everything. She felt so far removed from the things that had happened to her that she felt in control now. When Chas finished her account, she looked up and met Brian's eyes.

"Well, first let me say that I'm so sorry this happened to you," Brian said in a firm but kind tone.

"I'm going to have to ask some questions that may seem personal or even like I don't believe you, but I want you to know and trust definitively that I do believe you and I do trust your account of what took place."

"Okay, I will answer anything I can—you can ask whatever you need." Chas had expected questions, so this wasn't shocking, but it was nice to hear that Brian believed her.

"Okay, so I know you talked to me about your time at Restorative Hope both in 2006 and a few weeks ago. I am most interested in your time spent there in 2006. Would there be any proof that you were there—invoices your parents paid? We could subpoena them. Or perhaps an eyewitness who would be willing to come forward to testify about what was happening during your time there?"

Chas was fairly certain this program was a cash-based business—if it cost her parents anything at all—and she knew asking anyone from Restorative Hope to speak about what took place would lead to nowhere.

"I don't have either of those things, but I do have my journal that I kept while I was there in 2006. It has my counselors' notes in the margins."

"I understand this is a huge infringement on your personal space and internal safety, but would you mind if I looked at the journal?"

Chas was embarrassed about what was in there, but if Brian needed an account of what happened, this was the best she could offer. She didn't know this man, not really, but she felt at peace with him—safe, secure.

"It's embarrassing, but yes, you can see it."

For the next forty-five minutes, Brian sat in pure silence, reading every sordid detail of young Chas's life. From the kiss with Jess to her feelings about women to touching herself while thinking about girls. Her cheeks flushed, knowing he was seeing all of this, with the addition of Megan's comments telling her that this was unnatural, wrong, that she should be ashamed, that the feelings she was experiencing were Satan placing sin in front of her and her failing to resist the temptation. That these sexual desires should only be for her future husband, and she must remain pure for him.

Brian turned white, then green, and then red. His face went from looking shocked and sickened to pissed. *Good*, Chas thought. *Those are my feelings too.*

Finally, Brian closed the journal after reading her last entry and Megan's parting lines:

Chastity,

I'm so proud of your perseverance in becoming the model Christian woman. I can't wait to hear about you years from now, happily married and with a bunch of babies. You will make an excellent wife and mother. If you ever encounter a struggle with your inherent impure thoughts, you must be honest with yourself and return to Restorative Hope immediately. We can only help if you come before it is too late. Do not let yourself give in to temptation. Do not turn your back on God. Be a good woman. Go in grace.

With admiration,

Megan

Chas could still remember every word of it.

Brian looked up with a horrified expression in his eyes.

His next words made Chas want to die on the spot:

"Chas, I don't think you should get a divorce …"

CHAPTER 49
CHAS, 2016

"I think you qualify for an annulment on the grounds of religious coercion," Brian explained quickly, seeing the horror on Chas's face at his opening line. "Sorry, I didn't mean to worry you. I just think an annulment is what I would recommend, but the choice is completely yours to make."

"What's the difference? Does one take longer?"

"An annulment is a legal declaration that a marriage was *invalid from the very beginning.* One of the key grounds for annulment is *duress,* which means a person was forced into the marriage against their will and could not give free consent. While we often think of duress as a direct physical threat, like being forced to marry at gunpoint, the legal definition can be broader. It includes *psychological coercion* and *undue influence.* The context of conversion therapy could provide a compelling legal argument for this."

Here, Brian paused so Chas could process what he had said so far. "Your 'therapy' wasn't a choice; it was a form of psychological abuse that manipulated you into suppressing your identity, which directly led to you marrying Brian—and sorry about the name, by the way," he inserted, looking sympathetically at Chas.

"The threats to you weren't physical at that time, but they were severe: the loss of your family, social ostracism, and the fear of eternal damnation. These aren't minor pressures—they are fundamental threats to a person's well-being and sense of self. I don't think you could have been considered to enter this marriage with *free consent*. The grounds for annulment must exist at the time of the marriage. The psychological duress from your 'therapy' and your parents' manipulation directly led to the marriage, which means the marriage was flawed from the beginning, making an annulment a more appropriate legal recourse than a divorce.

"I can get you a divorce; it would end your marriage. An annulment, however, erases it. It is a legal judgment that you were never truly his wife."

Chas broke into a teary smile.

"Brian, if you could help me obtain that, I'd be forever grateful. I don't want to have ever been married to him, and knowing this could be irrevocably undone as if it never was—I *need* that."

Brian gave her a broad smile. "Let's do it."

CHAPTER 50
CHAS, 2016

Chas came home positively beaming. She barged in through the door, hoping that Alex was home. She was in luck. Alex was in the kitchen, cooking something for dinner that smelled positively divine.

"How did it go, my girl?" Alex asked. Seeing Chas's bright face, Alex smiled, knowing this was going to be good news.

Chas explained Brian's advice to pursue an annulment and how that would mean that, legally, she would never have been considered married to Brian. He would just be an ex-boyfriend, not an ex-husband. Chas's excitement was palpable. Alex wouldn't have cared if it was a divorce or an annulment, as long as Brian couldn't get to Chas again. She was relieved, but seeing the freedom Chas felt gave Alex the sense that this was much deeper than just the term being used and its legal ramifications. This meant something to Chas beyond what either of them could sense.

Chas gave Alex a peck on the cheek and wrapped her arms around her waist, standing behind her. Chas was shorter than Alex, so hugging her from behind was like the little spoon trying to be the big spoon, but it felt amazing to just be wrapped around her person.

Alex turned to face her. "Chas, I'm in love with you. I was trying to find the right time to say it, but I have been falling in love with you since the day of your massage, and I know that without a shadow of a doubt—I am fully, deeply, and hopelessly in love with you. I know this is incredibly soon, but ..." Alex reached into her pocket. She took Chas's hands in her own, holding something shiny between her fingers.

Chas gulped in air. She would marry Alex this minute if she asked, but she was surprised at the speed with which everything was unfolding. Chas looked closer at the shiny object. It wasn't a ring but a small gold pendant about the size of a dime with a white face featuring a tiny green beetle. The pendant was dangling from a beautiful gold bracelet.

"Alex, it's beautiful."

"Did you know that the beetle must shed its skin to grow? They create an entirely new exoskeleton underneath their present one. Then they break through their old shell, emerging in a soft new skin." Alex held her hands as she explained the bracelet's meaning. "This is you, my love. You're the beetle. You needed to shed your skin to grow. You did all of this quietly, building who you were underneath, and when you were ready, you broke free. I feel so blessed to be a part of your journey, and I fervently hope to remain yours forever."

That was so much better than any proposal. Alex was celebrating her. In that moment, Chas understood. She saw the journey she had been on, and she felt the warmth of Alex's love and admiration. This wasn't about a marriage, but about her rebirth, and Alex had not only been a witness to it but a catalyst. This was not a proposal; it was a celebration of Chas.

Chas's heart swelled with a confidence so profound that it had no room for doubt or fear. She looked into Alex's eyes, and her own words felt completely, perfectly right.

"I found my life when I found you. I love you, Alex. Will you marry me?"

CHAPTER 51
CHAS, 2016

"Chas, I'm never going anywhere, so my answer will always be yes."

Alex leaned down, giving Chas her first kiss as an engaged woman. Chas knew there were still many, many things to figure out. The annulment for one. What they each wanted for a wedding for another.

Alex pulled out of the kiss slowly, leaving their lips connected by a breath for several seconds. Neither wanted to pull away any further.

Chas spoke into Alex's lips. "I know it's so soon. I completely understand if you want a super long engagement to ensure everything feels right."

"Chas, I don't need a long engagement unless that's something you need. I do know we need to let the legal things settle, so I'm trying to be practical about that, but I would become your wife this minute if I could. I'm not worried about us not working out. I'm not worried about what people will think. I want to be your wife more than I have ever wanted anything. I want to wake up next to you every single day. I want to spend our time learning everything there is to know about each other and falling deeper and deeper in love as the years pass. I want to join our souls in every way possible."

Chas's heart was hammering. She had never been happier in her life than in this moment. She wanted to present Alex with something—anything. Alex had given her the bracelet, and then Chas had proposed with nothing to show her love in a physical, tangible way. The thought of it suddenly became an urgent need, a buzzing impulse that had to be acted on.

"Alex, I want you to call Kip and Mara. Tell them we're engaged and have them come over for dinner. I need to go out for a bit. I'll be back shortly."

"Okayyy?" Alex was clearly a little confused, and Chas knew she was killing the buzz a little. Alex wanted to stay in this moment and enjoy their newly proclaimed and committed love, but there was just something Chas had to do.

Chas kissed Alex deeply and then strode to her Jetta.

Chas drove to the closest jewelry store in Savannah, about forty minutes away. The entire drive felt like a single, breathless moment. Her mind raced, replaying every word Alex had said, the feel of the bracelet on her hand, and the incredible weight of being chosen and celebrated. She needed to give Alex something that held a similar, beautiful meaning.

Chas arrived at the jewelry store with only one thing in mind: Alex. She walked past the glitter of diamonds and sapphires, looking for something that felt solid and true. She found what she was looking for: a solid gold band with a small, intricate design carved into the ring. It looked to be a sun. The jeweler pulled it out for Chas to look at. She wasn't sure on size, but she felt like she would get fairly close based on knowing the exact size, shape, and feel of Alex's hands in her own. Chas was admiring the beauty of the piece when the jeweler explained, "This is a Celtic warrior band. It symbolizes protection and empowerment." If Chas was the beetle, Alex was the warrior. Chas was stunned. She had found the ring. It was the only one made just for Alex. Chas made her best educated guess at a size and purchased the ring.

When she arrived home, Mara and Kip were basically jumping around like kids. Chas giggled at their excitement, a little relieved they were so outwardly giddy. Mara was standing by the kitchen counter, pouring herself a drink and trying to steal bites of whatever it was Alex had cooked. Alex was swatting her hand away.

"So you're a lesbian for like a minute, and you've already tapped into your inner U-Haul lesbian?" Mara busted out laughing as she said this.

"Oh, Mara, love, behave yourself!" Kip chided her.

"What's a U-Haul lesbian?" Chas laughed in return.

"Oh, sweet baby lesbian, we have so much to teach you!" Mara replied exuberantly. "A U-Haul lesbian refers to a lesbian who needs a U-Haul within the first ten minutes of dating someone because they'll be moving in together."

Chas burst out laughing.

"Card-carrying member of the U-Haul club right here," Chas said with a wink. "Do we get discounts from U-Haul, or is there at least a secret handshake?"

Kip and Alex laughed loudly. "Mara, she's going to give you a run for your money," was Alex's reply.

Mara just grinned.

Chas had the ring in her pocket. She wasn't one for big displays and didn't like being the center of attention, but these were her best friends. She wasn't doing this for show or because she felt she had to. She just desperately wanted to.

Chas went to Alex, who was standing in the kitchen, dutifully plating up the dinner they would all share. Chas reached into her pocket and knelt to the ground. At first, she felt a little silly. She never thought she would be the one proposing, and she had already messed this up in spectacular fashion by proposing, then going to get the ring, and then proposing for a second time in the span of two hours, but she didn't care. This was Alex, and she would propose to this woman every day for the rest of her life.

Chas pulled out the ring and held it out to Alex, who was crying silent, joyful tears. "Alex, I love you. This is a Celtic warrior ring that represents protection and empowerment. You've given me both of those things in the time we have been together, and I've never felt more whole. I'm fully present in my love for you. And now, I've found a way to show you what you mean to me—my home, my strength, my warrior. This ring is for you, with all my love." Chas placed the ring on Alex's left ring finger.

It fit perfectly.

CHAPTER 52
CHAS, 2016

Kip and Mara left late in the night. They had all spent hours enjoying the chicken curry Alex had made, drinking wine, and sharing stories—mostly of Kip, Mara, and Alex after they had all met. Chas loved hearing about their adventures before she had come to the island, and she was thrilled to know that from now on, she would also have a starring role in these stories.

Alex came to sit by Chas on the couch. She looked blissfully happy. A sleepy smile crossed her lips. She was stunning.

Chas felt a burning low in her abdomen that crept down to between her legs.

Alex felt the shift in Chas as soon as it happened.

Chas didn't wait for permission. She knew if Alex wanted her to stop, she would tell her. Chas wanted to unleash herself on Alex. She didn't want to hold back. She didn't want to go slow. She wanted to shred her clothes and she wanted to feel soreness between her thighs for days so she would have a constant reminder of Alex's presence there. Chas pulled Alex's legs out from where Alex had curled them under herself. Chas had never experienced this need for release. It made her feel powerful. Strong. Beautiful. Fierce. She knew what she wanted, and she wasn't stopping to ask if she should express her wants. They had the kind of trust between them that she didn't need the constant reassurance. Alex looked truly shocked for about a millisecond, but then her smile turned feral. This would not be the slow, intimate exploration of their bodies—this was going to be something wholly different.

Alex grabbed Chas by the face and looked her directly in the eyes. "If either of us wants to stop or needs something different, we say it." It wasn't a question, but a bargain and commitment all in one.

Chas nodded as she bit down on Alex's lip. Hard enough to evoke a small whimper from her soon-to-be wife. "Tell me how you want it, Alex," was as close to a command Chas had ever given. This was a whole different side of her. She hoped it wasn't too much for Alex, but she wasn't slowing down to find out. They had their bargain.

"I want your mouth on me."

"Where?"

"Everywhere."

And with that, Chas came undone. All illusion of self-control shattered. Chas grabbed and ripped at Alex's clothing, trying to undress her as swiftly as possible. Alex stood to allow easier access. Chas stripped herself bare. There was a slight pause, a beat of a moment.

"Do what you want, babe. I'm yours." Alex.

Chas firmly pushed Alex back until her legs hit the edge of the table. Alex looked surprised at this sudden burst of heated passion, but not scared. She would not look away from Chas's eyes.

"Look at me, Alex. I'm yours, and I want you to look."

Alex obliged. Leaning back slightly with her buttocks pressing against the table and her arms placed behind her to support her weight, she stared at Chas's toes and took an agonizingly slow time making her way up Chas's body.

Chas swore she could feel everywhere Alex looked and lingered as if tracing her lines with a finger as she went. Chas was determined to withstand this moment and allow Alex her fill. Alex lingered on the apex of her thighs. Her hair had grown back fully and was unruly and more natural than when they first started seeing each other. Chas didn't care. She liked it this way, which meant she knew Alex would like it too. After an agonizing amount of time spent memorizing that spot, Alex moved her gaze upward. When she got to Chas's breasts, Alex's body responded, her nipples hardened, and her breath changed to more shallow puffs. *Yes*, Chas thought, *your body wants mine just as badly as mine needs yours.* Alex's eyes traced the larger circles of her breasts and then honed in on Chas's swollen nipples. Chas was coming to the end of her torturous wait. She just needed to be patient and allow Alex to make her way to her eyes. Finally, Alex's eyes locked with Chas's, releasing her. Chas lunged forward, insistent. Alex's eyes looked bright, alert, and expectant. She had never seen Chas like this, and she was ready to know what this Chas wanted and how she was prepared to take it.

Chas pushed Alex's torso back onto the table and propped her legs on two of the dinner chairs. At first, the chairs were close together, but Chas knew what she wanted. Chas slowly and deliberately slid one of the chairs further and further away from the other. Alex was lying bare on the table, and now her legs were being spread further and further apart. When she was spread as wide as Chas could get her while still keeping her comfortable, Chas traced small circles on Alex's inner thighs. Teasing higher and higher. Chas walked to the other side of the table, grabbed an unoccupied chair, and brought it between Alex's legs. Alex looked down at Chas sitting between her spread legs as Chas started feasting on her fiancée.

CHAPTER 53
CHAS, 2016

The days passed in a haze. Chas and Alex would separate to go to work, but when they returned home, their lovemaking commenced almost immediately. It was as if the day apart left them hungry, and the only way to fix that hunger was to spend the first part of their evening pleasuring each other. They had made love on just about every surface of the house. They had even considered taking their passion outside for a romantic tryst under the string lights. Everything remained new for Chas; each new experience was like learning about a whole new part of herself.

They had been living together for the last four weeks, and every day, the desire grew.

Today, Chas was more than eager to get home to Alex. Her mouth had been watering all day, and her underwear, having been soaked through, was completely useless at this point. She just wanted Alex to peel her out of these clothes and make her body quiver. It was something only Alex could do—send Chas into full-body quivering waves that rolled through her in ebbs and flows.

Chas bounded into the house and found Alex standing by

the kitchen counter, eating a bowl of ice cream. Perfect, Chas thought. Chas planned to stretch Alex out on the counter and slather her with the ice cream she was eating. Chas came over and boldly and deeply kissed Alex. Alex moaned and kissed back, just as hungry. Chas reached for the buttons on Alex's pants, imagining the sensation of ice cream on her own skin when Alex's hands stopped her.

Chas froze.

"Alex, are you okay? Did I do something wrong?"

Alex let out a little frustrated laugh.

"No, not at all, babes. I just started my period today, so it looks like we'll be playing a little one-sided. I can't say I'm sad about it—I have been dying to have you all day." Alex's face had a bright, mischievous smile.

Chas's face fell right along with her stomach. It was Alex's turn to worry and be concerned.

"Chas, I'm sorry, I still want to …"

Chas was trembling and starting to cry.

"Chas, what's wrong?!" Alex's voice was starting to give way to the panic rising in her.

Chas just shook her head.

"Chas, please, please tell me what is wrong. Whatever it is, we will deal with it together." Alex was imagining some horrible flashback from Brian or Restorative Hope. She knew Chas carried such trauma and had always wondered if she would ever have a reaction like this. She just wanted to help Chas by providing a safe, comforting space for her.

Chas's cries started to have sound. Now she was screaming. Alex helplessly held on to her.

"I love you," Alex repeated this over and over like a mantra to help Chas find her way back.

When Chas finally spoke through broken sobs and screams, their entire world shifted.

"Alex, I haven't had my period—I was due two weeks ago."

PART THREE

CHAPTER 54
ALEX, 2016

It took Alex hours to help Chas settle down, but she was finally resting. Chas had cried until she couldn't breathe and was gasping for air. Alex felt completely helpless. She wanted to take this pain and fear away from the woman she loved.

Eventually, Chas had exhausted herself and passed out on the bed, still fully dressed. Alex was just grateful she was resting and breathing normally again. She covered Chas with a blanket and turned off the lights in the bedroom.

Alex needed to work her own way through this revelation. She wasn't sure how she was feeling aside from relieved that Chas was resting. She needed to actually check in with herself.

Okay, Alex thought. *I love Chas. I want to marry her. That hasn't and won't change.*

I never really thought about kids. I knew I wanted a partner first, but that doesn't mean I don't WANT kids.

Alex paused her pacing.

This changes nothing for me and how I feel about Chas. I will support her no matter what she chooses to do from here.

Alex's shifting thoughts moved briefly to some logistical issues. She needed to book Chas an appointment with the gyno.

There wasn't one on the island, but there would be plenty of good options in Savannah.

Would Chas want to keep the baby, or would she want to terminate? Would she want to birth the child and then put it up for adoption?

Alex knew there was no point asking herself all these questions, and they were probably things Chas didn't even know herself. Wait a minute … they were assuming Chas was pregnant, but they had no confirmation. Maybe her period was just late? Although Chas's reaction led Alex to believe that somehow Chas knew. She knew her body well enough to know if there were subtle changes that she hadn't noticed until that moment.

Alex grabbed a piece of paper and wrote Chas a note in case she woke up soon.

Hi, my love,
Headed to the store. Will be back in 5.
I love you so much, Chas.

Alex grabbed the keys to her Jeep and headed to the market on the island. It was open until eight in the evening, and it was quarter to eight now. She could make it.

Alex ran into the store and headed for the personal hygiene aisle. Nothing. She went to the medicine aisle—sitting next to the tampons and pads were pregnancy tests. Alex grabbed three. *Best out of three wins?* Honestly, she had no idea what she was doing, but she knew neither of them would believe the test, whether it showed positive or negative. They needed at least two, and three felt safer somehow.

Alex checked out—thankfully, the clerk wasn't anyone she recognized—and headed back home.

When she entered the front door, Chas was sitting on the

couch, wrapped in a blanket, holding her note, and staring into space. Alex dropped to her knees directly in front of Chas.

"Chas, baby …" She didn't know what to say. *How are you?* was a stupid question. *Are you okay?* was equally lame.

Chas looked at Alex with puffy, red-ringed eyes. Alex hadn't seen her look so hopeless since the day she had turned back up in Tybee after being hauled off to Restorative Hope by Brian.

Alex could do this. They were connected—always had been. She just needed to steel herself.

"Chas, I love you. More in this moment than ever before." Chas looked skeptical and tired. "I'm going to be here every step of the way for whatever you choose. This changed nothing for me. I will love you if it is just you. I will love you if it is you plus one. I will love you no matter what decisions you make to do what's best for you. You aren't alone, and you won't be alone for any of this, unless you ask to be."

Chas finally made eye contact. Alex held her gaze.

"I love you, too," came Chas's small reply. She seemed so small and young in this moment.

Alex got off her knees and sat beside Chas. She rubbed soothingly along the small of Chas's back, just like she had done the day they met for the massage. Just like the day of the massage, she could feel Chas's tension seeping out of her body. She doubted she could release all of her tension—this was potentially life-altering news—but even seeing her relax a little brought Alex some measure of comfort.

They sat this way for a long while. Neither of them rushed to fill the silence, which wasn't awkward but heavy.

Then, Chas reached for Alex's free hand, and Alex grabbed onto Chas's outstretched hand and interlocked their fingers.

"We don't even know for sure I'm pregnant," Chas said, more to herself than to Alex. She was catching up to the place Alex had already been mentally. Chas looked at the clock on her phone, a deep frown creasing her forehead and mouth.

"What is it?" Alex prompted.

"The market is closed." Chas seemed on the verge of crying again.

"What do you need from the market, Chas? There are still places open in Savannah, so if it's something you need, I'll go get it."

Chas put her forehead to Alex's chest. Alex moved her hand from her back to gently stroke her hair.

"I need a pregnancy test."

Alex shifted the bag she had placed on the floor at her feet. "I thought you might want to find out when you woke up, so I went to the market before it closed and got these." She lifted the bag and placed it on Chas's lap. Chas didn't need to open the bag—when Alex released the handles, the contents were left exposed.

Chas smiled slightly. Alex loved that smile and wanted to keep doing whatever it was that induced it. "Thank you, Alex, but why did you get three?" Chas asked with a wry smile.

"I wasn't sure how accurate these things are, and I figured you and I wouldn't believe it anyway," Alex replied.

"I don't even know how to take one of these," Chas said.

"Neither do I," Alex offered, "but we can learn together if you want."

Chas smiled again. The smile didn't reach her eyes, but Alex caught a glimpse of her girl in there.

"Okay."

Alex opened one of the tests and pulled out the instruction manual that was folded into a neat little square. When she unfolded it, the page was actually as big as a medium-sized poster, and the writing was tiny. *What on earth could they be telling these women to do that took that much writing?* Alex flipped the page over, and the instructions continued on the back. Jeez, she did not want to sit here and read a novel to figure this out, but she would. She started reading the directions, and Chas picked up the box and turned it over in her hands.

"Alex, *these* instructions on the back look way easier than whatever you're reading."

Alex looked over, and on the back of the box, only three steps were listed. Had the situation been different, Alex would have laughed. Why would they include all those lengthy pages if you could just do this in three simple steps?

"Great." Alex tried to sound cheerful.

Alex read the box. Chas would need to pee on something called the wick. Alex dumped the test out of the box and into her palm. Following the instructions, she removed the cap. Then Chas needed to pee on the wick, and then they had to wait three minutes and check if there was one pink line or two. One pink line meant not pregnant. Two pink lines …

Alex realized the likelihood of Chas having enough urine to pee on three sticks back-to-back would be low. She went to the kitchen and started rummaging in the cabinet for her cups. She found what she was looking for—a Solo cup.

"Chas, if you want to do this, you'll need to pee in this cup, and then we will dip the wicks of each of the tests in there, and then wait the three minutes, and then we will know."

Alex was very careful to use "we" as much as she could. She needed Chas to feel her presence and intentions through her actions.

Chas simply nodded, got up from the couch, and took the cup from Alex's hand. A few minutes later, Chas called Alex to the bathroom.

There was a cup of Chas's pee sitting on the bathroom counter, and Chas was just staring at it.

"Do you want to dip these, or would you like me to?" Alex asked, holding up the pregnancy tests.

"Can you do it?"

"Of course."

Alex removed the three caps, dipped each stick in the cup, and then replaced the lid. Alex took the cup, dumped it back in the toilet, and threw the cup in the bathroom trash can. Now they waited. Chas looked anxious.

"Do you want to wait in here, or would it be easier to wait in the bedroom or the living room?"

"Let's go to the bedroom."

Alex intertwined her fingers with Chas's and went and sat on the bed. Three minutes came and went. Then five. Then ten. Alex was not going to pressure Chas into anything. When she was ready to review the test results, she would. After fifteen minutes, Chas nodded.

"Alex, if you don't want to …"

"Chas, do you want me to go look first?"

Chas only nodded.

Alex went to the bathroom door. She didn't even need to get close to the three tests; she could see from the door that each test had two bold pink lines.

Alex walked back to the bedroom. Chas wouldn't meet her eyes and was looking down at her toes. Alex knelt down beside her and placed her hands on Chas's.

"It's positive, isn't it?" Chas said.

"Yes."

Chas nodded her understanding. Alex wasn't exactly sure what to say or do. She stood and kissed Chas on the head.

"Would you like to lie down in bed?"

Chas nodded again.

Alex lay down on her side and waited for Chas to lie down beside her. Once Chas lay down, Alex curled her body around hers, shielding her from the world and the weight of all of the decisions that were waiting for them. They could face those together tomorrow.

CHAPTER 55
CHAS +1, 2016

Chas woke the morning after, still feeling the shock of disbelief. She was pregnant—with Brian's child.

Chas had clients that afternoon, but she still had a few hours before she had to be "human" again. So, she opted to rot in bed. At least that was comforting and kept her from facing any strong realities just yet.

Alex had been so supportive when the tests came back positive. Chas couldn't imagine the state she would be in had Alex been nervous or shown doubt. This isn't what Alex signed up for. She had agreed to marry Chas, but they hadn't even talked about kids. Chas would completely understand and accept if Alex didn't want to continue things with her, but that wasn't like Alex. There was immense comfort in knowing that Alex wouldn't leave, circumstances be damned.

Chas looked over at Alex's empty spot. No note, which meant Alex was probably still in the house—likely in the kitchen making breakfast, or maybe she had gone to work already and just didn't leave their customary note. Chas prayed that it wasn't the case. She thought that if Alex had left, and there was no note, it would be a sign that things had, in fact, shifted between them. Chas was starting to break out into a cold sweat, worrying herself sick at the thought.

"Hey, sleepy muffin." Alex was standing in the doorway of their bedroom with a tray. Memories of their first night, and the flower Alex had picked for her, flooded back to Chas. She wanted to go back to that morning. Chas smiled and sat up in the bed.

"I have a blueberry bagel with plain cream cheese or a cinnamon raisin bagel with butter—your pick, my lady," Alex said in a silly accent.

Thank God she's being normal. Chas didn't have it in her to banter, but this was helping more than Alex could know. The sense of normalcy when in reality, EVERYTHING had changed in a single night.

Chas picked up the cinnamon raisin bagel and smiled. "Thank you, Alex."

Alex snuggled her nose up to Chas's ear, hidden within her curls. Chas's skin prickled at that familiar sensation, but recalling her reality shut her body down. She wasn't sure how long it would take for her desire to return, but that burn she usually felt was extinguished for the time being.

Alex withdrew slightly and kissed her cheek and then her forehead.

Chas and Alex ate in silence until Chas realized it was getting later in the morning—Alex should be gone by now.

"Did you have a cancellation?"

"No, I took the day off so we could be together." Alex's smile was tentative, like she had more to say or like she expected Chas not to want her around.

"I hope you don't mind ... I called the salon and told them that you were ill and wouldn't be making it in today. I'm sorry if I crossed a line with that one or if you wanted to go in. I just ..." Alex trailed off.

"No, thank you. That's great, actually. I don't really want to leave this bed, maybe ever again."

"Okay, well…. I also took the liberty of calling an ob-gyn in Savannah and asking for their soonest available appointment. They have an appointment today at 2 p.m. We can cancel if you want. I just wanted you to have the *option* to go and find out more if you wanted to. If you aren't ready or don't want to, then I'll call and cancel—no biggie." Alex's words were coming out faster than normal. It was like she was expecting Chas to be mad at her thoughtfulness.

Chas paused for a beat, trying to decide if she wanted to go or if she wanted to cancel the appointment and give it some more time. Alex waited patiently, quietly, and without showing any signs of pressure, one way or another. Chas knew it was never going to get any easier, and she did have the day off, and it would be nice to get some basic answers so her imagination stopped running away with all the awful things that could be happening.

"I'd like to go. Alex, will you go with me?"

Alex looked relieved. "I would *love* to go with you, my girl."

Chas stayed in PJs the majority of the morning and early afternoon, but as half-past noon rolled around, she threw on a pair of Alex's old sweatpants that were a few sizes too large for her and a graphic T-shirt. She pulled on her Adidas sneakers and sported her normal messy bun. She honestly looked a little rough, but she didn't care today.

Alex drove them to the OB-GYN office. She parked and waited for Chas to make the first move to get out of the vehicle. Chas reached for the car door and slid out of the seat. She was on some sort of strange autopilot, but at least she was somewhat functional.

Chas walked into the clinic, filled out the paperwork, and provided her ID and payment. She didn't have insurance. If she was pregnant, she would need to fix that.

The receptionist gave her a form to fill out with her past medical history and her last period, and it asked if she had depression, difficulty finding food, or had housing concerns. Once this was filled out, she kept the clipboard on her lap and waited, Alex at her side.

A few minutes later, the tech called out Chas's name: "Chastity Jacobs." Her heart sank as usual at the name. Alex squeezed her hand in reassurance. *That's just a name—it isn't even mine. Not really.* Chas started walking toward the girl who had made the announcement. She looked behind her to make sure Alex was with her. Chas locked eyes with her—a silent plea. Speaking soul to soul the way that only they could. She didn't realize Alex would want to wait for her invitation—she just assumed she would come with her, but Alex always gave Chas the option. Chas needed her. Alex received her silent plea and immediately stood up to join her.

The tech took Chas's vitals and weight. Chas had gained ten pounds since her last visit. Not a ton, but still, she had been the same weight for years. They had Chas pee in a cup and then took her to the room where they would be examining her. They gave her a "vest" made of a paper towel and a blanket made of the same material. They requested that she remove all her clothing, put on the vest with the opening to the front, and use the blanket to cover herself. Alex watched her go through the motions as requested by the tech. She didn't feel the need to fill the silence with chatter. Chas was grateful for that. It would have only made her more nervous. She just needed Alex's calm and grounding presence.

The doctor came in a few minutes after Chas had adjusted herself on the table. "Hi, Chastity, I am Doctor Beddor. Your urine results show that you have very high levels of the pregnancy hormone, so you have a positive pregnancy test. Is this your first child?"

"Yes."

"Okay, well, I'm going to tell you how the first appointment goes so you know what to expect. Some aspects are similar to your annual gyno visit, but with some differences. We'll do a breast exam to check for lumps as usual, but I will also squeeze your nipples to make sure there is no discharge. It's early in the pregnancy, so we would not expect to see anything yet. I will then have you slide your bottom to the end of the table and place your feet in the stirrups as you would for your annual pap, but instead of inserting a speculum, I will insert my fingers and feel for your cervix. I will also use my other hand to apply pressure on your abdomen to try to get an approximate size of your uterus. After that, we will move on to the ultrasound. When was your last period due?"

"A little over two weeks ago."

"Okay, it will be too soon to see on an abdominal ultrasound, so we will need to do a transvaginal. The ultrasound tech will administer this part. They will insert a wand into your vagina with an ultrasound probe on the end; it will allow us to see your uterus, baby, ovaries, and cervix. Do you have any questions before we get started?"

Chas didn't have any questions; she was mostly just feeling overwhelmed by all the information and the very real probability that they were about to find a baby inside her. Alex got up from the chair in the corner and came to hold her hand.

"Ah, I'm sorry—I should have also introduced myself to you," Dr. Beddor said, noticing Alex for the first time. "Is this your partner?" he asked Chas.

"Yes—she's my fiancée."

"Great! I'm so glad you can be here …" he trailed off, waiting for Alex to fill in the missing information.

"Hi, I'm Alex."

"Okay, friends, let's get started."

Dr. Beddor completed all the steps in a very efficient

fashion. Once it was time for the ultrasound, he dimmed the lights in the room so Alex and Chas could see the screen.

The ultrasound tech inserted the probe and was wiggling it around inside of Chas. It wasn't painful, but it wasn't pleasant either. Chas kept her eyes glued to the screen, expecting to see a baby pop up out of nowhere. The tech kept fishing and kept their face completely neutral, which was infuriating. Chas had no idea what was going on, and the only thing she could make out were black circles and gray stuff. Nothing at all that looked like a baby. Chas was doing her best to be patient, but her patience was wearing thin.

At last, the tech removed the probe and turned on the light, and then left the room. Dr. Beddor removed his glove and told Chas she could sit up. Alex assisted her into a seated position, and Chas fought against the stupid paper-towel vest to keep it shut.

The moments felt taut. Something was wrong. She could feel it. The baby was dead or gone or something else—maybe it was stuck in her tubes.

Dr. Beddor smiled broadly. "Chas, I want to show you the recording we just took and walk you through the findings. Do you see these two black circles in this field of gray?"

"Yes," she and Alex both said and nodded in agreement. That was the only thing she could really see.

"Well, there are two circles because you have two embryos. You're going to have twins."

CHAPTER 56
CHAS +2, 2016

Thank goodness Alex was in the room. Chas didn't hear anything after the word "twins." Dr. Beddor was busy showing Alex a little flashing thing on the recording they had made, and he was saying something about heartbeats. Chas couldn't focus on anything other than her abdomen and the knowledge that there were babies growing inside her.

"Babies"—more than one.

Finally, Dr. Beddor walked out of the room, leaving Chas and Alex alone again. Presumably, this appointment was done, and Chas was supposed to get dressed and walk out of this room and back into the world as if nothing had changed. But everything had changed.

Alex hadn't missed a beat. She knew Chas was stunned. Alex reached out for Chas, pulled her into a warm embrace, and said something that Chas didn't hear or couldn't register. Alex pulled the paper garments off Chas and helped her put her bra and underwear on, and then her sweatpants and shirt. Alex intertwined their fingers and guided Chas out of the room and to the receptionist. Alex and the receptionist spoke for several minutes, and then Alex paid for the visit. Chas was sure that the receptionist mentioned an amount, but she didn't hear that either. The only sound she perceived was a whooshing sound that became a regular beat in her ear—her own heartbeat.

Alex loaded Chas into the Jeep and buckled her seatbelt around her. Then she started to make the drive back onto their island—back home.

Chas registered briefly that Alex was on the phone as they were traveling. What a strangely normal thing to do at a time like this.

Time didn't seem to exist anymore—they had just left the doctor's office, but somehow they were already pulling up to the house.

Alex did everything she had done to get Chas home in reverse now—she unbuckled her, helped her out of the Jeep, and then linked their fingers and guided her into their home. Alex sat Chas on the couch and laid a blanket over her legs.

I'm not feeling anything. Is that normal when you find out you're pregnant? Am I already a bad mom to these babies?

Chas was starting to get the beginnings of her thought processes back. She registered Alex grabbing things from the kitchen in a somewhat hurried fashion. Chas couldn't really remember how she had gotten here—vague flashes of Alex helping her move around from the doctor's office to home played through her mind's eye.

Chas was coming back to her body.

"Alex." Chas's voice came out in a croak that sounded like she had been asleep and was just waking up. When had she last spoken? Had it been minutes or hours?

Alex's head snapped up as if a gunshot sounded through the house. She strode over to Chas and perched on the couch beside her.

"Chas." It wasn't a question but rather confirmation that

Chas was coming back to herself and had been somewhere else for an untold amount of time.

"Alex, I'm so sorry."

"Chas, honey, why are you sorry?"

"I know this isn't what we planned for. I completely understand if this changes things for you. You didn't sign up for this, and it wouldn't be your fault at all if you needed to end things here."

Alex gently placed her hands on either side of Chas's face. Chas's gaze dropped, and she wouldn't meet Alex's beseeching eyes.

"Chas, my love is not conditional. It wasn't for if you were a certain way and stayed that way forever. My love is going to chase you relentlessly until the moment one of us leaves this Earth. It will be yours through every life cycle, every change. It was never and will never be contingent on something you did or did not do."

Chas's eyes finally met Alex's. There was relief in Alex's eyes —Chas was coming back. Chas's eyes looked glassy, but she could see Alex meant every word she had said.

"Alex, I want to keep them."

"Chas, nothing would make me happier than to be a mom with you. This may be a large ask, and if you need or want to say no, it won't change anything for me. Chas, can these little ones please be our babies? Can we raise them together?"

Chas was so relieved that she couldn't find the right words to express how much she needed to hear that. She knew she didn't have to or need to express it. Alex's soul spoke to hers in ways she didn't fully understand but was learning to trust.

"Alex, I would love nothing more."

The rest of the day was spent lying on the couch, with Alex stroking gentle circles on Chas's lower abdomen. Alex knew Chas hadn't heard a single word Dr. Beddor said after he had announced that she was carrying twins.

She was filling Chas in on what she had missed.

"So the babies are actually seven weeks along, and they are about the size of a blueberry or a grape. They look like they're developing normally, and they even showed us the little flicker of each of their hearts, so that was the flashing on the screen. We will need to go back in a month. We will have monthly visits until a little later in the pregnancy, or if anything changes and we need to go more often. I didn't know your past medical history, but I told Dr. Beddor that you didn't have any known risk factors for carrying the babies. If you do have something, we will need to call back and let them know, and we can go back sooner."

It was starting to fully sink in. Chas was a mom, and Alex was a mom, too. They were parents. Chas was scared, but excitement was starting to leak into the fear and take up space in her heart and mind.

"I did make one other call when we were on the way home," Alex said a little hesitantly.

Chas remembered thinking something about Alex being on the phone while they were in the Jeep. She couldn't put together what she had said, even though she had been sitting right there. It was like her head had been underwater at that time.

"I called your lawyer," Alex said tentatively.

"I want to make sure we protect you and our babies."

Holy fucking hell. She forgot—how could she forget? She didn't just spontaneously grow these babies in her belly. She would never be rid of Brian—he would have rights, she was sure. He was going to poison these babies to believe all of the garbage she had grown up with. Brian was a firm believer in all of that homophobic doctrine. Chas's stomach clenched. She rested her hand lower on her abdomen.

"Alex, we can't let him hurt them."

"I know, my love. It won't happen. I won't let it." Chas knew that Alex wouldn't lie about something like that. She knew Alex was the warrior. She had earned the ring Chas had picked. She would protect and empower them all. These babies would not be raised to believe they could not be loved for being who they are—no matter who that is.

CHAPTER 57
CHAS +2, 2017

It had been several months since the pregnancy was discovered. In that time, Chas had several more prenatal visits to the gyno. Everything was developing normally, and today was the day they would find out the babies' genders. The doctor believed the babies were fraternal twins—they had two separate amniotic sacs with separate placentas. The doctor told Chas this wasn't an exact science, more like an educated guess, but to find out if they were truly identical, they would need to conduct DNA testing after birth. Chas couldn't care less either way; they were healthy, and that was more than enough for her.

Chas was standing in front of the full-length mirror in their bedroom, completely nude, running her hands back and forth over her abdomen reverently. She couldn't feel the babies moving just yet, but her body was changing dramatically. Her belly could no longer be mistaken for a little extra weight. It was clearly a pronounced baby bump. Her breasts were engorged, and they were much heavier than her pre-pregnancy form (much to Alex's delight). Initially, Chas wasn't sure how she would feel about her body changing, but the larger the twins grew and the more her body changed to allow for that growth, the more radiant she felt. She had one of those pretty bumps. It stuck straight out from the front, and her belly button was starting to flatten and would probably turn to an outie at some point. She had a thin little brown line that went from her belly button down to her pubic hair. Chas loved watching her body change. It was a healthy body that was strong and very busy growing two perfect little humans.

"Chas, are you ready to go?" Alex called from the kitchen. She was collecting snacks for the ride into Savannah. Chas's hunger had been unreal lately. She would eat and feel full, and then thirty minutes later would be craving more. Alex had quickly learned to have snacks handy if they were leaving the house for any length of time.

Alex had taken off from work today so that she could go with Chas to her anatomy scan.

Chas dressed quickly in her new, stretchy maternity jeans and an XL-sized T-shirt. It was late spring, but Chas's favorite thing to wear were those jeans—*Why don't women wear maternity jeans all the time? These are so comfy!*

Chas came into the kitchen and found Alex slipping at least six different types of snacks into a snack bag. Chas had to chuckle a little at this sight. Her fiancée was doing great, keeping up with her and her needs. It was just funny to see how ridiculously over-prepared Alex was on the snack front. Alex glanced up, taking in Chas. Ever since Chas had developed the beginnings of her baby bump, Alex has been staring at her so intently. At first, it worried Chas that Alex wasn't appreciating the changes in her body as much as Chas was, but after one night catching Chas looking at herself in the mirror, Alex came and wrapped her arms around Chas's nude form. She put her hands around her and held her blooming tummy. The gesture was so sweet, and Chas could see—this body had the exact same effect on Alex as her prenatal body had when they first met.

Alex loved Chas, and Chas felt her love growing at a rate to match the twins. The larger they grew, the more Alex's love grew as if she was swelling with it, ready to shower them the minute they made their arrival. They were due in the fall, so they had plenty of growing to do—Chas was scared that by then, Alex might burst with all the love welling up in her.

"Hey, babe," Chas said. "You ready to see our babies today?"

"I don't think I have ever been more excited to go to a doctor's office in my life."

They piled in the car—Chas, Alex, and the seriously overloaded snack bag—and set off for Savannah.

Dr. Beddor had the same kind and caring manner as always.

"Hi, mommies to be," he said by way of greeting. It was his new favorite way to greet them. Each time, it made both Chas and Alex beam with pride.

"Are you two ready to see what we are having or do you want to let it be a surprise?" Dr. Beddor was putting on gloves and was pulling up the abdominal ultrasound machine next to Chas.

"We want to know!" Chas and Alex said in rushed unison.

Dr. Beddor chuckled. "Okay, let's see if we can get these babies to cooperate and show us what we want to see."

Dr. Beddor took the ultrasound gel from the warmer on the wall and poured some of it onto Chas's stomach. Chas loved the feel of the warmth on her skin, like she was rubbing hair gel or warm aloe vera gel on her skin, but without a sticky mess afterward. He placed the wand in the middle of the puddle of gel and started wiggling it around.

Chas's patience had never been great, but today it was even shorter than usual. She was dying to know. She didn't care either way, but somehow knowing their gender allowed her to think of them as more real, more human. They could start talking names, planning their room. It would get things rolling.

Dr. Beddor was working the wand in a burst of circles and straight lines, pushing in a little here or there, and taking measurements using the computer as he went. He told Chas and Alex that the babies both had strong hearts, their heads were the right size for their stage of development, and he didn't see any signs of anything to worry about. One of the twins was a little larger than the other, but that wasn't uncommon with twins, according to Dr. Beddor.

"Ah, okay, here we go … baby A is a … girl! See these three little lines right here—that is considered the hamburger sign and will develop fully into female genitalia," Dr. Beddor explained. Alex and Chas grinned widely. Alex had tears of sheer joy in her eyes. A girl. They were having a baby girl!

"Alright, mommies … baby B is … also a girl! Here is the same hamburger sign for this little one."

Chas and Alex wept together the most happy and joyful tears anyone could have ever wept. The twins were girls. They were having GIRLS!

CHAPTER 58
CHAS +2, 2017

It had been a week since they found out they were having girls, and Chas and Alex were in full "girl mom fever." They spent their nights speaking of the tiny humans that would join them and started tossing around potential names. One day, they would refer to Baby A as Polly and Baby B as Greta, and then the next day, Baby A was Alex Jr., and Baby B was Savannah. Chas and Alex loved this game. Every morning, they would each pick a name and play with it throughout the day.

Life was nearly perfect.

This week, though, they did have another legal hurdle to cross. Chas had been meeting with her lawyer, Brian, via phone calls and online Zoom meetings. They were nearing the conclusion of this legal saga. Today, her ex, Brian, would be served a "Petition for Declaration of Invalidity of Marriage." Chas loved how it was worded. Who knew a document's title could have so much power? Her ex would have thirty days to respond, according to Georgia law, and then if he didn't contest, they could move to a court hearing. Chas wasn't sure if Brian would contest. She hadn't seen or heard from him at all in the months since the incident at the beach cottage.

"Good morning, Odette," Alex said as she patted Chas gently on the belly. Baby A's name for today, apparently.

"I am thinking Ophelia may want pancakes for breakfast," Chas said playfully. Baby B was not to be outdone by her sister.

Alex leaned down to speak directly to Chas's stomach. "Girls, I'm rather fond of those names. Will you let us know how you feel?"

Chas felt it immediately. A flutter in her abdomen. Her hand dropped immediately to her stomach, and her eyes were huge and bright.

"What is it?" Alex asked excitedly.

"Alex, I feel them."

Alex's hands joined Chas's on her tummy.

"I can't feel them with my hands, but I can feel them inside me!"

Chas and Alex hugged and laughed. This pregnancy had had so many moments of joy, but this one may have topped them all for Chas. She just wished Alex could feel them too. It felt like she had a moth in her stomach. It wasn't trapped and trying to get out, but rather floating around, feeling out the edges of Chas's belly. She adored this feeling.

"Okay, that settles it. The girls have spoken. Odette and Ophelia. Our girls," Alex said with awe.

CHAPTER 59
CHAS +2, 2017

In the early days of the pregnancy, Kip and Mara had been over the moon to find out they were becoming "Aunts". Alex had called them over, and when they arrived, Chas and Alex were wearing matching T-shirts that said "always read the fine print," and then in tiny little writing were the words "We are pregnant." Then in tinier writing, the words "with twins."

During that visit, Kip decided they wanted to be an "Auntie" as that felt most right and natural to them, but they didn't want to be called Auntie by the babies. They wanted to be called Kip. Mara was obscenely excited. She announced that she would surely be the favorite aunt and would be the one to teach them how to order drinks at a bar and how to pierce their own eyebrows. Chas knew she was 100% serious and threw Alex a look that said, "You're going to stop this one, right?" Alex laughed and promised Mara that she could teach them how to drink at a bar, but after they were twenty-one, and that the piercing(s) would need to be done in a tattoo shop, not over a kitchen sink. Mara looked a little disgruntled but said, "Fine, as long as I get to take them!"

Last week, when Chas and Alex had called them on speakerphone to announce the gender of the babies, Kip and Mara had both squealed when they found out "we" were having girls—they were both insistent that these babies were theirs, too.

Today, Kip and Mara were coming over to help Alex and Chas paint the nursery and put together cribs, changing tables, and gliders.

"Let me see my babies!" Mara yelled out when she entered their house. Always entering with the force of a tornado, Mara came directly to Chas, who was rocking a tube top over her swollen breasts and baggy short overalls on top of that. Mara looked heartbroken to see Chas's attire. As soon as Chas started showing, it was Mara's greatest pleasure to put her cheek against Chas's belly and talk to the girls "so they would know she was there." Chas laughed heartily at Mara's downtrodden face. She unclipped her overalls and slid them down to her ankles, leaving her in a tube top and underwear with her belly protruding out. "Oh, thank you, Chas baby!" Mara squealed in excitement. "Hello, girls, it's Auntie Mara here. I'm going to make you the most beautiful nursery! I'll make sure there isn't too much pink—we all know your moms can't be trusted," she said in a conspiratorial whisper to the babies she couldn't see.

"Hey," Chas said, indignant, "you do know I can hear you, and I'm the one who let you use your little telephone method to talk to them in the first place."

Mara looked a little sheepish and kissed the belly that housed her nieces. Then she straightened up and kissed Chas on the cheek, too. "You know I'm right," she said with a wink. Chas gave her a half-hearted kick on the bum as she walked away. Now, it was Kip's turn. Kip also loved talking to the girls but was never one to pressure Chas to allow access (unlike Mara, who practically demanded it). Kip knelt down on the floor and rested their hands on Chas's budding belly. They looked up at Chas. "You three are growing so beautifully," they said with reverence. "Thank you, Kip." Chas loved their love.

"Hello, my darlings. It's your Kip. I hope you're enjoying yourself in there. We're getting ready for you!" Kip placed a gentle kiss on the stretch of Chas's belly between their resting hands.

Then Kip stood up and went to gather tools with Mara and Alex. Chas pulled up her overalls, and the four of them got started on the day.

"So what are we calling Baby A and Baby B today?" Mara asked.

"Oh," Alex said casually. "The girls officially have names."

Mara looked positively ticked and flipped out her arms, palms up, as if to say, "Well, what are they, you idiot?"

"Baby A is Odette, and Baby B is Ophelia," Alex continued, after drawing out the moment a little more to Mara's chagrin.

Kip made a warm humming sound. "Those are lovely, you two."

Chas smiled proudly.

Mara looked a little confused.

"Okay, Mara, out with it. What's wrong with those names?" Alex said impatiently.

Mara rolled her eyes as if this should be so obvious. "I've been looking at the origins of baby girl names for the last week. I memorized as many as I could, but I don't know what either of those means."

Chas's smile broadened.

"Ophelia means help, and Odette means prosperous."

Alex whipped her head around and stared in amazement at Chas. She hadn't thought to look it up, but given Chas's history with her own name, she would be uniquely sensitive to the meaning of a name. "Prosperous" and "Help"—the two most fitting words in the English language for the journey that had brought them here.

To Chas, in this moment, Alex looked like the sunshine she smelled of.

CHAPTER 60
CHAS +2, 2017

Kip, Mara, Alex, and Chas completed the nursery in one day. Having that much help not only made the process go much faster and more smoothly, but it also made Chas realize just how lucky they were. Their family was beautiful—it was happy, healthy, and full of love. It didn't matter that it didn't necessarily look like everyone else's family. As far as Chas was concerned, every family would be incredibly blessed to look like this.

The nursery went in the old spare bedroom directly across from Chas and Alex's bedroom. It now housed two Jenny Lind–style cribs with spooled wooden elements that fit in with the vintage feel of the rest of the house, a dresser with a changing station on top, and two baby gliders (one for Chas and one baby and one for Alex and the other). The nursery didn't have a theme necessarily, but Chas wanted it to be strong for her girls. One of the cribs had bumpers that were a deep green with a floral pattern that had an occasional glimpse of a cheetah or leopard (Chas was never quite sure how to determine the difference between the two cats). The other crib had the same exact bumpers, but in navy blue. They hung various prints from a mix of vintage stores that together evoked thoughts of a fierce woman. Strong and determined—two things she hoped for her girls to become.

The next day, Chas was standing in the nursery and just soaking it all in. In a few more months, they were going to have babies in here. Dr. Beddor had already prepared Chas and Alex for the fact that the twins would likely be born earlier than if it had been a singleton pregnancy. They should expect to go into labor anytime from thirty-four weeks along or later. Alex already had an emergency go-bag sitting by the door at all times. Chas's skin warmed up, thinking about Alex and their girls. Chas would love to stand here for the next eight hours, but she was still working in the salon in Savannah and needed to get going, or she would be late. She planned to work there until she went into labor. Alex said she would take four weeks off after the babies arrived and then would go back to work two to four weeks before Chas was released to return to her work. Kip and Mara were going to begin working opposing schedules and would be watching the girls anytime both mommies were at work.

Chas headed into Savannah and arrived a few minutes before her first client was scheduled to arrive. One of the receptionists came over to Chas's station with the phone in hand. "Chas, it's for you." Chas was surprised. The receptionists handled any hair-related calls and all scheduling issues. It wouldn't make sense that someone was asking for her directly.

"Hello?"

"You fucking dyke!" Brian screamed down the line.

God. Chas's stomach rolled. She was going to throw up. Her hand instinctively dropped to cover her girls.

Chas didn't respond. There was nothing to say. She thought of hanging up, but she didn't want Brian coming here. He still didn't know she was pregnant, and she planned to keep it that way for as long as humanly possible. Chas's lawyer warned her that Brian may react this way and to try not to rise to it. Don't give him a reason to contest this annulment.

"I just wanted to call and say I am not contesting this annulment. I don't want you. You misrepresented yourself when you married me. You were supposed to be a good Christian; you had been fixed. I didn't sign up to deal with your unnatural, sinful perversity." Brian's words were dripping venom, but he wasn't screaming anymore, just speaking as if he was spitting every word down the line. As if he were throwing his words like knives.

Chas didn't have anything to say. She was just glad he said he wasn't contesting.

"Oh, and just so you know, I'm happily seeing a woman who's an actual Christian woman, and we're happy. I told her all about how my wife left me for a dyke, and she couldn't believe it. She actually loves me and doesn't want to fuck a bunch of women."

Just let him get this out. Don't fight. Stay quiet.

"So, looks like I'll be seeing you in court soon so that I can finally be done with your whorish behavior for good."

With that, Brian hung up.

Chas knew her face looked like something was wrong because several of her coworkers were now surrounding her, looking concerned. The temporarily abandoned clients at their stations were also staring in Chas's direction.

Chas needed to breathe. Her babies needed her to be strong. As harsh as Brian's call had been, it wasn't upsetting her to the point of dizzying nausea. Chas had just realized that for her plan to work out, she needed the annulment before the babies were born. They lived in Georgia, where the law was that if she was unmarried, she would not have to put the father's name on the birth certificate. It wouldn't prevent Brian from seeking legal rights to the girls, but it would slow him down considerably. She would be seeing Brian soon, and then he would know. Brian was going to see Chas, and the swell of her stomach would give them away.

CHAPTER 61
CHAS +2, 2017

It had been six weeks since the phone call with Brian. Although Chas was dreading every single second of today, she was so very thankful that the day had finally come. They were going to court for the annulment hearing. Chas would not be alone. Alex, Kip, Mara, and their lawyer, Brian, were all going to be there with her.

Her hearing was at 2 p.m., but their lawyer, Brian, had requested she arrive at 1 p.m. to make sure they were ready the second the judge called the court into session.

Alex hadn't said much this morning, but in true fashion, their souls were connecting. She provided silent comfort through frequent touches of reassurance, and Chas returned them. It was like they couldn't stand not being connected today. Hands twisted together, arms wrapped around each other, legs crossed, and feet leaning into each other. Every time one body part released contact, another part was linked. This wasn't something either of them talked about or agreed to. It just happened.

They left the house at half-past eleven. Alex would not let them be late, no matter what the traffic was like. Alex stopped and picked up Kip and Mara on their way off the island. The car ride passed in near silence, but the tribe was together. There wasn't anything they couldn't face as long as they had each other.

Chas and her tribe walked into the courthouse at 12:15 p.m. and made their way through security, which was understandably very strict.

Chas was wearing a simple black dress that went to her knees. Mara had joked that she looked like she was going to a funeral, and then said that maybe that was fitting after all—it was the death of a "fucked up marriage," in her colorful terms. Chas had intentionally picked a dress that was a few sizes too large. It was pointless, though. Maybe at a passing glance or from the back, you wouldn't notice, but the second Chas was facing you, it would become very apparent that she was very pregnant.

Chas felt exposed in a way she hadn't felt before. The tribe had formed a small circle around her, almost like they could all collectively hide Chas's bump. She loved them all the more for trying. Thankfully, Lawyer Brian found her before ex Brian made his appearance. Lawyer Brian asked the crew to follow him to the second story of the courthouse, where family court was held. He pulled them to a small alcove that had a few benches forming an L shape. Brian asked Chas to position herself with her knees angled toward him, and he would sit facing out. Alex, Kip, and Mara would form a shield of sorts to try to keep Chas's secret hidden for as long as possible.

When they assumed their positions, Lawyer Brian spoke in a very hushed tone. Everyone in the courthouse was very quiet—it felt similar to a library, but if that library was full of tension.

"Okay, I'm going to ask this once, and I'm going to explain it once. I need you all to listen. Are any of you prone to outbursts?" Brian said.

Chas, Alex, and Kip all looked at Mara.

"Jeez, okay. Yes, I'm prone to outbursts," Mara admitted, a little annoyed at her friends for calling her out, but now was not the time for lying.

"Okay, what's your name?" Lawyer Brian asked.

"Mara."

"Okay, Mara, this is very important. You cannot, under any circumstances, have any form of outburst. If you do, the entire party may be removed from the courtroom. The judge will not tolerate any show of emotion or support from anyone in attendance. It's my job to protect Chas. You're officially off protection duty until we walk out of this courthouse. If you don't listen and you do have an outburst, you may be pulling Alex away from Chas, and then we'll really be up shit creek." Lawyer Brian waited for Mara's acknowledgment of his words.

Mara gave one quick, determined nod. Kip reached for her hand and squeezed it. Chas caught the gesture and reached across Alex for Kip's hand. Before anyone said anything else, the tribe had all linked hands: Chas with Alex, Alex with Kip, and Kip with Mara. They would face this united.

"Okay," Lawyer Brian went on, "Chas, you know that he may try to contest once he sees that you are pregnant—we talked about that when he called the salon."

Chas nodded. She had mentally prepared for that possibility because the likelihood was high.

"No matter what happens in there, you just sit quietly and try your very best to remain calm. Look anywhere but at him. Look at me or look at your girls if you need to. You won't be able to see Alex because she will be behind you, but she's there, I promise." Lawyer Brian had become like a pseudo-father figure in this whole ordeal. He knew what she needed to feel safe, and he did everything he could to prepare her for what was coming for her.

"We did have one stroke of luck," Brian continued. "We have

Judge Gordon. She's very pro-LGBTQIA+. She will not tolerate any hate being spewed."

They waited in their huddle until 2 p.m. arrived.

At five minutes until two, Chas saw Alex tense. Chas was angled away from the hallway in front of the courtroom. With Alex's body tensing, Chas knew her ex had arrived and was looking directly at her. Chas would not give him any satisfaction. She would stay seated and hidden from view.

They had a plan. Chas just needed to stick to the plan.

Ex Brian and his lawyer entered the courtroom.

It was time.

Chas sent up a prayer.

God, please let this plan work. Please protect me and our girls. Amen.

CHAPTER 62
CHAS +2, 2017

Chas felt sick. Her body was trembling, and her spine felt like a wet noodle.

Lawyer Brian led Chas into the courtroom. As she was walking down the aisle, she saw Alex, Kip, and Mara all sitting on the front bench directly behind where she would be. She caught ex Brian staring daggers at Alex. His lawyer must have also given him the no-outbursts speech because Chas could see him straining with the effort of not spewing hate across the aisle at Alex. Alex was either unaware or didn't care because she only had eyes for Chas. She was following Chas's movements from the back, closing in on her place in the courtroom. Lawyer Brian was walking in front of her—another strategic move to hold off the inevitable.

Chas looked behind Brian, and her brain lurched at what she was seeing. Richard and Susan Montgomery were sitting on the bench directly behind her ex. *What the fuck.* They hated her so much that they wanted to publicly watch her endure this. She had a renewed sense of burning under her skin.

As Lawyer Brian stepped through the little swinging wooden gate that separated the public from the people involved in the case, he stepped to the side, effectively blocking Brian's view of Chas, but they both knew it wouldn't last for long. Just a few more minutes were all they needed for the plan to be in motion.

Chas slid into her seat to the right of Lawyer Brian, who was sticking that dad-bod belly out a little extra far today, attempting to mask Chas's own belly.

The judge walked in.

"All rise," the bailiff commanded.

"The honorable Judge Gordon presiding over the case of Jacobs v. Jacobs. The court is now in session."

The judge opened questioning to Lawyer Brian. "What are the grounds for the annulment?"

"Religious coercion prevented my client from entering this marriage of her own free will," replied Brian in a smooth, professional voice. "She was unable to give consent with the threat of religious persecution."

"What evidence do you have to support this claim?"

"Permission to approach, your honor?" Lawyer Brian picked up Chas's journal.

This was it—no turning back now.

Her lawyer shifted and then moved up to place the journal in front of the judge.

Ex Brian looked at Chas, who was no longer obstructed from view. His eyes bulged, seeing her secret on full display, and then he took the bait ...

"Oh, fuck no!" Brian stood up and screamed in the courtroom. "My child will not be raised by a bunch of whoring dykes!" His scream was at a fever pitch. It was bloodcurdling.

The whole court erupted into a frenzy of yelling and motion. Brian's lawyer was pleading with him to sit down and be quiet. Chas's parents stood up to see if Brian was actually right. They were struck still when they saw their daughter and her budding belly. The bailiff was making his way over to Brian's side of the courtroom. The judge was slamming her gavel and looking truly pissed. Chas sat stock-still. She didn't look at her parents or Brian, but down at her belly, stroking soft circles over it as if trying to soothe the girls.

Thankfully, Alex, Kip, and Mara kept their end of the bargain. None of them rose to the insults being hurled in their direction. She was sure that Mara was biting her tongue nearly off to keep her mouth shut.

When Chas looked up, her lawyer gave her a soft smile. They had planned this. If they wanted to show religious coercion, the only evidence they had was Chas's journal with her own words from all those years ago and the notes from the counselor, but they could not prove it.

They just had to get him to show himself.

The judge was commanding the bailiff to take Brian into custody for disorderly conduct and contempt of court.

"I will not have my child raised in this perverse lifestyle you have chosen! They will not be raised by a bunch of freaks!" Brian was screaming as he was led away in handcuffs.

CHAPTER 63
CHAS +2, 2017

The courtroom settled once Brian was removed, but the tension was thick. The judge looked haggard, and Brian's lawyer looked a little ridiculous standing by himself at a table, trying to establish that his client was a loving husband and now wanted to contest the annulment.

Thankfully, Judge Gordon was having none of it. She read portions of the journal without a single reaction to any of it.

"There is enough evidence in this journal alone that demonstrates the case for religious coercion causing duress that prevented Mrs. Jacobs from freely consenting to the marriage. The demonstration from Mr. Jacobs has only served to further solidify that there was no recourse for Mrs. Jacobs, and the coercion continued into the marriage."

She paused for a bit and continued. "Therefore, I'm granting this annulment. A decree of annulment will be entered and filed with the court."

"I would like to add one more thing," the judge said, looking directly at Chas. "The psychological abuse you suffered is not only unacceptable but also a criminal action. I am glad to grant this annulment so that you can regain your agency."

The gavel slammed, and the judge stood up and left the courtroom.

Chas turned to her lawyer and finally gave him a full smile. She leaned in and hugged him. "Thank you for helping me through this."

"You know, if you were my kid, I would want someone out there helping them. I'm sorry this was done to you, but it has been my greatest honor to help undo what I was capable of undoing."

Chas turned around to see Alex standing up. They leaned over the half-wall separating them and hugged. Kip and Mara joined in and sandwiched Chas in tight.

It was over.

Chas was just about to walk through the little swinging gate to exit the courtroom when she stopped suddenly. Richard and Susan were standing at the end of their row, as if waiting for Chas. She looked back to make sure Alex was tracking all of this —of course, she was. Alex moved swiftly to the center of the aisle, leading out. She opened the gate, swinging it toward her and turning her back to Richard and Susan, giving Chas a human barrier between them.

Chas moved swiftly in front of Alex and reached for her hand. Their fingers intertwined. Kip and Mara had taken up their positions at Chas's back. Richard and Susan were trying to push into the aisle when Kip and Mara smashed into place, forming their shield.

"You were my daughter. You would think you could have told us you were carrying Brian's child. You were raised better than this, Chastity," Richard had rushed into the aisle and was speaking loudly over Kip and Mara's shoulders. "You know better than this. I can see you think you are in love with this woman, but it's lust, not love. You can't love someone of the same gender. You know this. We are so disappointed in you. We pray for you to find God again."

Chas tugged on Alex's hand, cueing her to stop.

"You have told me my whole life that I'm not worthy of your love unless I conform to your religious doctrine. I do not believe in that ideology, so your beliefs have no further hold or power on me. I don't need to find my way to God—that sounds more like a *you* problem. I carry God with me always. He loves me. As I am. Which is more than I can say about either of you."

She turned on her heel and stormed out of the courtroom like the badass she was.

CHAPTER 64
CHAS +2, 2017

Later that night, Chas was lying in bed, and Alex was tracing circles around the girls growing inside her. The babies were wriggling around like crazy. Chas was enjoying their wild dance moves.

Alex sat up. "Odette just kicked me, and I felt it!"

"Babe, there's no way to know it was Odette and not Ophelia," Chas replied with a giggle.

"It was Odette. Oh, wait, now they are both going at it!" Alex flattened her palm and spread it wide across Chas's belly. She let the girls dance and kick her hand until the whole family of four drifted off to sleep.

CHAPTER 65
CHAS +2, 2017

"Babe, are you ready to go?" Alex called for Chas through the house.

Chas had made it to thirty-eight weeks with the girls. At their last appointment (the day before), Dr. Beddor told Chas and Alex it was time to induce. The girls were large enough and fully developed, and twin pregnancies have a higher risk of complications for both mom and babies if they are carried to term.

Chas was standing in front of the full-length mirror, nude again. It was still her favorite thing to do. Her belly was so huge and so stretched that it felt like it might pop from one of the girls' kicks or jabs. Now the girls were so big that when they moved, it was actually visible through Chas's skin. It was a wild thing to see—a little eldritch even, but magical nonetheless.

"Girls, it's time to come out and meet us—Mom and I are so excited to hold you and love you from now until forever."

Alex walked in during Chas's pep talk with the girls.

"How are my three best girls doing?"

"Nearly ready. I just want to see myself like this one last time."

Alex gave a soft, almost-moan of agreement. She worshiped Chas's body this way, holding their babies.

Alex came up behind Chas and wrapped her arms around her, low toward her hips, just under her enormous belly. Alex lifted up gently. This was one of Chas's favorite sensations that Alex had taken to doing every day for a few minutes. It gave Chas's body the smallest reprieve. Alex was holding their girls (still inside of Chas), but the pressure of their weight was lifted for a few minutes, and it gave Alex the chance to hold them in the way she could.

"Mmm." Chas was savoring this feeling. "It's going to be strange to see my body when they are no longer in there. I think I may miss this a little. Although I'm not going to be sad to be able to sleep normally again."

"Your body has done an exceptional job of taking care of them, but I'm so ready to meet them."

"Me, too."

Chas took one long, last look at her body holding her two girls inside her. She scanned the firmness of her breasts and was imagining the girls nursing. She scanned her bulbous form and smiled.

"Let's go have some babies."

Alex grabbed their go-bag and placed it in the Jetta's trunk. It was full of everything the Internet had said they needed and some ridiculously cute outfits for the girls. Alex opened the door for Chas, and she waddled her way into the seat, leaning it back to allow her lungs a little more room since the babies occupied most of her chest cavity at this point.

They pulled out of the driveway and stopped at Kip and Mara's house. Both were waiting, neither one even attempting to contain their excitement.

"Our babies are coming!" Mara practically squealed.

After the forty-five-minute drive to the hospital, they were admitted, as Dr. Beddor had explained they would be.

They took Chas and Alex up to the labor room, which would be converted into her birthing room and then her recovery room. She was at a hospital where they didn't move you to a different floor or ward—you got to stay where you were the whole time—an idea Chas liked a lot. It felt like a safe little bubble for them all to get to know each other in those early hours.

The nurses pulled the curtains, leaving Mara and Kip on one side while they hooked Chas up to monitors, IVs, and everything else, but that didn't work. Mara just jerked the curtain back and said, "They want us here," to the nurse who had attempted to obtain some privacy for Chas.

Chas gave the nurse a look that let her know she was sorry for the behavior, but said, "They are going to be here for all of it, so I don't mind them watching."

"Okay, hon."

The nurse started the meds that would start labor contractions through the IV. They would have her start contracting, and then when her cervix was dilated to about 4–5 cm, she could have the epidural placed, as Dr. Beddor had promised.

"I am not one of those crunchy moms—not that that is a bad thing. I just want to be able to tolerate the pain so I can be present in this moment to greet my children," Chas had told the doctor during their last visit.

Dr. Beddor had explained that they were planning a vaginal delivery for both girls, but given that they were twins, it was standard procedure to have an OR at the ready just in case it was needed.

Chas was a champ through labor. She made it to 4 cm and was given her epidural. Kip, Mara, and Alex stood sentry and switched duties involving running to get her ice chips and or wet towels for her head and neck. Chas was doing great, but she was so hot.

When the nurse came to check her next, she was at 8 cm. Not too far to go.

"I want this gown off me."

"Okay, babe, let me help you out."

Alex released the ties from the back of the gown, and Kip lifted the gown off Chas, leaving her bare.

"Kip, can you get me a cold, wet rag?"

"Sure, Chas, baby."

Kip returned with the wet rag seconds later and handed it to Chas so she could place it wherever she needed it. Chas uncurled it and laid it as an open square across the center of her chest.

"Nobody mentioned labor was this hot," she tried to laugh, but it missed the mark. "It feels like I need to go to the bathroom. I may need to go number two. Alex, can you go get the nurse to help me?"

Alex left swiftly and returned a few seconds later with the nurse. Chas went to sit up to try to go to the bathroom, but the nurse stopped her.

"I need to check your cervix."

"But I feel like I really need to go now."

"That is actually a great sign, and it may just be your body signaling it is time to push."

Chas lay back down and allowed the nurse access to check her cervix.

"Yep—looks like it's time to push; we are at 10 cm. Great job, laboring mama. I'm going to step out for a few seconds to page Dr. Beddor. He's in the hospital, so it should only be a few minutes. Do not push until I come back in here."

True to her word, the nurse returned a few seconds later, and then Dr. Beddor was entering the room within a minute or two.

"Hi, ladies—are you ready to meet these beautiful girls?" His grin was wide and excited.

"Yes!" Chas, Alex, Kip, and Mara said in unison.

Dr. Beddor laughed and said, "Okay, family. Let's do this."

CHAPTER 66
CHAS +2, 2017

Kip held one leg, and Alex held the other, with Mara holding Chas's hand. Dr. Beddor was seated on a stool between Chas's legs.

"Okay, on the next contraction, I'm going to tell you to push. I want you to take a big breath of air, and then I want you to bear down like you're trying to go to the bathroom. I know you can't feel everything, but you should feel some pressure low, as if you need to make a bowel movement."

"Ugh," Mara made a face. "I mean … birth is beautiful?" she said with a look that clearly said "Sorry!"

Dr. Beddor laughed. "If you do have a bowel movement, you won't be any the wiser—we will clean you off and remove everything before you even know what happened."

"Not helpful," Chas and Mara said in unison. Mara broke out in a huge grin at that.

"Okay, Chas, here it comes," Dr. Beddor said, watching the monitor. "Okay, push, push, push, push, push … Good job. Take a couple of deep breaths. You did great! We're going to do the same thing on the next one." A minute later, they repeated the sequence, with Dr. Beddor coaching Chas on how hard and long to push.

The excitement in the room was palpable; everyone was expectant.

"Okay, let's let this next contraction pass, and then we'll go again."

This rhythm of pushing for two contractions and resting for one continued. Chas was starting to wear down, but she was desperate to see her girls.

"Chas, do you want to see your baby's head?"

"Yes."

Dr. Beddor summoned a mirror. Alex and Kip helped raise Chas's upper body while supporting her legs, and Mara was still holding firmly onto her hand.

"Okay, Chas, on this next one, I want you to push as hard as you can. You're going to be able to see your baby's head crowning."

"One, two, three … push, push, push, push."

Dr. Beddor was continuing the mantra, and Chas was pushing with all her might, all the while keeping her eyes on the mirror. *There she is.* Chas could see black hair emerging from inside her. Chas's body was stretching, and the baby's head was moving closer and closer to coming out of her, but she ran out of steam and relaxed out of the push, sucking in a breath of air. The baby's head sucked back inside her. *No.* She wanted her out. She wanted to hold her in her arms while they waited for her sister to join her in the world.

"I want to go again on the next contraction."

"Okay, Mama, we can do that."

"Okay, here it comes, one … two … three …"

Chas pushed again, giving it everything she had. There was the baby's black hair pushing through the center of her. Just a little further, and that baby would be with her. Chas curled harder on herself, and the baby's head was out. The contraction relaxed, but the rest of the baby was still inside her. The doctor turned the baby.

"Okay, Chas, last one, and she will be here."

"One, two, three ..."

Chas watched the mirror, and to her immense relief, the baby's shoulders came, and then she slid free from Chas.

Dr. Beddor placed a clamp on the umbilical cord and passed Alex the scissors. Alex cut the cord linking the baby to Chas. The nurse lifted the baby from Dr. Beddor and walked up to the head of the bed for Chas and placed the baby on her bare chest.

"Okay, Baby A has been delivered," the nurse said.

"Odette. Her name is Odette," Chas said, out of breath.

At the same moment, Chas felt a sudden warmth between her legs.

"The sack for Baby B just broke."

Then the heart monitors on Chas's belly started beeping loudly.

"Baby B's heart rate is dropping."

Dr. Beddor looked at Chas, who was clearly starting to panic. He didn't offer reassurance or say everything was fine.

The nurse who had brought Odette to Chas took her back immediately.

"What's happening?" Chas was panicked.

Alex, Kip, and Mara were exchanging worried glances.

Dr. Beddor reached inside of Chas. He removed his hand suddenly and looked directly at Chas.

"Chas, we have to take you to the OR now. The umbilical cord is prolapsed, and your baby's heart rate is dropping. We have to get her out."

CHAPTER 67
CHAS +2, 2017

"Can I go with her?" Alex's voice sounded desperate.

"I'm sorry, but no," Dr. Beddor replied, sounding genuinely sorry. The nurses were a flurry of limbs in the room. Suddenly, there were tons of them running around, disconnecting things and putting up side rails on Chas's bed.

Chas could see the panic on Alex's face. She hated it. She had to make it stop.

"Alex, it's okay. Stay with Odette. She needs you."

Alex leaned over the side rails and kissed Chas.

"I love you. You and Ophelia, come back as soon as you can, okay?" Alex was crying now. She was trying hard not to, but the tears were flowing freely.

"I love you," Chas cried over her shoulder as they were wheeling her out.

Kip and Mara were frozen.

The room was suddenly too quiet, and only one nurse remained with Odette. She had placed Odette in some sort of transparent bassinet and was wiping her down and checking things over.

Alex was a mess but couldn't find any words.

"Hi, Mom, would you like to put on a gown top so you can have skin-to-skin contact with your baby?"

Alex nodded numbly. This was supposed to be the happiest moment of her life. She couldn't reconcile the stark reality with how this scenario had played out in her head earlier.

The nurse helped Alex into a gown. Alex opened the gown to the front instead of the back and left her sports bra on. The nurse put Odette straight on her chest, and Alex curled the wings of her gown around her.

"Odette, your Mommy is coming right back—she will bring Ophelia with her." Alex wasn't sure if she was talking to Odette or herself in that moment.

Kip and Mara came to sit on the couch beside Alex, who had found her way to a hospital-style reclining chair.

Nobody said anything else.

CHAPTER 68
ALEX AND ODETTE, 2017

Alex was sitting in the hospital room with Odette held to her chest. The baby was sleeping peacefully. Kip and Mara were pacing the room in quiet circles.

"Alex, darling, I'm going to get something to drink for Kip and me. Can I get you anything?" Mara asked.

Alex just shook her head.

It had been over an hour. Why hadn't anyone come back to tell Alex what was happening?

As Mara reached for the door handle, the door opened.

It was Dr. Beddor. His eyes were red-rimmed.

God, please no.

Kip and Mara came to stand beside Alex. Alex stood still, holding Odette.

"Alex, I think you should sit down."

Alex's body must have heard the command because she sat, but she wasn't registering her own movements.

"Alex, we lost the baby."

"Her name's Ophelia."

Dr. Beddor stretched his hand to grasp Alex's.

"We lost Ophelia, and I'm so incredibly sorry. The prolapse

deprived her brain of oxygen, and by the time we were able to get to her, she was gone. We tried to resuscitate her, but we just couldn't bring her back."

Mara was sobbing, and Kip was holding her, letting their own tears flow.

Alex couldn't cry yet. She had to focus.

"Where's Chas?"

"Chas is okay. She's in recovery, waking up."

"Does she know?"

"No, not yet. We will tell her once she's fully coherent."

"Please don't tell her alone. Can I please be with her?"

"Yes. We can make that happen. I will need to take you to her in recovery. We can't bring her back to the room until she passes all the post-op checks."

Alex passed the still-sleeping Odette to Kip, whose entire shirt was wet from a mix of their and Mara's tears.

"Kip, take care of Odette. We'll be back soon."

"We can call the nurse to take Odette to the nursery if you'd rather—" began Dr. Beddor.

"No, thank you. Kip is her aunt—there's nobody who will treat her better."

Kip smiled with Odette in their arms, tears flowing down their cheeks. Alex steeled herself and turned to the doctor.

"Take me to Chas."

CHAPTER 69
ALEX, 2017

Alex followed Dr. Beddor down several hallways and into a restricted access area. Dr. Beddor used his ID to open the door.

Already, Alex felt the upcoming moments weighing her down. She wanted to be with Chas, and she wanted their girls with them, but the reality that only three of them would be walking out of here was a slap in the face and a knife to the gut. In all of their preparation and planning, they hadn't even discussed the possibility of not coming home with the twins. This was a certainty of their future, something they had planned everything beyond this moment to include—two girls. They were going to raise two girls: Odette and Ophelia. Alex's throat closed at the thought of her daughter, who was no longer here with them.

"Dr. Beddor, wh– where's Ophelia?" Alex stammered out.

"She's being cleaned and wrapped up by the nurses so that you and Chas can spend some time with her if you choose," he replied solemnly. "Chas is in recovery, as I mentioned, but she's in a private room so that you all can spend time together. The nurses have ways of capturing the memories if you choose to—

we can take a lock of her hair, or footprints, or hand prints—we can take pictures of the three of you. It will be up to you and Chas, and what you need for what happens next."

The only thing Alex registered from the information he shared was this: Ophelia was getting taken care of. They would see her. She had hair—Dr. Beddor offered to cut them a lock of her hair.

Alex swallowed. She knew she couldn't say anything to thank Dr. Beddor for taking such good care of Ophelia and preparing for their needs without breaking into a million pieces.

Dr. Beddor finally came to a stop in front of a room. There was a nurses' station directly across from the room with several nurses milling about it. At the sight of Dr. Beddor and Alex, all the nurses stopped their work and turned to face Alex. Each one covered their heart with their right hand—the only tribute or acknowledgment they could give. Nobody said a word.

"Alex, do you want me to tell Chas, and you be there to support her?"

He didn't offer any alternative plan, but Alex knew the alternative. She had been thinking about it since the moment she asked to be with Chas.

This is the worst news either of them would ever receive. She couldn't let Chas hear it from anyone else. It had to be her.

"I will tell her."

"If it's okay with you, I'll stay in the room to answer any questions Chas or you may have as you navigate this."

"That would be great—thank you."

"Okay, Chas is coming out of the anesthesia, but she still isn't fully coherent. It may take another few minutes for her to be aware of everything. I will stay with you the whole time."

"Are you ready?"

No. But Alex nodded.

Dr. Beddor quietly pushed through the door to the room.

The windows were open, so the sunlight was providing a quiet, soft glow, not like the bright, demanding fluorescent lights of the hallway. The nurse who was monitoring Chas saw Dr. Beddor enter, Alex in tow. At the sight of Alex, she made the same motion (her hand over her heart) and left the room so that they could have their privacy in these initial moments of grief.

Chas was lying in what looked to be a new bed with pristine sheets folded neatly around her, with a lightweight knit blanket covering her from her chest down. Thank God she knew Chas was okay because at this moment, Alex could not imagine losing both Chas and Ophelia. Her throat was closing at the thought. Alex had never had a panic attack, but if she had to imagine what one would feel like—this was dangerously close.

"Can I touch her?"

"Yes, I would encourage it—talk to her, and she should start to come around and respond to your voice."

Alex crossed the room to be with her partner. Her whole universe had expanded with the arrival of the girls, but the very center of that universe was lying in that bed.

Alex gently picked up Chas's hand and intertwined their fingers—a familiar comfort for them both. Alex took in what she could see of this beautiful and brave woman she loved so deeply. Chas had an IV in her left arm and a tube that was hissing slightly in her nose, presumably providing oxygen.

"Did she have trouble breathing?"

"No, it's standard practice while a mom is in recovery and for the first few hours, just to ensure we have stable oxygen levels. She won't remain on it unless she needs it after the first two hours."

Alex used her other hand to stroke the back of Chas's hand that was interlocked with her own.

What do you say to someone who isn't fully back with you? She wasn't sure how much Chas could hear or understand, so she didn't want to freak her out and say she needed her or that Chas needed to wake up.

"Chas, baby, you did such a great job being so strong for our girls." She brushed a kiss over the place she had just been making small circles. "Odette is with Kip and Mara, but I wanted to be here when you woke up. I miss you so much. Take your time waking, my love—I'm right here for when you are ready."

At the sound of Alex's voice and the feel of her hand, Chas started to stir. It wasn't like when she usually woke up all sleepy and doe-eyed in the morning. Her movements were jerkier and more forceful. Alex looked back at Dr. Beddor for reassurance.

"She's okay. It isn't uncommon for people coming out of general anesthesia to have a period of restlessness or disorientation. It won't last long. You can keep talking to her, and it will help."

"Babe, I ..." Alex had abruptly run out of things to say. She wanted to provide reassurance, but she was not going to lie. She wanted to tell Chas to come back to her now so she wouldn't be alone with this knowledge for another minute, but she simultaneously wanted to keep Chas away from this news for as long as possible.

She tried again, "Baby, I .... I love you." That was the only thing that felt right and true in this moment. Instead of filling the silence with any other words, Alex repeated this phrase over and over. It became her prayer, while also a guiding light for Chas to come back to.

After a few more minutes of restlessness, Chas reached up to the nasal cannula, trying to pull it out of her nose.

Dr. Beddor stepped in. "Hey, Chas, I'm glad you're coming back—I need you to leave this in your nose, okay? It's giving you oxygen while you recover." Dr. Beddor replaced the tubing and gently guided her hands back down to the bed.

Alex started expectantly.

Chas opened her eyes and locked them with Alex's. She did not look startled, but confused at first, and then relieved to see her.

Alex's heart shattered. She wanted to smile and provide her with that reassurance that all was well and that they were just recovering and would soon be reunited as a family of four, but she couldn't. She couldn't give Chas false hope, but she also didn't want her to panic before she was fully present with Alex. This was like walking a tightrope the thickness of floss. You were bound to fall.

Alex managed a wobbly smile. Chas saw it and looked confused. She reached for Alex's face with her free hand. Then Chas remembered …

"Alex, where are the girls? Where are Odette and Ophelia?"

Alex's eyes welled. *Damn it.* She wanted to be strong. She *needed* to be strong for Chas, but now that Chas was here with her, she was fighting a losing battle to reach out to her person for some comfort of her own.

"Chas." Alex's voice broke fully. "It's Ophelia … honey, she didn't make it. She passed away."

Then, Alex's control broke, and the tears started flowing in fullness. Soundless streams down her face and onto the bedding covering Chas.

"No," Chas muttered at first.

"No. No. No. NO." Now, she was breaking into a scream.

Alex stood up and curled herself around her fiancée. Her person. The very center of her heart.

Chas cried and cried and cried. Alex just held her through it all. While Chas's reaction was loud and broken and sounded like a wounded animal, Alex's was silent and still. She was breaking in her own way, a rip deep within her gut, her heart, her soul.

Dr. Beddor remained in the room with them, neither offering to help nor providing reassurance. Just a presence for when they needed him. Alex knew he had cried for their baby girl—she could tell when he entered the room to inform Alex—but when she looked to him now, he was standing still, bearing witness for them.

Chas's body was shuddering. Shivering. Coming undone. It lasted for what felt like an eternity, but time didn't exist in this moment. It wasn't welcome here.

As Chas's breathing slowed, and her body regained some voluntary movements, Alex continued to hold on to her. She had climbed into the bed at some point—she was unsure when—and was lying on her side, barely able to fit into the space while Chas was on her back, staring blankly at the room. Alex knew she couldn't hold Chas in their usual way—her body needed recovery as well—but this body-to-body comfort was a way for them to communicate without words until one of them was ready to speak.

"Where is she? Where's our baby? Where's Ophelia?"

At this point, Dr. Beddor broke his silent vigil over them to say, "She's with a nurse. I can have her brought here if you want to see and hold her."

"Yes!" It was a gasp of air, not quite a word.

Dr. Beddor would not leave them. He fiddled with what looked like a pager. Within two minutes, a nurse arrived, pushing a bassinet that looked completely different from the one Odette was placed in. Instead of being clear and mounted on a wooden stand, this one was on a metal cart and appeared to have high purple walls shielding Ophelia from view.

Dr. Beddor took the cart from the nurse and allowed her to leave. He pushed the cot over to the side of the bed Alex was on. Alex climbed out of bed and just stared at her daughter. She could be sleeping. She looked so small in this big bassinet.

"Would you like me to set your bed up so that you can hold her?" he offered to Chas.

Chas nodded, silent tears now flowing down her face to match Alex's.

Chas was placed in a semi-reclined seated position, and Alex was able to sit catty-corner on the bed with her right leg outstretched on the floor to keep her in position. She curled her left arm behind Chas's back, supporting her shoulders.

Dr. Beddor picked up Ophelia and placed her in Chas's waiting arms. Alex used her right arm to form a bassinet shape around Ophelia. Her body felt cold, but she was wrapped in a hospital blanket that matched the one currently on her sister. This was it. The moment they had been waiting for, but not at all how they had imagined.

They were holding their daughter.

CHAPTER 70
ALEX, 2017

They spent the next several hours holding their baby girl and talking to her. Dr. Beddor had left some time ago, and they were alone for the most part. The nurses were a constant, but not an intrusive, presence. They would come by at regular intervals to check on the three of them. Chas was in recovery, so they would make sure everything was okay with her, but then they would linger a moment to check on them in the more important ways. They were a force to be reckoned with, these nurses. How they could walk in and out of the room, knowing the heavy sorrow that awaited them within, but still remain calm, reassuring, and understanding was something Alex couldn't understand, but was immensely grateful for.

They took foot and hand prints and a lock of Ophelia's hair, raven black just like Odette's. All these mementoes were placed in a little album. They helped Alex and Chas bathe her. These moments, while tender, were some of the hardest of Alex's life. She could see them taking a toll on Chas as well. They were in this together; one without the other would have surely collapsed under the weight of the grief.

Chas went to wrap Ophelia in the standard hospital blanket

after her bath, but several of the nurses came in with something small and white.

"We wanted to offer you this dress for Ophelia," the nurse holding the white garment said quietly.

Alex held the gown in her hands. It felt like silk, like the material of a wedding gown. The fabric was thick but soft. It was clearly made with love and for this exact purpose.

The nurse, catching Alex's brief inspection of the gown, explained, "We partner with an agency that turns wedding gowns into dresses and suits for babies who have passed away while in the hospital."

What a painfully beautiful thing, Alex thought. Ophelia would never get the chance to wear a wedding gown. This was the only outfit she would ever wear. It was a beautiful gown.

Chas and Alex dressed Ophelia in her new gown. She continued to lie silently in their arms.

CHAPTER 71
ALEX, 2017

After hours in recovery, Chas was asked if she wanted to be moved back to their original room to rejoin Odette and their family.

Chas looked panicked when the nurse made the offer, but the nurse quickly explained, "We will bring Ophelia with you, so you can all be together for as long as you wish."

Chas's body visibly relaxed at the offer.

"Yes, I need to see Odette."

The hospital team wheeled Chas down the hall with Ophelia's bassinet wheeled before her so she would have constant eyes on her daughter. Alex was beside her. Whenever they would pass any member of the hospital staff, Alex noticed the staff would all make the same gesture the nurses in recovery had—their hand held against their heart. Nobody offered words of comfort. They just made the sign as a symbol of their understanding.

It's strange to be caught in a moment of grief, Alex realized. The world around her was going on as if nothing had happened, while her entire existence had been fundamentally altered. This small gesture from the hospital staff was an acknowledgment.

The world was going on, but they were being seen in this moment. Their grief was being acknowledged by these people. They knew. There was beauty in that.

They entered their original hospital room to find Kip and Mara sitting on the couch, leaning against each other for comfort. Their eyes were puffy and raw.

Odette was in her bassinet right beside the aunts who were keeping vigilant eyes on her, making sure every breath was steady, and Odette was safe. Odette's blanket had been replaced with a purple one, and there was a card on her bassinet with her name, Odette Montgomery (the middle name was left blank), her date of birth, weight, and length at birth. Below all this information was a purple butterfly. Alex instinctively knew the meaning. The reason Odette's blanket had been changed: She was a twin who had suffered the loss of her counterpart. She had grown in the womb with another human growing right alongside her, but now that she had entered the world, she was alone. Sure, she would have her family, but her twin would not be continuing the journey with her.

Kip and Mara stood up as Alex, Chas, and Ophelia entered the room.

The aunts huddled around the purple bassinet holding Ophelia (keeping her body cool so they could stay with her longer)—purple to match Odette's blanket and butterfly.

Alex reached in and lifted her daughter. She offered her back to Chas. Chas looked wrecked. They all did. Chas gently shook her head.

"Kip and Mara can have some time with Ophelia if they want it."

Mara reached out for her, needing to hold the baby she had communed with all these months. She had always wanted to be skin-to-skin with them. Mara held her. She didn't cry (although she had obviously cried for hours). She just looked at her with the tenderest and softest expression on her face. Alex had never seen that look on Mara before. It felt wrong—Mara, the bold and assertive punk of a baby sister, was nothing but a soft, silent picture of grief as she held her niece, who would never get to go drinking or get that eyebrow piercing she had promised her.

Kip went to Odette and picked her up from the bassinet—the protective aunt. It wasn't that Kip didn't want to hold Ophelia or see her. Kip had been charged by Alex to take care of Odette. Alex was sure in this moment that Kip hadn't left Odette's side for even a moment since Alex had left the room earlier.

Kip walked over to Chas and Alex and held out Odette to them. "The nurses brought me a bottle to feed her a few hours ago—she took it like a champ. She has been asleep ever since."

Alex reached out her arms toward Odette.

The difference between her daughters was another slice at her heart. While Ophelia was cool and still, Odette was warm and wiggly. This realization that Ophelia was supposed to be doing the same things caused a lump to form in Alex's throat. She tried and failed to swallow it down. Instead, a gasp escaped her.

Chas looked knowingly at Alex and stretched her own arms out toward Odette.

The six of them were all trying and failing to reconcile reality with the vision they had had coming into the labor suite. This wasn't how it was supposed to go.

CHAPTER 72
CHAS, 2017

The next several days in the hospital were a blur. There was a mountain of logistical things to take care of. Thank God for Alex, because Chas was still only half present in this world. The other half was trying to stay with Ophelia.

At some point, a nurse had come in to assist with the birth certificates. She needed the girls' full names: Odette Hope Montgomery and Ophelia Alex Montgomery. Alex broke when she heard the girls' full names. They had been so busy calling Odette and Ophelia by their first names that they just glossed over the fact that they needed middle names. Chas chose them in the moment—Ophelia would have Chas's last name, but she belonged to Alex just as much as she belonged to Chas. "Alex" was the only choice for a middle name for their daughter.

When it was time to put in the father's name, Chas opted to leave the field blank. These girls would eventually know their father. Chas was sure she wasn't done with Brian, but she was going to stall his progress as best she could for the safety of her daughters. Daughter. Only Odette would eventually meet Brian.

They also made the arrangements for Ophelia's funeral. They decided to have Ophelia cremated so that they could keep her ashes until they were ready to release them in the sea surrounding the island they loved. They did keep her little white gown.

Kip and Mara had stayed for most of the journey, but at some point, they offered to return to Chas and Alex's home and remove one of the cribs and a glider if they felt that would make their transition home any easier.

The truth is, this would never be any easier. But Chas was touched by the offer. It was hard to make that decision. It felt so final. This was the last physical evidence that Ophelia was missing from their lives.

Chas and Alex talked it over and ultimately decided that it would be helpful for Mara and Kip to remove the crib and glider. Chas initially wanted to keep it, but then she thought about the future. If she came home and the crib was there, and there was no baby to fill it, she would be gutted anew. Then, after time—who knows how long—she would need to take down the crib and glider. She couldn't ever imagine a time when she would be okay doing that. It would be better if she relied on them to take care of this part. She was at the limit of her emotional strength.

Today was discharge day. It was the day that they were taking Odette home. Just the three of them facing this new, unexpected life.

"Okay, I have put the car seat base in the car. It took both Kip and me to get that sucker in there, so it's staying put until Odette is in college," Alex said with an attempt at levity.

Chas smiled.

Alex scooped Odette out of Chas's arms.

"There she is, my little one!"

Alex was just as broken as Chas was, but they both couldn't help feeling some joy when Odette was near.

"It feels wrong to be happy when I'm with Odette," Alex had shared with Chas one of the first nights.

It really did feel wrong, but neither mom could hold that baby girl and feel anything other than gratitude that she was with them. She was present and real, a true pillar of hope in the storm of grief they found themselves in. That is how she had decided on her middle name: Hope. It was what she was providing them.

"Well, at least we know it's right—Kip has been studying the manual and watching instructional videos for the last few days," Chas offered in reply.

Alex burst out laughing when she recalled how paranoid Kip had become with the car seat situation.

Almost immediately, she looked ashamed and then started crying.

"Come here, Alex."

Alex walked over and sat on the bed beside Chas, still holding Odette.

"It's okay to laugh when things are funny. It's okay to start to feel normal." It was the same speech Chas had been giving herself.

"Will we ever feel happy—like truly happy again?" Alex asked in a voice quivering with grief. "I should have taken more time to be with you during the pregnancy. I should have held them more while they were inside of you. I didn't know the time was limited."

"You were very present for me and the girls during the pregnancy, Alex. You did soak up the time you had, and you cherished it well, but knowing what we know now makes it seem like we should have done things differently to really spend the time with her. I don't actually believe that's true, though. I wouldn't have wanted to know she wasn't going to be with us. We had the best pregnancy and the sweetest moments that we will always remember."

Pausing for a bit to look into Alex's eyes, she continued, "And yes, I do think we will find our way back to happiness."

CHAPTER 73
CHAS, 2017

Later that day, the trio arrived home. Chas was not able to lift anything, and getting in and out of the car was a workout all on its own. Thankfully, Kip and Mara were home to help them get settled. Kip came to get Odette in her car seat while Alex assisted Chas to the sofa. Mara brought in the bags from the car, piling them up in the living room so Alex could go through them all later.

Now that they were out of the car and the motion had changed, Odette started crying. Kip picked her up and rocked her gently in their arms. Odette was having none of it. Her cries were insistent.

"I think she may be hungry, Mama," Kip said, handing her to Chas.

Odette had taken to breastfeeding beautifully. She latched right away and never seemed to have difficulty with Chas's flow during letdown. Out of everything Chas had learned how to do during her hospital stay (how to bathe her, how to burp her, how to change her diaper, how to change her clothes), breastfeeding was her favorite part. It was something only she could provide, and it was a special, sweet, quiet time between the two of them.

Chas raised her shirt and unsnapped her nursing bra, allowing her nipple to be viewed in the room. It was already leaking little white drops of milk, having heard Odette's demands.

If you had told Chas a year ago that she was going to be the type of mom who just whipped out her boob in a public place, or even a private place with family around, she would have been scandalized. But that was the exact type of mom she was, and it brought her great joy. She was proud of feeding her daughter. It was not a sinful or shameful act but a beautiful moment of a mother providing for her child. She totally understood all those arguments on social media saying that women should not have to be "covered or secluded" to feed their children. For this moment, her nipples were not a sexual part of her body—they were a life-sustaining necessity for Odette.

Kip and Mara watched reverently as Chas manipulated her huge breast and held Odette like a football, gently guiding the dripping nipple into the baby's mouth. Seeing her latch always made everyone in their tribe a little misty-eyed. Odette was perfect. She was doing everything she was supposed to do. The stark reality that Ophelia was not there to join her somehow made even the smallest things Odette did seem monumental to the group.

Odette was nursing away contentedly while the group sat in the living room, just watching her. Nobody knew exactly what to do, but they were all there to figure it out together. It really would take a village to raise this child.

"I really want a shower."

"Okay, babe, we can do that. As soon as Odette is done nursing, I will go with you, and Kip and Mara can hang with Odette."

The doctor had told Chas that she could take a shower once

she returned home, but that she would need to use a mild soap and shouldn't soak the incision directly. Chas still had a bandage on her lower stomach (tucked underneath the flap her belly made). This could come off when she showered and would not need to be replaced, according to the guidance she had given.

While in the hospital, the nurses had helped her to and from the bathroom during her hospital stay, and Chas could see remnants of iodine on her skin when she would lift her gown and pull down the mesh underwear the hospital had provided, but she hadn't been able to take stock of her body as she had before the labor. She could feel her deflated stomach. It felt saggy and empty—so different from when the girls had filled her womb with wiggles and warmth and magic.

Chas wanted to be clean, but mostly she wanted to appraise herself. She needed to see the physical reminders of where Ophelia had been.

Odette finished nursing on one nipple ten minutes later, so Chas switched her over to the next.

After another fifteen minutes of nursing, Odette was nearly back to sleep with Chas's nipple lying gently in her mouth. Chas removed it and tucked her breast away, buttoning up her bra and then pulling her shirt down to cover herself.

Mara stood up and reached for Odette. Kip looked a little disgruntled, but it was technically Mara's turn. Mara caught the look. "Kip, I thought maybe you should be on standby if Alex or Chas needs help in the bathroom." Kip's face immediately relaxed and became determined. They would be ready for whatever Chas or Alex needed.

"Honey, are you feeling up to the shower now, or do you want to wait a while longer?"

"I'm ready."

Alex assisted Chas toward the back of their house. Chas

started to head to the bathroom, but Alex gently tugged her toward the bedroom.

"It will be easier to change in the bedroom—our bathroom is so small, I figured getting in and out of clothes may be easier with more room to maneuver."

Alone in the bedroom, Chas realized Alex hadn't seen her body yet (other than her breasts when Odette was feeding). Alex didn't know that her belly was flaccid and flopped over on itself. There was a beat of self-consciousness, but it passed quickly.

Alex gently removed Chas's shirt over her head. Chas could smell her underarms when she lifted her arms. She needed this shower. Then Alex helped her take off the nursing bra. Apparently, these are more complicated than the average bra because Alex actually used two hands to free her. If her breasts were swollen before, they were near bursting point now. She could see the blue of her veins showing through the stretched skin there. Then Alex moved to help her take off her pants. Chas was still incredibly grateful for maternity pants. They provided just enough light pressure over her abdomen to help her feel like her skin was being held together with these pants. After removing her pants, Alex wrapped her in a towel and walked Chas into the bathroom next door. Chas sat on the toilet and peed and allowed Alex to help clean up the pads and undergarments. Under ordinary circumstances, Chas would have been mortified, but she didn't have the strength to even worry about something that trivial anymore.

"Kip, can you bring the squeeze bottle that should be sitting on the very top of the diaper bag?" Alex called out.

A few seconds later, Kip passed the squeeze bottle through the sliding bathroom door.

Alex filled the squeeze bottle with warm water and held it out for Chas. Chas grabbed it and squeezed water on her still-sore vagina. The doctor told her not to wipe for the next two weeks. She had had a vaginal birth and a C-section and had the after-care for both to contend with.

Alex turned on the water and made sure it was not too hot. Chas really wanted scalding water, but now was not the time for that. Just a warm, gentle shower for now.

Alex stripped down bare. She was going to be with Chas. There was no way Chas was going to be alone for a single second of this journey.

Alex helped her stand off the toilet. Then she bent over and started peeling the bandage from Chas's abdomen. The tape pulled at the skin, and it stung a little, but nothing too bad. After the bandage was freed, Alex inspected the incision for any signs of infection, as the doctors and nurses had told them to do. Chas couldn't see the incision because of the belly flap, and she was too afraid to lift it for a look. Her skin felt like it was barely holding her organs inside.

Alex got in the shower first and put a small hand towel at the bottom of the shower to prevent Chas from slipping. Then she reached out to help Chas in. Chas lifted one leg over and then the other. Alex had Chas face the wall, and then she slid in between Chas and the shower curtain to allow Chas access to the water.

It felt amazing on her skin. Like the first shower after a long, sweaty walk or a day at the beach. It was washing away so much more than dirt. It was clearing Chas of the feel of the hospital on her skin.

Suddenly, Chas jolted, which really wasn't the right thing to do—her incision burned, but she didn't think it tore.

"What is it? Are you hurt?"

The tears returned to Chas. "I'm washing off the only skin that will have ever touched or held her, Alex. Why did I do this?"

"Babe, I know it feels that way, but you will always have

Ophelia with you. Your skin will always remember her there. It doesn't mean you can't wash. Your body knows she was here."

Alex held Chas, as they both cried, letting the water wash over them.

CHAPTER 74
CHAS, 2018

A few weeks had passed. Both she and Alex were still on maternity leave (although neither of their professions actually paid for it), but this was ending for Alex soon. They had enough saved for them both to miss work for about five weeks and then some more for Chas to miss an additional six weeks, if she needed.

The days passed in a blur. There was the horrible, tremendous grief that greeted them every morning and waited for them every night, but then there was also Odette.

Odette was a perfect baby. She cried when she was hungry or wet, but the majority of the time, she was content to stare at whichever adult was holding her in their arms. Odette was rarely put down. She had swings, a bouncy seat, a Moses basket, a bassinet, and a crib, but unless they were all sleeping for the night, she was almost always in someone's arms.

Kip and Mara had returned to work, but they were now on opposing schedules, so one of them was typically at the house. After the first week, Mara and Kip started leaving a little earlier in the day to allow Alex and Chas some time together and with Odette. The new normal, while painful, was finding its rhythm.

They were deep into winter now, and the new year had come a few days after they had returned home from the hospital. The air was crisp and cold most days, so Chas stayed inside with Odette in the warmth of their little home. Today, though, was slightly milder than it had been. It was still cool, but the kind that feels good on your skin (until the wind blows, at least).

"Babe, what do you think about taking a walk with me to the beach when Kip arrives today?" Alex asked.

"Kip has arrived for today!" they announced, walking in the front door with a beaming grin and immediately searching for Odette.

Chas had just finished nursing, so Odette was in a post-feed stupor—very relaxed and a little sleepy. Kip strode over and waited patiently for Chas to offer up their niece. Chas grinned, seeing Kip's utter failure at keeping the impatience off their face. She didn't have it in her to make Kip wait—she lifted Odette a little, signaling Kip could swoop in and collect her.

Odette loved her aunts. The smell of any one of them could settle her into sleep within a few minutes. She was much beloved.

"A walk on the beach actually sounds nice."

"I have got Ms. Odette taken care of," said Kip. "You two go and get some fresh air."

Chas slid on her favorite shoes and a jacket and reached for Alex's hand. They interlocked their fingers and headed one block over to the beach access point nearest to Alex's house.

The sea oats were gently swaying in the wind. The sky was not the clear blue of spring and summer, but the light gray of winter. There was something reassuring about that. It was as if the whole world was in mourning over the loss of Ophelia. Chas didn't want to see the sunshine and hear the birds chirping happily just yet. She needed the melancholy of the winter to support her through the worst of the grief.

Chas and Alex walked hand in hand. Chas tugged her toward the place where the ocean met the sand. A little over a year ago, she had swum in this same winter sea. She recalled the feeling of it on her skin and desperately wanted that feeling now. Alex caught her shift.

"Babe, you can't go in. The doctor said six weeks, and it has only been four."

Four weeks without Ophelia. That is how Chas kept time now. How long she had survived without her beautiful daughter.

"What if I just go in till my thighs?"

Alex gave an exasperated huff but knew better than to fight her on this. She knew Chas needed it, or she wouldn't have asked.

"Okay, but we go together."

The sea was calm, almost flat. The area where the waves broke was close to shore and so small that they may have even overlooked it.

Chas pulled off her maternity jeans (rolling them up to her thighs wasn't a logical choice—they would still get wet and be horribly uncomfortable). Alex followed suit. Thankfully, Tybee in the winter months was a ghost town. Nobody was around to see them.

Chas took the first tentative step into the water. It was cold, but not as cold as the last time she had taken a winter swim.

Alex followed Chas as she moved deeper and deeper into the water. Chas wanted to go under. She wanted to feel this water hold her. The water had always helped her. It had provided her a safe harbor when she needed it, and she needed it now.

"Babe, I know you want to, but we really can't right now."

Chas knew Alex was right. She knew it would put her at risk of infection or something going wrong with the incision. Chas stood in the water, allowing it to ripple around her thighs. *Two weeks. In two weeks, she could have the water all around her if she wanted.*

CHAPTER 75
CHAS, 2018

The next two weeks passed even more rapidly than the first four. Alex had returned to work last week and seemed to be finding her rhythm there. She hated missing the days with Odette and Chas, but was so excited and practically giddy when she finally got to come home to them.

Today, Chas had told Kip and Mara that she was good and that they should take a break for the day. Kip looked more put out than anything, but Chas knew they had both been working and helping nonstop for the last six weeks. They needed a reprieve, even if they didn't think so themselves.

Chas woke up with Odette (earlier than she would have liked —it looked like Odette may be a morning person like her mom, Alex). She collected Odette from the bassinet in their room, where she slept next to their bed. Chas stripped off her shirt and positioned Odette to have easy access to her left breast and nipple. Odette fed greedily, causing a swift letdown for Chas.

"Oomph; hey, little lady, that hurts a little."

The sensation of pins and needles subsided, and they found their rhythm. They completed nursing in lockstep; they had done it so many times now. Odette drained the left breast and then gave a sharp, demanding cry, at which Chas positioned her to nurse from the right. These sweet moments were holding Chas together. Odette was the glue holding Chas to this world and preventing her from drifting off to the one beyond with Ophelia.

There was a sharp knock at the front door. Chas walked to the door with Odette still on her breast, feeling a little cross, knowing already it was Kip who had dropped by to check on her and see Odette. Chas swung the door open. It wasn't Kip. This was someone she didn't recognize.

"Chastity Montgomery?"

"Can I help you?"

"Are you Chastity Montgomery?"

"Yes."

The stranger held out an envelope, which Chas accepted.

"You have been served."

And with that, the stranger walked away.

Chas was left dumbfounded, standing at the front door with Odette nursing while the man walked away from her. What was he talking about?

Chas returned inside and sat on the couch. She propped Odette up so that she could nurse while Chas had access to both hands. Chas ripped into the tan envelope.

IN THE FAMILY COURT OF THE SECOND CIRCUIT STATE OF GEORGIA PETITION FOR PATERNITY SUMMONS: PETITIONER BRIAN ADAM JACOBS

Brian was coming for Odette. Chas knew it would happen, but she wanted more time. She needed more time with Odette, to just be their family. Odette was what was holding her together.

Chas pulled out her phone with shaking hands and opened her text thread with Alex.

"Hey, can you call when you get a chance. Not urgent." Chas didn't want her to be freaked out that Odette was hurt, so she said "not urgent," but she knew that this was one of the more urgent moments of her life.

Thankfully, Alex wasn't buying the "not urgent" thing. She called immediately.

"Chas, what's wrong? Is Odette okay?"

"I was just served papers—Brian is petitioning for paternity so he can establish his rights."

"I'm on my way."

Alex was home within ten minutes, and Kip walked through the door five minutes after that.

"I didn't want the day off anyway, Chas baby." Kip came and scooped Odette up.

Chas should have had some idea about what to do next. All she could think about was the sea. She wanted to be in the sea.

"What can I do?" Alex sounded as desperate as she was.

"I want to go for a swim."

"Okay, we can do that."

Kip looked alarmed and searched Alex's face, trying to figure out if both moms had lost it or just the one.

Alex gave a knowing nod to Kip, who gave a quick nod in return. They had Odette taken care of. Alex needed to take care of Chas. They would divide and conquer.

"Do you want to get into a swimsuit?"

"No."

"Okay, let's go."

Chas walked as fast as she could—one block, then about a hundred yards down to the sea. As soon as her feet touched sand, Chas was stripping her clothes from her body. Last time she was in her underwear. Today, she would have nothing between her and the water. She needed this. She was *not* hiding from herself, from Alex, or from the truth of her situation.

Soon, Alex caught on to what was happening. She stripped to her underwear and bra. She was going in with Chas.

Chas knew Alex would come in, too. If she was going, her partner in all things would be going with her.

The water had returned to the icy knife's edge it had been

last winter. It wasn't the mild, pool-like water it had been two weeks ago. Today, it was biting. Chas thanked God for that. She needed the physical pain to help center her in reality. This was her reality. There was no escaping it. Only enduring it.

The water brushed past her ankles, then her knees, then her scar, then her navel, and finally over her breasts, covering all but the upper portion of her neck and head. She pulled her hair tie from her hair and let the curls fall. They grazed the water, their tips dipping below the surface around her shoulders.

Alex was with her, she knew, but for this moment, it was just her in the water. Making the same bargain they made last time.

"Be brave and true to yourself," the water called. "It will work out in the end."

She was no longer running from her feelings. She was seeking clarity and strength from her most trusted source: herself and the ocean.

Chas smiled as she went under.

CHAPTER 77
CHAS, 2018

Odette was now six months old and growing rapidly. The family of five (including Kip and Mara) had found their rhythm for the most part.

Chas and Alex had learned to manage the grieving process while juggling the intrusion of the legal world.

Chas and her lawyer, Brian, were united in their plan. They were going to grant permission to obtain Odette's DNA, definitely proving she was Brian's, but they were going to wait until the case went to court in an effort to convince the authorities that Brian should not have any custody given the events that had transpired (him taking Chas back to Restorative Hope to fix her to be the wife he wanted, the assault when things did not go his way, his final explosion in the courtroom upon seeing her pregnant form, and his subsequent arrest for contempt of court and disorderly conduct).

"I believe we have a strong case for denial of his parental rights. We're going to argue that Odette's safety and the risk of further harm are factors that cannot be ignored or even compromised with. Odette's well-being is going to be the crux of the case. If he would do all of these things to you, who was supposed to be his partner at the time, then what would prevent him from inflicting the same harm on his child? I will explain that the risk is not only physical but psychological, and that his religious doctrine and ideology would make him an incompatible and psychologically damaging co-parent."

Chas and Alex nodded, hearing Brian explain the plan for the twentieth time. They had been meeting via phone and Zoom over the last six months, but now that they were going to court in a week, Brian had asked them to come into Savannah to walk through everything one last time in person.

After everyone was in agreement, Chas and Alex hugged lawyer Brian.

"See you in a week, ladies. When all this is done, I want to have a dinner to celebrate where I can finally see Odette."

As uncertain as things were, Chas was remarkably calm. She had put all of her faith and trust in God. He would protect her, Alex, and most of all, Odette.

"Is there anything else you need or want to do while we're in Savannah?" Alex was headed to the car.

"Alex, I think we should get married."

Alex barked out a loud laugh. "Chas, my love, why do you think I said yes when you asked me? I think we should get married, too."

Then, Alex caught the serious look on Chas's face.

"What do you mean exactly, Chas?"

"I think we should get married today. Right now, actually."

CHAPTER 78
ALEX AND CHAS, 2018

Chas and Alex were on an emotional high. They were doing this. Alex called Kip, who was at the bar, while Chas called Mara, who was with Odette at their house.

"Kip, is there any way you can get your shift covered?"

"Is everything okay with Odette?" Kip practically shouted into the receiver.

"Yes, sorry! Odette is fine. Chas and I are getting married! Today—actually, now! Can you come?"

"I wouldn't miss it for the world. Give me an hour or two, and I will be there."

Kip asked a very practical and logical question that Alex and Chas had missed thinking about in their excitement. "Hey, who did you get to marry you on such short notice?"

"Shit!" Alex let out a hushed, frustrated huff to keep Chas from hearing. She was on the phone with Mara, asking her to come and bring Odette.

Alex's stomach sank. She needed and wanted to do this today.

"Alex darling, do you need an officiant?"

"Do you know anyone?" Alex was trying not to let go of the hope that this could still happen.

"Actually, I do, but they are on the island. Are you set on having it in Savannah?"

"Let me talk to Chas, but go ahead and let them know we will meet them and pay them whatever they want."

"Okay, darling. Call me back once you have told Chas about the change in plans."

Alex hung up and quickly ran to Chas, completely out of breath.

"Chas!"

"Babe, I'm on the phone with Mara. She is going to bring Odette—"

"We need to have a slight change in location," Alex cut in.

"Okay, but why?"

"We need to get married in Tybee. Kip knows an officiant. I hadn't thought that part through yet—sorry, I was putting the cart before the horse." Alex looked a little flustered, but glad that she could offer a solution to the problem.

Chas felt a warm spread from within. She knew what she wanted and needed to do now. Chas felt God intervening and pointing her in the direction she needed to go.

"Alex, we get to get married on our island."

They shared excited smiles before Chas got back on her phone.

"Mara, we're coming to the island. Do you think you could have Odette ready in a dress? We should be back in the next two hours. We will call when we are headed back."

Mara shrieked—Chas wasn't sure if there were any actual words coming from her mouth or if they were just sounds. She was taking that as a yes.

"Okay, talk soon," Chas hung up on Mara mid-squeal.

Alex texted Kip, informing them that they were getting the license and then heading back down the island.

Alex and Chas filed for the marriage license at the Chatham County Probate Court. Thankfully, not too many people were waiting for their license on a random Tuesday afternoon in June. They were in and out with the license in twenty minutes.

Alex took Chas to a little boutique in the historic district—it was one that Chas had been to before when she lived nearby.

Outfits and a marriage license in hand, they got back in their car an hour later, headed for Tybee.

CHAPTER 79
CHAS AND ALEX, 2018

The plan was to meet Kip at the beach access near Alex's house. They would walk out on the sand with Kip's officiant friend, and then they would get married with their two best friends and their daughter there to witness.

When they arrived back at the house, they went into separate bedrooms to get dressed.

Chas had picked out an off-shoulder royal blue dress cut just above her knees. It hugged her curves in the best way.

Alex had opted for a button-down shirt and slacks, leaving the top button undone.

Neither had shown the other what they would be wearing. Even if they didn't coordinate, they would each be comfortable in what they selected, and that was coordination in its own right.

"You look … stunning," Alex said when she first caught sight of Chas.

"Thank you!" Chas flushed at the compliment and the way Alex's eyes were roving over her body in the dress, taking in every last curve and swell.

"Okay, I agree, but that look you're giving her is just gross,"

Mara remarked, having walked in on their exchange. "There's a baby in the room, for Pete's sake!"

"Are we ready to do this?" Alex's excitement was filling her up and overflowing.

"Alex …" Chas said, a little hesitantly.

"Oh no, do you want to call it off? We can. There's no pressure …"

Chas held up her hand to show Alex she was on the wrong train of thought.

"Alex, this is one of the happiest days of my life. It will be a day I remember for the rest of my life. I know we can only have Odette here with us physically, but I believe Ophelia is here, too. How would you feel about spreading her ashes during our ceremony?"

Alex's eyes welled with tears. The tears were a mix of joy and awe for the strength of her bride, the mother of her children.

"I can think of nothing more perfect than that."

CHAPTER 80
CHAS AND ALEX, 2018

They brought Ophelia's ashes with them to the beach access.

When they crossed the boardwalk that led over the dunes and to the beach beyond, they saw Kip standing with two other people they did not recognize.

"Hey, Kip …"

"Alex, Chas, meet Jeremy, your officiant, and my partner," Kip said with a sly grin.

"What?" Alex, Chas, and Mara said in perfect unison.

"We have been seeing each other for a few weeks, and I was planning to introduce you all soon, but it turns out today is the day!" Kip said with a look of joyful humor that they had kept this secret from the tribe.

They all took turns introducing themselves to Jeremy, Chas, and Alex, hugging him, Mara shaking his hand while holding Odette on her hip, and supporting her with her other hand.

"Okay, but what is Mark doing here?" Mara jumped in, asking about the other visitor who was clearly known to Kip and Mara.

"This is Mark," Kip said, flipping their hands as if they were Vanna White, and Chas and Alex had solved the puzzle. "Mark is a regular at the bar. He's always showing me pictures he has taken for his business. He's a photographer. Usually, he takes pictures for marketing campaigns, but he has a nice camera, and he knows what he's doing, so it totally counts."

"Thank you, Kip!" Chas and Alex sandwiched Kip in a hug. "We literally couldn't have done this without you."

"I know, I'm pretty handy when it comes to making connections—it's the bartender in me," Kip said with a wink.

The group made their way to the place where the ocean met the sand. Chas and Alex were standing in the water with Jeremy standing in the sand, looking out over the ocean to face them.

Kip, Mara, and Odette stood to the side of Jeremy, looking at Alex and Chas. Mark was everywhere, it seemed, clicking away on his camera.

The moment was perfect.

"Alex, I think it's time."

Chas was still holding the small urn that contained the ashes of their second-born daughter, Ophelia.

No words can convey the sadness a parent feels when they lose a child. It is an ever-present grief you learn to navigate, and then you learn to live with.

Alex nodded, and Chas began to pray as she released Ophelia's ashes into the water surrounding them.

"God, please continue to watch over us and guide us. I know Ophelia is with you, and I take comfort in knowing that we will all be reunited again when the time is right. Amen."

The last of Ophelia's ashes flowed into the water. The water was warm. It offered a small caress to their ankles.

In their moment of profound sadness, they also had immense happiness and joy. Chas remembered back to their time in the hospital, when Alex had asked her, one day, if they would ever be truly happy again. This was it. The balance they had found. The grief was there, but the happiness had returned, too.

CHAPTER 81
CHAS 2018

Chas had always written poems when difficult feelings were stifled inside her. Since finding Alex, her feelings had flowed as freely as the water that held their daughter—but on their wedding night, Chas wrote a poem to Ophelia.

We Held You

We held you in our hearts,
a whisper in the storm.
A love so fierce and tender,
in a tiny, perfect form.
We held you for a moment,
With silent, falling tears.
We knew we'd hold your memory
through all the coming years.
Now, in her living gaze,
a new love sets us free.
Our home is safe and warm
You are here in her, and with me.
Love, Mommy.

EPILOGUE: ODETTE, 2047

Odette stood before the full-length mirror, a vision in white, the soft lace of her gown shimmering in the late afternoon light. Her heart hammered with the joyful anticipation of marrying the love of her life, but in this quiet moment, her thoughts drifted to the two women who had brought her into this world, loved her fiercely, and guided her every step.

A soft knock preceded the opening of the door. "Ready, sweet pea?" Chas's voice was warm, a familiar melody that had comforted Odette her entire life. She looked up to see her Moms entering the room, their faces radiating pride and a hint of shared memory. Chas, elegant in a deep emerald suit, linked arms with Alex, who beamed in a tailored navy ensemble.

"Almost," Odette laughed, turning to embrace them both. Their hugs were a grounding force, a silent reminder of the unwavering foundation they had built for her.

Chas stepped back, her eyes softening as they lingered on Odette's dress. "It's perfect, honey," she whispered, her fingers tracing a delicate, almost invisible, embroidered butterfly nestled within the lace of the bodice. This was the detail only they knew. A small, subtle patch of fabric, carefully sewn into the dress—a piece of the delicate white gown Ophelia had worn on the day they said goodbye. It was Odette's quiet way of carrying her sister with her, a secret shared between three hearts.

"She's here with us, isn't she?" Odette asked, her voice thick with emotion, knowing exactly who Chas was thinking of.

Alex squeezed Odette's hand. "Always, sweet pea. Always. Every step, every joy, every triumph—she's right there, cheering you on."

They stood together for a moment, a tableau of love spanning decades. The raw grief that had once defined their early days had softened into a gentle, enduring ache, a testament to a love that had proven itself capable of holding both immense sorrow and boundless joy. They had not just survived; they had thrived, raising Odette in a home overflowing with acceptance, laughter, and the ever-present, loving memory of her twin.

Another knock. "Are we clear to enter? We heard a lot of sappy sniffling in here." Mara's voice, accompanied by Kip's knowing chuckle, announced their arrival.

Kip, now with distinguished silver at their temples, and Mara, just as vibrant and irreverent as ever, burst into the room. Kip's eyes immediately found Odette, brimming with affection. Mara, ever the practical one, quickly scanned the room. "All right, everyone in place? No last-minute jitters, Odette? Because if so, I've still got that eyebrow piercing kit in my bag."

Odette rolled her eyes, but her smile was wide and genuine. She pulled both aunts into a hug. Kip and Mara, the anchors of their extended family, who had literally moved a crib and held a baby, had been as constant and loving as her Moms.

"It's time," Alex said, her voice steady but laced with strong emotion.

Chas took Odette's arm, her touch firm and reassuring. "Are you ready, my love?"

Odette looked at her Moms, at Kip and Mara, at the shimmering butterfly hidden in her dress. She saw the unwavering love that had carried them all through unimaginable loss into a future brighter than they had ever dared to dream of.

"I'm ready, Mama," Odette said, her voice clear, her heart full. "I'm more than ready."

Together, the three of them, their unbreakable bond forged in pain and celebrated in joy, stepped out of the room and towards the waiting aisle, ready to walk into the next beautiful chapter.

ACKNOWLEDGMENTS

This book would not exist without the incredible support and expertise of many dedicated people.

First and foremost, my deepest gratitude goes to Robin Schroffel. You are truly a force of nature. Thank you for your exceptional work as my editor, cover designer, and interior formatter, and for your invaluable guidance through the entire publishing process. Your skill, patience, and dedication transformed this manuscript into the book you hold in your hands.

To the amazing friends and family who took the time to read the earliest, messiest drafts: thank you for your honesty, your encouragement, and for helping me find the true heart of this story. Your critical feedback was indispensable.

To my wife—you are my constant anchor. Thank you for tolerating my single-minded focus when I was deep in "writer mode," for keeping me fed and watered, and for reminding me that the world exists outside the pages. This book is as much yours as it is mine. And to my kids, thank you for sharing your time and your attention with the characters I created. Your presence makes every triumph meaningful.

Finally, to the beautiful cities of Savannah and Tybee Island, Georgia: thank you for sparking the initial need to write this story. The beauty of the coast provided the perfect, safe, and lovely home for these characters, and my hope is that I have done them justice.

ABOUT THE AUTHOR

SK Holt writes compelling contemporary gay romance that delves into the heart of modern relationships and identity. Her debut novel, *Her Name Was Chas*, is a tender and unforgettable story of finding love and self-discovery. A native of South Carolina, SK lives with her wife, their children, and a demanding trio of French bulldogs. When she isn't working, she can be found unwinding with her family by the ocean, her favorite spot for inspiration.

www.ingramcontent.com/pod-product-compliance
Lightning Source LLC
Chambersburg PA
CBHW050026120726
47903CB00006B/1929